Color of Blood

···

Saint Lakes Book Seven

April Kelley

Hard Rose Publishing

Contents

Prologue

Ladon Somerset had perfected the art of sneaking. It had never crossed his mind until he decided time was with his mate was important enough to lie for it. It proved difficult in a house full of shifters, anyway. They smelled and heard things better than other beings, so it hadn't been worth it before. It wasn't as though impatience was going to make him shift any faster, so he made the most of it.

Every time Ladon tried to force the shift, his dragon part went silent. He was just a wet butterfly halfway out of his cocoon. His dragon barely hatched.

Ladon kept his steps light as he made his way across the living room floor. When he entered the kitchen, he held the edge of the door and gently let it slide back on its track.

Was he a late bloomer? He might be, or maybe something was wrong with him that he was nearly twenty years' old and his dragon still hadn't come out. If he'd had his first shift already, life would be grand. No sneaking necessary. By human standards, he was an adult, but he wasn't a human. He was a dragon shifter, and that meant he had to wait to bond with his mate.

It wasn't as if he couldn't feel that part of himself. Even as he crept down the stairs to the first floor, his dragon flapped his wings in excitement at just the thought of seeing Magnus again. Ladon's back itched where wings would someday sprout, and his muscles jumped.

Sucking in a breath, he turned to see if they were there, but no dice. Damn it.

It was as he turned that he saw Ramsey standing against the kitchen counter with a cup of coffee in hand and his arms crossed loosely over his bare chest. He seemed as if he was the picture of calm, which was deceiving. Ramsey had a lot of stress, what with the impending battle with Stavros and the humans possibly behind the bigger problem.

Ladon had some thoughts on how to protect the clan. He wasn't sure if anyone would listen, but he wouldn't have minded discussing them with Ramsey sometime soon.

After he spent time with Magnus. He had priorities, after all.

His hands shook, so he shoved them into the pockets of his jeans. His mood shifted with the wind. The swings were difficult on everyone, not just him. Mom said it was perfectly normal, not that it made it okay for him to be a prick one minute and happy the next.

As much as Ladon wanted to keep his tone neutral, he couldn't. "If you're here to tell me I can't go out, save it. I'm going anyway. I might not have had my first shift yet, but I'm still an adult. I'll do what I want."

Ramsey's eyes turned into his dragon's, but he didn't show any other outward sign of anger. "Nope. I trust him not to bite you."

Ladon growled. The sound rolled out of him, unexpected and unwarranted. "But you don't trust me."

"Your dragon is so close you're not thinking clearly. You'll shift soon." Maybe that was why Ramsey didn't stop Ladon's challenging behavior. Knowing it would happen didn't help improve his attitude.

Ladon leaned against the table and crossed his arms over his chest. "How long have you known I was sneaking out?"

Ramsey smiled. "Couple weeks. Don't worry, Mom doesn't know, and neither does Garridan. And they won't hear it from me or my recruits."

"Let me guess, Shawn and Lucas."

"I would never recruit Lucas. He can't keep his mouth shut to save himself. It was Shawn and Sage."

Ladon smiled for the first time since his adventure had begun. "Interesting pair. I could see how those two nosy shits would work well together."

"My thoughts exactly." Ramsey grinned. "They did a great job."

Ladon's muscles lost their tension. He hadn't even realized how much stress he'd carried until it disappeared. "So if you're not here to tell me I can't see Magnus, then why are you waiting for me?"

"I need to talk to Magnus. Was wondering if you'd let me steal a few minutes with him."

"Has to do with the humans knowing about us?"

"Yep. Shawn found something on the computer, and I'd like Magnus to look into it." Ramsey winced and looked away. "It means sending him out again."

Ladon growled. The tension returned until his shoulders came up to his ears and his whole body felt like one big knot. "It's dangerous for him to go by himself. After I shift, I'm going with him."

When Ramsey met Ladon's gaze, his eyebrows drew together. "I doubt that."

"Why?"

Ramsey took a sip of his coffee. "We'll talk about it later."

As much as Ladon wanted to read between the lines, he wanted to get to Magnus more. "I'll go get him. He always waits for me in the middle of the back meadow."

"I know."

"Right. Guess we're not as stealthy as we thought."

"*You're* not. Magnus, on the other hand, can stand two feet behind me and I'd never fucking know."

"What got me caught?"

"You making coffee so early every morning. You're not a morning person and the stuff you make is as thick as tar." First one up made the first pot. It was a house rule, so Ladon always made it on his way in from seeing Magnus.

Ladon wasn't exactly a genius when it came to anything in the kitchen. Both Sage and Mom had tried to teach him how to make the simplest things but failed. "There go my skills as a spy."

"Stop making coffee if you don't want the parents to know. They find out, and we're both in trouble."

Ladon moved away from the table, closing the distance between them. He hugged Ramsey. "Thanks for having my back."

"Always." Ramsey returned the hug.

"I know." Ladon let him go and took a step back. "Sorry for being such a dick lately."

"You want to make amends you can clean the gutters. Mom keeps hinting for me to do it."

Ladon nodded. "I'll do it tomorrow." He liked yard work and fixing things anyway, so it wasn't a hardship.

Ladon needed a few minutes alone with Magnus before going into the house, so he stopped him on the back stoop before Magnus could pull the door open, tugging on his hand.

When Magnus turned, he had a look on his face that he reserved just for Ladon. It tightened Ladon's chest muscles every time, making his heart ache just a little.

That smile Magnus threw over his shoulder was sexy and unexpected. "What?"

"Just wait a sec." Ladon tugged on Magnus' hand again, silently demanding he come closer.

Magnus grinned. "You're keeping the Alpha waiting." Despite what he said, Magnus willingly came into Ladon's arms.

When they had first met, Ladon had been the same height as Magnus. Since his first shift was so close, he had grown several inches. Magnus could lay his head on Ladon's chest.

Magnus sighed and relaxed.

"You seem tired. And I needed a hug."

"I needed one too."

"Maybe we should take the night off from seeing each other." Ladon ran a hand down Magnus' back.

"No."

"If you need sleep then I think we should."

"Are you asking or telling?" Magnus spoke with a bit of humor laced through his tone.

"I'm asking."

"Since that's the case then I want to spend time with you. Besides, if Ramsey wants to see me, I'll probably be out of town for a while."

"Which is why you need the rest."

"So it was a demand."

Ladon narrowed his eyes. "No."

"Yes, it was."

"Magnus." Ladon winced at the harshness in his tone.

Magnus chuckled. "Fine. Then we hang out like normal. You're my best friend, so it's not a hardship."

Ladon winced. He knew they had friend-zoned each other but hearing it aloud erased everything else that had been between them, including the mating pull until Ladon wondered if it had ever existed.

Did he still feel the longing? Did Magnus?

Before Ladon could protest, the sliding glass door opened, and Ramsey stuck his head out. "I need five minutes. That's about all. Ladon, you come too."

"Sorry, Alpha," Magnus said.

Ramsey smiled.

Magnus pulled away from Ladon and followed Ramsey into the house.

Ladon followed them, right into the office. He wasn't sure why Ramsey let him in on their little meeting. Ramsey didn't do anything without a solid reason. He also wouldn't disclose that reason until he was good and ready.

Ramsey sat on the couch, instead of behind the desk. Magnus sat in the plush chair, so Ladon chose the arm of the chair.

Ramsey picked up papers from the coffee table and handed them to Magnus, who took them.

Magnus read through the stack. Ramsey's next words pulled at Ladon's attention. "Ladon, I'd like you to read through them next."

Ladon nodded.

Magnus met Ramsey's gaze. "This is a website about paranormals."

"Yes. A man named Wesley Swenson runs it."

"But it sounds like a lot of what the humans are saying is speculation."

"Yes. Shawn gave us a printout of the forum mostly. If you flip to the back couple of pages, you'll see the most important parts."

Magnus did. He read for only a few seconds before addressing Ramsey again. "The senator Wesley works for, I know him. His name is James Fowler. He's a human. Nicolono had me investigate him a couple of years ago. He's one of those that thinks the government should control every aspect of the world. Scary guy. I'm surprised he got elected."

Ramsey shook his head. "If Nicolono hired you, then this senator is probably the human at the core of our problem."

"Yep." Magnus handed the papers over to Ladon. "Sorry I didn't put it together until now."

Ramsey just waved his hand, dismissing Magnus' apology. "I need to know what their next move is. We need to get ahead of this and quickly before they make a move that could hurt the clan."

Magnus nodded. "I'll leave in a few hours." He met Ladon's gaze as if asking permission.

"You can leave whenever you want, Magnus." He didn't have to like it, but there wasn't much he could do. Magnus was good at his job and Ladon didn't have a right to keep him from it. At least not yet. When he finally shifted, and they bonded, Ladon would have a few things to say about Magnus going alone. Ladon had never liked that aspect.

Magnus grinned and never said a word.

Ladon turned his eyes to the papers in his hand. "Stop it."

"I didn't say anything." And there was the humor in Magnus' tone again.

"You didn't have to."

Magnus just chuckled.

"I'm not bossy."

That just made Magnus laugh even harder, which probably meant he didn't mind the bossiness very much.

Chapter One

Magnus Bridger tapped a finger on the steering wheel. The morning sun hadn't quite made it over the horizon, so the streetlights still illuminated the sidewalk.

He parked on the curb in front of a small yellow house.

All the houses were similar except for the colors. They looked as though some grandmother cut them out of sugar cookie dough and placed them on the street all pretty before decorating them. They were all square, one-story buildings with manicured lawns.

The neighborhood catered to the working-class set. Working-class people who came home every day from a foundry. They took a shower and ate dinner while they watched a game show on television.

Wesley Swenson's house was four up from the yellow one on the right. A light was still on in one of the two windows Magnus could see from his vantage point.

Wesley was a creature of habit. Most people were, even paranormals. Routine was what made the world go around. Or so it seemed. It was also what made people complacent and open to criminalization.

Not that Magnus planned on doing anything but snoop around inside. Still, breaking and entering was a crime punishable by jail time, not that he'd get caught. He broke into houses enough to be good at it.

It surprised Magnus that someone like Wesley Swenson, who worked for a politician, would live in the neighborhood. Not that he knew how much a politician's assistant made per year. He hadn't researched that information because he didn't feel as if it were pertinent to his investigation. He clearly didn't live above his means, which made him responsible with his money.

The house wasn't even empty yet, and already his heart lodged in his throat just thinking about getting out of the car.

He picked up his phone and dialed Ladon's direct number. Just talking to him would help calm Magnus.

It rang three times before he answered, which was odd. Usually, Ladon answered after the first ring. What was even odder still was the fact that he was out of breath. "You okay."

"I'm better now." The affection came through in every syllable he spoke. "Head injury."

Magnus stiffened and, instead of the calm he wanted to achieve, his lungs seized. "Fuck." By the gods.

"I'm fine. Well, I am now. I shifted right before the battle. That probably saved me from a bigger injury."

Shit. "It happened? Nicolono finally struck?"

"Yeah. We almost lost, but Wingspan and the council saved our asses at the last minute. The bear enforcers probably saved us the most. They all think Fane is the god of swords or something. Fane is one fierce little vampire. They aren't wrong about that."

Magnus let out a breath and rubbed at his chest as if relieving the ache. "I want to come home. Be with you."

"I want that too. More than anything." Ladon's voice got a husky quality Magnus hadn't ever heard before. And then he got all growly. "Just finish the job. You'd feel like shit if the humans did something to paranormals while you were home."

The only thing that would have made him feel like shit was if Ladon had gotten hurt irreparably and Magnus was off breaking into some political asshole's house. "I don't care about all that. My best friend got hurt."

"You just feel bad for not being here." Yeah, that too but Magnus wouldn't confirm or deny it. He must have been quiet too long because Ladon said, "Magnus."

"What?"

Ladon just chuckled, and that was enough for them both to know the truth. "You gonna talk or are we gonna sit in silence for the rest of the phone call?"

"What color is your dragon?"

"Bright green. I look like a giant tree."

Magnus chuckled. "I doubt that. I bet you're pretty."

"Dragons aren't pretty."

"Your human form is." Everything about Ladon was pretty, even his wide shoulders and his height. All that dark hair that curled around his neck, and green eyes with blue flecks in them added to his attractiveness.

Magnus hadn't allowed himself to think of Ladon in those terms for so long it felt foreign. In a lot of ways Ladon was still very young. He might've been twenty years' old and, with his first shift out of the way, he was physically ready to bond, but none of that changed Ladon's maturity level. And it didn't change the fact that Magnus had gotten comfortable with the friendship they had cultivated.

It wasn't the time to have the conversation, so h
phone call. "I have to go."

The light in Wesley Swenson's house flicked off, adding to
darkness outside. The garage door went up a second later, and Wesley's
car pulled out, backing onto the street.

"Can I call you tonight?"

"I'll call you. I need to report back to Ramsey anyway."

"Be safe."

"I will."

"One more thing."

Magnus smiled. "What?"

"I shifted. You realized what that means, right?"

His heart beat a wild rhythm for a completely different reason other
than being nervous. "Yeah. I know."

Wesley Swenson's house wasn't exactly Fort Knox. Magnus decided
to go in through the back door which led into the garage. It was locked
but had one of those nubby door handle locks that turned in the
center. It took less than a minute to get inside.

Magnus had a small flashlight that lit up just enough of the garage
for him to see it was like any other. There were shelves against the back
wall with boxes lining the top. Wesley kept gardening tools haphazard-
ly lying on the middle shelf within reach. Given the manicured flower
beds, he must've liked to garden.

There were no other tools lying around, so apparently Wesley
wasn't Mr. Fix It.

Magnus tried the door leading into the house, expecting it to be
locked, but the knob turned easily. The door led into the kitchen. The
room was as normal as the garage. Clean except for the mug sitting on
the counter next to the sink.

Magnus clicked his flashlight off and ducked when he passed in front of the window over the sink. He didn't want to risk being seen by nosy neighbors.

The kitchen opened up into the living room. A hallway went to the right. Magnus decided to check that out first. He sucked in a breath when he looked into the first door on the right, which stood open. Wesley had covered the walls with cut-out newspaper articles and pictures.

Magnus decided to start on the wall right inside the door. Wesley had taped an article about a giant bird next to the light switch. An altered picture accompanied the article. The picture contained a drawing of some half-reptile, half-fowl type creature. The human who had seen the creature, saw a dragon shifter but didn't know jack crap about paranormals, so they made something up in their head about feathers and pre-historic birds.

With cameras and cell phones in every person's hand around the world, it was only a matter of time before real photographs, and video evidence came about. Hell, there was already, but not enough for most to believe it. The pictures Wesley had accumulated certainly spoke the truth.

Wesley had other photographs as well. As Magnus scanned the next wall, the dragon shifter articles and pictures turned to vampires. One in particular caught Magnus' attention because the vampire in the picture had been a part of Nicolono's coven. His name had been Gary, and he'd died a few years ago trying to capture Lucas, the only male witch in existence. Neither Magnus nor Lucas had been part of the Saint Lakes clan then. In the photograph, Gary leaned over a human female as if to kiss her. The photographer had taken the photo from a higher vantage point, probably a window in an apartment building a few floors up, so the distance was noticeable, but Gary's fangs could still be seen, even in the dim street lighting.

The frozen moment of time was the exact reason why single vampires kept bloodwhores or bagged blood.

The next section involved warlocks. How someone had managed to capture a warlock inside a dome on camera, Magnus would never know, but there it was in full color. The warlock inside was a blond male who wore glasses and a fedora hat. He appeared human down to the way he dressed. An unsuspecting human might've considered him just like them.

The next photo was of a warlock with a flame in the center of his palm. The warlock stared at the flame with wide-eyed fear that told Magnus his story better than words. Humans had raised the poor warlock, so he'd probably discovered his magic by accident.

The next wall had a picture of a small paranormal town. The town could have been any human town anywhere with the normalcy of it, if not for the bobcat walking along the side of the road and the two hawks circling above it. Given the fact that the shifters in the pictures were a mixed bunch, there was a likely possibility other types of paranormals besides shifters belonged to the town's clan as well.

He pulled his phone out of his pocket and snapped a picture before turning to the other walls. He sent them to Ramsey right away with a message stating where he'd taken them. Ramsey would put two and two together and come up with the fact that most humans might think Wesley was a crazy fanatic but, given who Wesley worked for, his evidence proved dangerous.

Magnus turned to the desk that sat in the center of the room. There was nothing on it but a pad of paper and a pen. He turned the pad around and read what, presumably Wesley had written. Wesley had scribbled Virgil Tiago and Delano Archer's names.

Magnus recognized both names immediately. He took a picture of the notepad and sent it to Ramsey.

Virgil Tiago was Fane's father, and Fane was Ramsey's mate. Magnus hadn't met him yet, but Ladon had talked about him. The way Magnus understood it, Virgil was an asshole who had sold Fane to human scientists. And Delano was the brains behind Nicolono going rogue on Saint Lakes. Both vampires knew about the human experiments if Wesley knew enough to write their names down, and that made them part of the problem.

Magnus left the room, making his way back the way he had come. He'd seen enough to know he needed to find out if his hunch about Senator Fowler was true. If someone as influential as the senator was involved, the situation had gone from bad to worse.

It was one thing for some weirdo scientist to experiment on paranormals as long as they did it behind the backs of all the major movers and shakers. Magnus could've chalked it up to human curiosity, even if the scientists experimenting were assholes who hurt people. But if the human government was involved in any way, that changed the game.

Chapter Two

L adon Somerset could feel his mother's eyes on him as he lifted his coat from the hooks to the right of the back door. He felt her watchful gaze in his bones. She gave him the Mom look, with her eye narrowing and his lips pursing.

"Where are you going?" Mom pointed a wooden spoon at him. "You don't need to see the carnage outside."

Ladon put a boot on before he replied, "I helped make that mess. I can help clean it up." He slipped on his other boot.

Mom put the spoon back into the pot and stirred whatever it was she'd made. For once, she'd created a good smell, which told him she'd cooked a meal, instead of bubbling up some spell. Her spells held the worst odors.

"It's not spilled milk. You're picking up the dead."

Yeah, Ladon was well aware. Regardless, he still needed to help. "I'm part of the clan."

"You're newly shifted. You may not be able to control your reaction. Bennett had trouble after he shifted."

Ladon wasn't Bennett.

He had a hand on the door handle when he met her gaze. "I can smell the blood from upstairs in my room. I could probably smell it from three miles away, and so can every other shifter. I'm fine."

It wasn't the smell of blood that urged him outside to help, but that of decay. He would upset her if he told her that, though.

The odor had set in over the last few hours until it covered every molecule of air. His shifter senses had kicked in with his first shift, so even though the bodies weren't quite twenty-four hours old, he could still smell the rot beginning.

Mom sighed. "As long as you promise to come in if it gets to be too much."

And that was the real reason she didn't want him to go out there. She worried about him breaking down.

"Okay, Mom. I promise." It might've been hard for him, but it was harder for those who had lost family members and close friends. Their clan might have been small, and they were all grieving, but some had lost more than others. He was one of the lucky ones because his family remained intact. Gabriel had sustained a major injury, and Fane had almost died, but both would recover. So many couldn't say that.

And what about the vampires? They were Saint Lakes' enemy, but not everyone's. Someone out there cared about them.

The aftermath would leave more than physical scars for far too many on both sides.

Ladon pulled the door open and was about to step out, but her next words stopped him. "You're stronger than Garridan and Ramsey. You realize that, don't you?"

Ladon sighed and shut the door again. "I know." He closed the distance between them, holding out his hand for her to take. Sometimes having a witch for a mother made his inner turmoil shit a lot easier to explain, and he wasn't one who kept things from his mom.

He allowed her to see what he thought of being Alpha. It could mean pissing people off. Not every decision was a popular one. And he certainly didn't want to take the position away from Ramsey, who was a good leader.

Mom's forehead wrinkled when her eyebrows drew together and then she smiled. "You'll make a good Alpha. And don't worry about Ramsey. He'll do what's right."

She let go of his hand and turned back to the stove, returning to her pot.

The sour smell of bodies breaking down proved so much stronger outside. He put his hand over his nose and mouth before getting a good look at the backyard.

A lump formed in his throat, bringing tears to his eyes. Nothing had prepared him for the sight of so much death littering the ground. Not the smell from inside or fighting the battle hours before.

The warm spring air had defrosted the soil underneath the dead, turning everything to mud, even the few bits of visible dirt and trampled grass. Body fluids seeped into the ground, mixing with the dirt past the permafrost. It created a cancer, growing into boils under the earth's surface.

There was a grayness to the entire scene that he couldn't see with the naked eye, but he felt it deep within his soul. The cloud wove its way through everything and everyone, even those living and helping clean up the carnage. It wrapped around all of them, dragging them down until nothing remained but numbness.

Except Ladon's presence was new so the numbness hadn't quite taken hold and he didn't want it to. He wanted to feel, even if the ache in his stomach reached his heart and squeezed it until he bled internally.

He couldn't lose what pieces of empathy he had because he had helped create the carnage. He could justify it as self-defense, and that was warranted, but he'd still made a living, breathing individual dead. He couldn't take that back, so he wouldn't let the cloud wrap him up in numbness.

Several of the Wingspan clan were still around, helping to clean up and so were the bear enforcers. It warmed something inside Ladon to see them helping during the aftermath as well, although their help during the battle had been enough.

Kristin and Josh lifted the body of a vampire over to a pile. For mates who had rejected each other for years before bonding, they certainly worked well together.

What would become of them, Ladon didn't know, but they were all stacked together as if they meant nothing.

Something about that didn't sit well with Ladon, and he growled. Kristin met his gaze. Her eyes widened as if Ladon had directed the growl at her specifically. She dropped her gaze, turning her head to the side, giving over to his dominance.

Josh looked from her to Ladon before following Kristin's lead.

He wanted to tell them both to knock off the submissive pose, but he didn't because Mom's point about him being an Alpha still sat in his belly.

Nothing stopped his eyes from shifting, not even the tears that gathered.

His hands shook, so he put them in his coat pockets. It probably seemed as if he did it because he was cold, which was fine. Whatever. The lie worked. Instead of addressing their behavior and his own, he closed the distance between them and asked, "How can I help?"

Kristin shook her head and scowled. "Uh…why are you asking me?"

Ladon sighed. He knew what she meant. She was ready to take orders from him and didn't understand why he wasn't leading. Or rather, her eagle didn't understand. "I'm not your Alpha."

"You're the only Alpha out here right now. And you clearly have a problem with how we're doing things, so you tell me."

Ladon averted his gaze. "Sorry. Dragon's going nuts for a couple of different reasons."

"By the gods, little brother. Just lead."

Ladon was surprised to see Tim there helping. Tim had a body across his shoulder and must have heard the conversation because he stopped halfway to the vampire pile and turned to face them. He seemed to wait for Ladon's direction as well.

Ladon sighed and pulled his hands out of his pockets. "Fine. Line them up." He pointed to a spot where the field beyond met the edge of the yard. "Put them in the field. They may have families who will want to put them to rest. We need to honor that."

"Yes, Alpha." She smirked at him, trying to lighten the mood by teasing, but nothing could do that under the circumstances.

She and Josh took the body to where he'd indicated without a fuss. Tim led the way.

Damian, Owen's mate, picked up a clan member and slung him over a shoulder as if they were a sack of onions. "Where do you want the dead clan members, Alpha?"

Damian was a stranger, having swooped in and saved Owen's life during the battle. No one knew him very well, and that included Ladon. The only thing Ladon knew was that Damian had defected from Nicolono Stavros's coven around the time Forrest's mate, Angel, had.

"It's Ladon, and in any clear spot inside the yard. Mom has a spell on the yard still, so the clan can come inside the perimeter but the vampires who want to collect their dead can't." Ladon pointed to one side.

Damian shrugged as if he didn't care about the explanation. He did what Ladon commanded, nonetheless.

Ladon wanted to take exception to his lack of emotion but didn't know him well enough to know if he buried the emotion or honestly didn't feel it.

Owen seemed to think it was the latter if the look on his face was any indication.

The last time Ladon had seen them together, they'd been cuddled up on a bed all cozy, while Ladon had nursed a head wound that had left him in a bad mood. He didn't have a clue how things between the two mates had turned sour so quickly.

Owen's lips turned up in disgust as he watched Damian carry the body across the yard. Owen had the feet of a vampire and walked backward while Vaughan carried the head. "He's such an unfeeling jerk."

He might have mumbled, but everyone heard. They were all paranormals with powerful senses, although Ladon was still getting used to his.

"I feel something for you." Damian didn't stop what he was doing but flung the body down with little finesse. He turned and picked up another closest to him.

"Well maybe I don't want you to," Owen yelled across the yard. They put the body next to the others and started across it again.

"Too fucking late." Damian's eyes glowed blue, and he grinned, showing his fangs.

"Can you be more careful with the bodies? Sheesh." Owen rolled his eyes.

"They're dead. It's not like they can feel it." Damian bent down and picked up another. He was a damn machine.

"You're a psychopathic creep."

"Keep calling me names." Damian grinned. "I like it."

Ladon decided to intervene. "Owen." He waved him over.

Ladon met Vaughan's gaze as Owen made his way across the yard, stepping over bodies as he closed the distance. Vaughan gave him a smile that didn't meet his eyes. There wasn't a teasing quality to it but rather a weariness, as if he were soul-deep tired but couldn't bring himself to go inside.

Ladon understood. "I'll be over to help in just a sec."

Vaughan nodded and waited with his arms wrapped around his middle.

Owen stood in front of him, grabbing his attention. "What?"

"Will you go find Forrest and tell him to call the council? They might be able to help us locate the vampires' families."

Owen nodded and walked past him to the house. He gave Damian one last narrow-eyed stare.

Ladon shook his head at Owen's attitude but let it slip out of his mind as he got to work. Vaughan grabbed the feet of a body and waited for Ladon.

Ladon cleared his throat and shored himself up before grabbing onto limp arms. The flesh held the cold of winter that went to the bone, leaking to Ladon's palms. He had a sudden urge to let go and run back into the house. Instead, he looked down into the face of the dead.

The body belonged to a clan member. The woman was only a couple years older than Ladon and had been a cheerleader in high school. Ladon didn't remember much else about her, other than she had been pretty in a girl-next-door sort of way.

Her limp body hung between them. Her long dark hair brushed over the trampled grass and muddy wetness. Gravity pulled her head down, exposing her neck as if she'd submitted to death.

Ladon met Vaughan's gaze. "I had econ class with her in high school."

"It doesn't get any easier."

Chapter Three

Wesley Swenson plastered a fake smile on his face when the outer door opened. When it came to politics, everyone faked something, and everyone lied. They all told themselves they sinned for the betterment of the people.

Even Wesley did what he had to do to keep the senator's campaign money flowing, which was why he pretended to welcome Dr. Perkins' leer.

There was nothing about the smug little turd Wesley liked. It wasn't even the better-than-everyone attitude or the fact he always came in and demanded Wesley bring him a latte. It was the way he always spoke about God in some way as if silently calling Wesley a sinner for being gay right after he finished flirting.

Wesley had penciled Dr. Perkins into the senator's schedule last week and even then his stomach bit at his guts.

"Dr. Perkins. The senator is expecting you. You may go in whenever you'd like." *And get away from me*, was what he wanted to add but didn't.

Dr. Perkins came around Wesley's desk, standing about a foot away, trying to intimidate him.

Wesley moved his chair back and stood. His skin crawled underneath his clothing, making him itch.

Then Dr. Perkins licked his lips. Dr. Perkins was even more dangerous than that lizard bird he had seen as a child. That thing had picked him up and flew him several feet before putting him down again. He had bruises on his arms for days afterward.

Wesley didn't wait for Dr. Perkins to harass him further, not that he ever took it to the next level, but he wasn't about to stand there.

Wesley went around the other side of his desk. As far away as possible. "Coffee?"

"Latte. Yes."

Wesley gave the guy another fake smile. "Right away, sir."

The senator's office door opened and out walked Senator Fowler with a flourish. "Wesley, Coffee."

"Yes, sir."

Senator Fowler held out his hand to Dr. Perkins with a smile.

The doctor took it, shaking it before letting go.

"To what do I owe your visit?"

"I'm here to chat. If you have the time, that is."

"Of course. You paid to get me here. The least I can do is chat." The senator smiled at his joke. Wesley had worked for the senator for three years, and he had never once heard him laugh.

"I paid for you to enact legislation. I'm building you an army. You're supposed to do the rest."

Wesley didn't know what the doctor meant by *building an army,* but he knew the doctor studied paranormals. It was all hush-hush secretive, but it wouldn't stay that way as soon as the doctor found a way for the humans to survive when the paranormals attacked. The senator had promised Wesley.

The coffee machine was one of those that did just about everything. It would make any drink he asked for, and everything was digital. He only had to learn which buttons to press in what order. There had been a booklet that had come with the machine. All Wesley had to do was read it and follow directions.

The senator had never touched the machine or poured himself a cup of coffee for as long as Wesley had worked for him.

"Changing legislation isn't an easy thing, Jeff." The senator probably said that with a smile on his face, although he couldn't say for sure with his back turned. He didn't have to see them to know the senator never showed negative emotions. The man could schmooze anyone into thinking he was all ears, listening to whatever crap they had to spew. But Dr. Perkins' comment had pissed him off. Wesley could tell by the way the senator used the doctor's first name.

He jumped when a hand touched him on his shoulder. Dr. Perkins stood behind him and to the right. "Are you going to stand there staring at the cup of coffee you made me, or can I drink it?"

Wesley wanted to roll his eyes but restrained himself. Instead, he picked up the full cup and handed it over. "My apologies. Daydreaming gets me sometimes."

One corner of Dr. Perkins' mouth turned up into what would have qualified as a smile but for the calculation in his eyes. "Forgiven."

Wesley just started on another cup of regular coffee for the senator, who was a no-frills type when it came to the drink.

"Shall we take our chat into my office?" The senator eyed Wesley as he put a hand to the center of Dr. Perkins' back, pushing him toward his office.

When Dr. Perkins turned his back, Wesley gave the senator a smile as a silent thank-you. The senator didn't acknowledge it in any way, which was fine by Wesley. He didn't expect it.

Wesley knocked on the senator's closed office door before entering. The black liquid sloshed against the sides of the cup when he moved. Wesley held his breath when he thought it would escape. When it stayed in its cage, he let out his breath, giving his lungs a break.

Wesley went through the door and to the senator's desk, setting the mug down.

"Pitting them against each other was my father's solution. I'm smarter and what I've learned is that paranormals have the same intelligence as humans, Senator."

"We can call them out. Wesley has collected plenty of evidence. We can certainly bring it to the media." The senator met Wesley's gaze. "You'd turn over your evidence, wouldn't you Wesley?"

"Whatever you need, sir." He'd do anything to keep himself away from those savages. Wesley put the coffee in front of the senator and turned.

Dr. Perkins shook his head. "Don't do anything yet. Not until I get the formula perfected."

Whatever went on in Dr. Perkins' lab wasn't a good thing for anyone, humans included. Wesley rather liked just telling everyone about paranormals and letting the chips fall where they may.

"We'd have sanctions. Laws put in place to protect humans from paranormals. If we told people." Yes, laws were what they needed.

Dr. Perkins sighed. "Let me do the thinking, James. You're not good at it."

Wesley rolled his eyes. He felt he could, considering his back was to both men. He wasn't in danger of getting caught.

"You pay me to think, Jeff."

"I pay you to do what I say. The money will stop flowing if you don't."

Wesley turned to see senator's expression. He held the door open and stood in the opening.

The senator sat forward with his arms folded on the desk inches away from the coffee cup as if he was praying to the coffee gods. "I have a working relationship with paranormals. Wealthy ones with more money than you. I'm certain one of them supplies your lab with the drugs you use on your little experiments." Vergil Tiago was the paranormal's name. He had his own agenda, which mostly included greed. He fed the senator's campaign and in turn the senator turned a blind eye to all the environmental wrongs his company did. It was a pretty basic arrangement. "I don't need your money, Jeff."

Dr. Perkins stiffened, the loss of power stinging. To his credit, he never said a word.

"I need your science. And on that note, I'll be taking a tour of the lab next week. I'd like to see your progress. You seem good at turning humans into vampires but you're failing with the shapeshifters. I'd like you to tell me why." Dr. Perkins opened his mouth to speak but the senator stopped him by raising a hand. "Next week, Jeff."

Dr. Perkins shut his mouth and nodded.

From the way the senator spoke, it was clear he had the upper hand. The senator always kept his cool and had several aces up his sleeve. "Wesley, you'll come with."

Wesley turned, meeting his gaze. He shook his head. "No, thank you, sir."

The senator gave him a knowing look. He smiled. "It wasn't a question."

Wesley swallowed. The senator knew he didn't want to see paranormals, even if they were held in captivity. He made Wesley go just to torment him.

Chapter Four

L adon carried the cordless landline phone around the house and had his cellphone in his pocket. He covered all the bases. Magnus should have called him a day ago. The fact that he hadn't left all kinds of worry and questions. The questions were too early to answer.

The lack of communication made Ladon's stomach turn into knots and a million speculations run through his mind.

All he wanted to do was bond the shit out of Magnus until they were both exhausted, but Magnus had become a phantom in Saint Lakes. Ladon could only imagine him in his world. Even his voice was a memory.

Ladon ran his thumb over the back of the phone. The plastic was cool to the touch because of being outside for so long.

The battle had made time stretch until the moments before and after separated on a string like photographs. Ladon had to walk miles to get to the ones with Magnus in them.

The clan fanned out across the yard. The battle had reduced the grass to a dirt pit, but the families had claimed their dead days ago. The paranormal council had claimed the enemy's dead. The mud was the last skeleton left.

Several clan members carried the battle in their injuries as well. Lynn Osmond carried black bruises on her cheek. Being a shifter, she should have healed days ago, but it wasn't a normal wound. Ladon wasn't a doctor and couldn't say what sort of internal injury she had but she'd taken more than just a punch. The side of her neck was also a mural of scars and mangled flesh. She was the worst one, but several others limped around.

Etgar Blackburn had a bite mark high on his neck that had scabbed over. He'd probably shifted a half dozen times, and the scar still hadn't faded. He also had crutches keeping him upright.

Ladon leaned into Ramsey, who stood next to him. "Why did you make Etgar come? Dude can barely stand."

Etgar had graduated high school with Ladon. The two weren't friends so much as acquaintances. In a clan as small as Saint Lakes, rumors spread like lightning strikes in a storm, and he had certainly heard the ones about Etgar floundering a bit since graduation. Etgar was as big as a wolf shifter came and had muscles for days. He had been the stuff of legend in high school. Good at every sport and smart. The rumors suggested he had a drug problem—some drug shifters were getting addicted to. Ladon figured the rumors were false. There was something else going on with him and whatever it was, Etgar kept the truth close to his chest.

"I didn't make him. He insisted." Ramsey winced and pulled Fane into his side. "He lost his brother in the battle."

Ladon winced. "Shit. Okay." Etgar and Chuck had been closer than siblings. Ladon didn't remember a time when those two weren't together. They were close in age and for shifters that wasn't always the case. Ladon and his brothers had decades separating them, although that had more to do with being adopted than anything else. Still, some shifters waited years between births.

Ladon walked over to where Vaughan sat on a lawn chair. "I need the chair. Can you get up, please?"

He thought for sure Vaughan would argue, but he just nodded. He stood before folding the chair and handing it over to Ladon. "Giving it to Etgar?"

Ladon smiled. "Yeah. Dude looks miserable."

Vaughan nodded. "He fought hard, though. He was good at it, considering he doesn't have any experience."

"Natural ability, maybe."

"Maybe. You'll probably have to push him into fighting after this, though."

Ladon would have to push him? Ladon wouldn't push anyone into anything. He didn't have that in him. He wasn't a bossy dick. And even if he were, it wasn't his place because he wasn't the Alpha. "You mean Ramsey will have to."

"I mean you."

"Why me?"

"Just wait and see." Vaughan gave him a knowing smile and folded his arms over his chest.

Ladon rolled his eyes. "Whatever. Keep your damn secrets."

Vaughan chuckled but otherwise didn't say anything, which was weird considering Vaughan normally couldn't keep his mouth shut. He always had a comeback for everything. Vaughan must have figured out why Ramsey had called the meeting.

Well, Ladon had his theories too. He would bet money Ramsey intended to step down as Alpha, which meant Ladon would become leader.

He sighed.

He wasn't ready. He knew it even if no one else did. Shifters and their damn instincts. They all felt his strength, pegging him as an Alpha, but never once considered whether he was ready for the role.

He didn't even have a proper job, and wasn't that something he needed to be a bona fide adult? Shouldn't he pay his own bills first? He still lived at home with his mother. And yeah, okay, maybe the rest of his siblings did too, but that was out of necessity because of the battle. They'd all move back to their own homes at some point. Bennett and Lucas already had.

Vaughan must have sensed his stress because he grabbed Ladon around the shoulders and pulled him into a hug. Ladon put the chair down, leaning it against the side of the house.

"How did you know?" Ladon whispered so only Vaughan could hear, although he strongly suspected Bennett, who sat with Lucas in the chair next to them, heard every word.

"That Ramsey's about ready to announce he's stepping down?"

"Yeah."

"Ramsey doesn't have it in him to be Alpha. Never has. He fights to keep calm most of the time. Now that he's mated with Fane, he won't be able to take the responsibility."

Ladon pulled away. "And you think I will." He met Bennett's gaze. He gritted his teeth. His eyes shifted to his dragon. "I'm too fucking young, and you all know it."

Bennett raised one eyebrow and shifted his own eyes, not liking Ladon's challenge. Ladon didn't know why he'd directed it at Bennett in the first place. "You have a lot to learn. I'll agree with you there."

"What if I suck at it and get kicked out of the clan?" There, his main fear was out.

"You're bringing a clan member a chair because he's injured. You're already off to a good start, so stop worrying." Lucas curled into Bennett and never opened his eyes as he spoke.

Vaughan gripped the back of Ladon's neck, patting him twice before letting go. "You'll do great, Alpha."

By the gods, the title held more maturity than Ladon had. He was mature enough to admit that, if only to himself. "Not Alpha yet. Not until Ramsey announces it."

"Well, he's about to, so brace yourself." Vaughan let him go.

Ladon sighed and picked up the chair again, walking it over to Etgar. Etgar immediately dropped his gaze, tilting his head to the side in submission.

Ladon sighed. One shift and everyone in the clan saw him differently. He'd gone from Ladon the youngest Somerset to Alpha. How the ever-loving fuck did that even happen? "You don't have to do that, man. Seriously."

"Can't help it. My wolf demands it. You know how us wolf shifters are. Giving over to the hierarchy of the clan is in our DNA." Etgar met Ladon's gaze with a smile.

Ladon unfolded the chair and set it on the lawn. He shook it just enough to make sure it was relatively level before gesturing to it.

"Thanks."

Ladon took the guy's crutches in one hand and kept a steadying hold on his arm as he hopped around on one foot, maneuvering himself. When he sat down, Ladon placed the crutches at Etgar's feet. "If you need anything holler. Don't try to do everything yourself."

Ladon began to make his way back to Ramsey, but Etgar's next words stopped him in his tracks. "I'm used to it, but thanks."

Ladon turned to meet his gaze again. "What do you mean?"

"I live by myself. Well, I lived with my brother but he..." Etgar averted his gaze.

Ladon sensed any kind touch would break Etgar into a million pieces. Etgar didn't seem like the type to give over to his emotions willingly, so instead of a comforting touch, he said, "You should stay here. I can go and get whatever you need from your place. Clothes and shit, but you need help while you recover."

Etgar waved a big, dark hand at Ladon. "I don't want to impose."

"No imposition."

Etgar nodded. "If you're sure, Alpha."

No point in fighting the Alpha comment. If he made a bigger deal out of it than he had already, he'd give away his unease to the entire clan, and that wasn't what he wanted right before Ramsey made the big announcement. "I'm sure."

Ramsey began talking, so Ladon hurried across the yard to stand behind him.

"The people we buried, sacrificed themselves so we could live, and I will forever be grateful." Ramsey cleared his throat before continuing. "I can't say we'll never have another battle. We're still caught in the middle of a much bigger war that hasn't even begun escalating yet. We all need to stay vigilant and fight when the time comes. I'll be fighting next to you. I promise you that. Just not as your Alpha."

Ladon sucked in a breath and held it. Even though he knew it was coming, hearing the words aloud threw him off. The whole clan went for a whirl none of them wanted.

His lungs screamed, and still, he couldn't manage to make his body do what was natural. He knew what was coming next.

The clan met Ramsey's comment with complete silence as if the words hadn't registered right away. And then they all spoke at once.

Ramsey continued after someone let out a high-pitched whistle. "Ladon will take my place. Because he's so young, I'll be close at hand for everything. Garridan will, as well. We'll be his betas for the time being, and when he's comfortable leading, he can hold a challenge or pick others if he chooses. If he wants us to stay on indefinitely, we're both willing to do that as well. The transition will go as smoothly as possible."

Ladon heart beat a high-speed chase.

"If you're stepping down, shouldn't we all get a chance at the Alpha position," Tim met his gaze. The corners of his mouth turned up and he winked at Ladon as if wanting to ease his worries. Maybe Tim could read Ladon's mind or maybe he just saw Ladon's and worried about the clan. Regardless of the reason for the comment Ladon welcomed it. And Tim did have a point. The Alpha position should be earned, not blindly turned over as if the Somersets were royalty. Every clan might have seemed like a dictatorship, but that wasn't the case. They might not have a voting system like humans, but they had ways of picking leaders.

Ladon smiled at Tim and nodded his thanks before taking in every member of the clan. He stood with hands clasped behind his back, trying to give off a feeling of calm authority even if he didn't feel it. "A challenge isn't appropriate. Not today after so many of us need time to grieve properly. We'll hold a challenge six months from now. Ramsey will stay Alpha until that date. The winner of the challenge will take over." Ladon met Tim's gaze again. "Satisfied?"

"Thanks for that, asshole. Six months? It'll feel like six years," Ramsey whispered back.

Regardless if Ladon wanted to be Alpha or not, Ramsey needed him, so he'd be there.

Ladon smirked. "Serves you right for throwing me out there like that. Not gonna do jack crap without talking to Magnus anyway." If Magnus ever came home.

Ladon willed his phone to ring.

Ladon heard the roar of motorcycle engines from far off. He knew Garridan's friend Rocky and his crew stayed at Forrest's cabins. They hadn't been formally introduced to the clan yet, although they had come to dinner a few days ago to meet the family.

Fane and Ramsey clung together, completely ignoring the continued closeness of that roar.

"They're here for a formal introduction." Ladon thought maybe pointing that out would get Ramsey to pay attention to something else besides Fane.

"Take care of that, will ya?" Ramsey rubbed his cheek across the top of Fane's head.

"What!" Ladon rolled his eyes and started around the side of the house. Ramsey would boss him around for the next six months. "Damn it."

When Ladon came around front, Rocky dismounted his bike. He had a bandana around his head and a leather coat on, with chaps. What a total bad ass. Sully and Bandos did too, but Rocky gave off an air of authority along with it.

"I totally want a motorcycle, man. Seriously."

Rocky chuckled, meeting his gaze. "You look like you can handle it."

Ladon smirked. "Of course, I can."

"I can hook you up."

"Cool." Ladon gestured with his head. "Come on. Formal intro for the clan and all that shit. Better to get it done."

Rocky nodded and took a couple of steps in Ladon's direction. Ladon turned, expecting them to follow but he saw Rocky stop and sniff the air where Ladon had stood. "Shit, kid. You're a strong one. I didn't notice during the battle."

Ladon sighed. "We were all kinda busy."

He was so over it already. The sooner everyone got used to the fact that he had finally shifted for the first time the better things would get.

He led them around the side of the house. Garridan gave them all one-armed bro hugs. Whenever Garridan hugged Ladon, it was with both arms meant to comfort, like a dad. And when Garridan hugged Sage, he wrapped his whole body around him, creating a cocoon.

Ladon smiled at the difference.

Ramsey cleared his throat, gaining Ladon's attention.

Ramsey's facial expression had Ladon realizing he hadn't met them yet. Ladon thought back to the dinner they attended and realized Ramsey and Fane had been at their cabin.

Ladon snorted out a laugh. All three men looked more like criminals than they did experienced investigators. All eyes turned to him, and he shrugged. "Ramsey looks like he wants to attack."

Ramsey growled and pulled Fane closer. If Ramsey had his way, Fane would wear him like clothing. "Strangers near my mate."

"They wouldn't be strangers if you would have been here a few days ago."

Garridan introduced them to Ramsey. "Ladon will be taking Ramsey's place as Alpha in the near future."

Rocky nodded. "Makes sense." Yeah, to everyone except for Ladon, apparently.

Chapter Five

Ladon drove, with Rocky in the seat next to him and Sully in the back. Escorting the new guys around in a car seemed wrong considering they could have taken those badass motorcycles, but at least this way they were able to talk.

Bandos would have come, but he was updating the computer system at home. Ladon knew as much about computers as the average person, which meant he could roam around on the Internet.

If there was ever someone who didn't give off the computer nerd vibe, it was Bandos. He had muscles on top of muscles and was as tall as every other dragon shifter out there, including Ladon. He had a baby face, though, and appeared even younger than Ladon. Ladon would've pegged him for around sixteen years' old if not for his size. Bandos was probably closer to Garridan's age.

All three of them had a quiet watchfulness as if they knew violence was right around the corner. They had seen a lot in their lifetime and remained guarded because of it. Ladon's protective instinct kicked in.

At the same time, they had a strength about them that spoke of how quickly they could kick ass.

"Is real estate your thing?"

Ladon chuckled. "Not hardly. Rock, paper, scissors with Ramsey and I won, so I get to drive you around, show you the town." Plus, Ramsey was far too into Fane to focus on anything clan-related, even something easy and fun like taking the new guys house-shopping.

"You won, huh. Seems like a shitty task to me." Sully had a red bandana over his long braids. He should have seemed like a mom doing housework, but somehow, the bandana made him even more badass.

"Naw. I like showing off my town." Plus, if he'd stayed home, he'd wait by the phone for Magnus. The worry killed him. And all he wanted to do was dial Magnus' cell number over and over until he finally picked up. That was a needy move, though.

"It's a pretty area. Nice place to finally settle down for a change." Rocky peered out of the window as he spoke, taking in the scenery.

Sully growled low in his throat. "You're the only one who wants to, boss."

"No one's making you stay." Every word Rocky spoke was through clenched teeth. They'd clearly had the conversation before if the pissed expression was any indication.

Sully snorted. "Like I'd leave you and Bandos. Fifty fucking years makes following your ass around every damn place a habit I can't break."

North Lake was on Rocky's side of the vehicle, so he had a nice view, what with the sun reflecting off the water and someone in a fishing boat with a line cast out. Ladon thought the fisherman might be Freda Calhoun. She worked nights at a hotel two towns over and had weekdays off most of the time. She enjoyed morning fishing on those days.

"Closer to sixty. Without an Alpha. Or a clan. Dragon shifters are as much a pack species as your kind, Sully."

"Don't stereotype based on my species. Not all wolf shifters want a pack or to settle down in one place."

Rocky turned in his seat so suddenly he would have startled Ladon if not for his scent changing. The anger flowed off him like a wave.

Ladon didn't mean to growl. It slipped out. Rocky's scent changed back just enough that the anger wasn't as threatening.

"Sorry, Alpha. I meant no disrespect." Rocky held his gaze down, tilting his head to the side. Being in the car made the gesture even more awkward than the situation was already.

"Nope. It's my fault. I reacted to your scent. It's hard to get used to the enhanced senses. Feels like a superpower."

"You could smell my anger?" Rocky's forehead wrinkled.

"Oh, yeah. It was unmistakable." So powerful a scent in overrode everything else inside the vehicle.

"Hm. Guess Ramsey was right to step down."

"What do you mean?" His eyes shifted back, and he lost the tension in his shoulders and back. He loosened his fingers on the steering wheel.

"Not everyone can smell emotions." Rocky gestured to Sully in the back with his thumb. "Wolf shifters have a superior sense of smell. And I think some cat shifters do too. But even they have a hard time with emotions. The fact that you can, makes you special."

Ladon wondered if that meant Ramsey would have stepped down regardless of meeting Fane. He hoped his nature hadn't forced Ramsey out of the position.

Strength got some shifters kicked out of clans. If Ramsey was any other kind of Alpha, that was what he'd do. Instead, Ramsey saw Ladon's strength as a benefit.

Ramsey was a good Alpha. He'd make a good second-in-command.

Instead of voicing his thoughts, he just said, "It's hard to get used to. The shifting and all the stuff that comes with it, I mean."

"I got your back, man."

"What he means is that he's as old as fuck and can talk you through a lot of the issues you might have." Sully's interpretation broke whatever tension was left over from their little argument.

Rocky chuckled at the same time he held up his middle finger above the seat. "Thanks for that, asshole."

"My pleasure. And why'd you get so pissed anyway?"

"Because my mate lives here. You riding me about staying feels like a threat to it." Rocky looked out of the window again. "Not that other things aren't threatening the mating already. Something is going on with him."

"Henri Carpentier." Henri had been to dinner when Rocky and his crew had come. The two of them had thrown sparks at each other that evening. "Henri's a turtle shifter. Older than me, so I don't know him that well. I only know he's super-smart. As in, he studies on purpose. He lives off a trust fund. His parents have a butt load of money, I guess. Henri's parents live in a big house on Dewey Lake, but they hardly ever come to clan meetings and Ramsey's never made them. Henri comes, though."

Ladon pulled into the driveway of a large cottage that he knew was for sale. It didn't have a sign in the yard because someone had stolen it last week and, Lana Graystone, the real estate agent, hadn't gotten around to putting it back up yet. There was no doubt in Ladon's mind it was high-schoolers trying to entertain themselves with a little petty crime because they were bored. Ladon had done the same thing when he was in high school.

The cabin belonged to a single man who had recently met his mate and moved in with her. Ladon had never been inside, but it was probably big enough for three grown shifters.

"Some Alphas make demands. Others don't." Rocky seemed interested in the house.

"I won't."

Rocky waved a hand even as he eyed a wooden fence that ran between two parcels of property. "It wasn't a judgment. Keep telling me about Henri." Rocky winced. "Please."

Ladon grinned. "Okay, like I said, I don't know much about him. Not really. He lives on the other side of this lake in a small cottage. Doesn't seem to have much to do with his parents. Seems like kind of a loner but Jules made friends with him." Ladon shrugged. "Jules could make friends with anyone, so that's not much of a ringing endorsement to the guy's social abilities. He's kind of awkward at clan meetings. Maybe he wants to be more social but doesn't know how."

Sully leaned forward and touched Rocky's shoulders, gaining his attention. "We said when one of us finds our mate we would stop our nomad lifestyle."

"Yep."

Sully moved to the door. "Then let's go look around. This could be the place for us."

The back door opened and then closed. Before Ladon knew it, Sully was standing at the front of the vehicle with his hands in his pants pockets.

Rocky let out a breath as if he were truly afraid Sully wouldn't stay with him.

"You three have a special bond."

"Yeah." That one word said more than anything could how much of a history they had. "Is this too far out for internet? Bandos will want Internet."

Ladon smiled. "I'll make sure you have Internet. And this isn't the only property for sale or rent. We can look at others."

"Nope. This'll do." Rocky got out and threw his arm around Sully's shoulder before walking to the edge of the water.

Ladon stayed in the vehicle, letting them have their moment. He wasn't trying to eavesdrop, but he couldn't help hearing their conversation.

Rocky pointed out across the water. "He's probably in one of those houses right now."

"Fly over and sniff him out." Sully's suggestion was a solid one, but for some reason, Ladon didn't think that was Rocky's style. He seemed the type to weigh every situation carefully before taking action.

"I need to find out why he has an issue with mating first."

"Need me to do some digging?"

"Yeah. It might be less of an issue later if you do the dirty work."

Ladon chuckled. There was no way it would matter if it were Rocky or one of his closest friends looking into Henri's past. It would still feel like an invasion of privacy, especially to a loner like Henri. But, whatever.

Chapter Six

Magnus sipped the gin and tonic he didn't like and pretended to be interested in the happenings around him. The gin burned his throat and tasted like what he imagined gasoline would taste like. His body instantly tried rejecting the liquid when his stomach churned. He had never been much of a drinker and didn't like bars overly much. Alcohol reminded him of his drunk mother.

He stood between two stools at the far end of the bar, leaning against it, facing the room. There weren't very many people in the place. Just the after-work crowd who needed to let the stress pour out of them one sip at a time.

Two clear groups separated the tavern. The blue collar, construction workers who probably worked on the site the next block over, and white-collar office personnel in business suits. He guessed that the construction workers didn't frequent the bar. They were only there because it was close. With the dark red wood tones and the top shelf liquor, the place screamed expensive.

Each little group seemed to hang around a table, spilling work-site secrets and bitching about asshole bosses.

Magnus turned again, facing the bar. He was one of two people not in a larger group. He gave the other loner the side-eye.

Wesley Swenson drank gin and tonic. It was the reason Magnus had ordered it. He figured the commonality might give him an automatic discussion topic.

He needed the guy's identification, which still hung clipped to his collar, and to do that he needed to get closer. Swenson had wiggled around enough that he had angled his ID card in such a way Magnus could see the magnetic strip on the back, but not much else. He hoped the card was work-related. Reason told him there was a high probability.

The emptiness of the bar meant Magnus couldn't just slide onto the barstool next to the guy. If he did, it would come off as Magnus wanting to take the guy somewhere and fuck. Magnus might not have liked bars, but he'd been in enough of them to know the etiquette. He'd also had to come on to a guy for information before. He wasn't above it. There were other, more platonic ways of getting what he wanted, and he'd grown accustomed to those since knowing Ladon.

If ever there was a person who didn't look as though they wanted to talk it was Swenson. It was a problem. One Magnus didn't have an immediate solution to.

Magnus wanted to snatch the ID from his lapel and run like hell, but that probably wouldn't work.

"Hard day?" He winced and inwardly cursed himself.

Swenson twirled the liquid around in his glass and gave Magnus a noncommittal noise.

"Me too, man." Maybe that lie would break the ice some. Magnus held up his drink. "Need this at the end of every long day."

Wesley held up his drink, giving him a weary smile. "Absolutely." He took a sip of his drink. "Lately, anyway."

"Boss bitchier than normal?"

Wesley chuckled. "No. About the same in that regard." Wesley studied Magnus for a full minute before standing and moving a seat closer. He opened his mouth to speak but then shut it again. He eyed Magnus before say anything. "You really want to hear about this?"

Magnus took a sip of his drink and fought the urge to make a face in disgust. "I'll tell you if you tell me. It's not therapy, but hey. Whatever works, right?"

Wesley smiled. "Right." He sighed. "Have you ever thought you knew someone and then they did something to scare you? On purpose."

Magnus shrugged. "I don't know. Maybe." Not really. Magnus was pretty good at reading people. He'd been around enough for human behavior to become predictable. He also wasn't naive enough to think someone was always on the up and up just because they had a kind word and a smile.

Wesley chuckled. "It shouldn't be so surprising. I work for a politician."

Magnus laughed. "Never trust a politician."

Wesley laughed harder, which gave Magnus the opening he needed to take the ID card. He reached over to undo the metal clip then stuffed it into his pocket.

Easy mark.

Magnus drained his glass and set it on the counter.

"What about you? Your boss?"

"I don't have a boss. Never have. I only like one person telling me what to do and that has nothing to do with work." Magnus grinned, thinking about the way Ladon fought his natural dominant tendency.

"One person telling...ooohhh. Right." Wesley chuckled again. "Completely understandable. Working for yourself must be nice."

"It is. I travel a lot, which sucks sometimes. Miss the boyfriend something terrible. Other than that, it's all good." The best way to lie was to tell just enough of the truth. That way there was less to remember.

"What do you do?"

Magnus' phone chose that moment to ring, which was a good thing. He didn't know what part of the truth he'd tell Wesley anyway. He smiled and pulled his phone out of his pocket. Looking at the screen, he noticed it was someone from the Somerset house, so either Ramsey or Ladon finally got pissed off enough to call.

Magnus winced just thinking about Ladon with his feelings hurt. He just hadn't had a free second.

"I have to take this." Magnus didn't wait for Wesley to respond. Instead, he answered. "I'm sorry, baby. I was gonna phone later."

"That's great, but I think Ladon would be pissed if he heard you call me baby." Ramsey had a bit of rare humor in his voice.

Magnus didn't even realize he used an endearment until he said the word. "Sorry. Hold on just a second."

"Sure."

Magnus moved the phone down, away from his mouth. "Nice meeting you, man."

"Nice meeting you too. My name is Wesley Swenson. Look me up."

Magnus knew damn well Ramsey had heard. Wesley had just made the conversation with Ramsey that much easier.

Magnus nodded once and turned toward the door. He didn't speak until he was all the way outside with the door closed firmly behind him. "Wesley's definitely caught up in something. He's not the leader of the charge. I think he works for the senator because he's the only one who would listen to his paranormal bullshit."

"Makes sense." Ramsey chuckled. "What's next?"

"I need to get into the senator's office. See what I can find out there. I'm hoping to finish after that, but we'll see where the information takes me."

"You won't be able to stay gone much longer. And I'll talk to you later. Ladon's standing over me, growling, which has to tell you something as I'm still the Alpha."

Magnus chuckled, but the laugh died when Ladon spoke. "You didn't call." Every word came out on a growl.

"I know. I'm sorry. I get caught up in the job. Found out a lot—"

"Look, if you don't want to be with me just say it straight."

Magnus sucked in a breath. "Where the hell did that come from?"

"As far as I'm concerned our relationship moved way out of the friend zone when I shifted."

Well, Magnus hadn't been around for that, so as far as he was concerned, they had a few things to talk about before changing things. Instead of stating that, he tried to end the conversation. "I have a job to do, Ladon."

"The next time you don't call, I'm coming to get you. I'll drag your ass back to Saint Lakes."

"Okay, one. Giving me an order is one thing, threatening me is another. And two. You don't need to come here. You'll slow me down." Magnus had parked down the block and around the corner. He made his way in that direction almost on autopilot.

Ladon didn't speak. Magnus would have thought the call had dropped if not for the breathing on the other end. "You don't want me."

"To come get me. Like I said, you'll slow me down."

"Fine. Forget me coming then. I'll send someone else."

Magnus stopped, his hand on the handle of the car he'd rented. He sighed and shook his head. "I didn't mean it that way."

Magnus was so focused on the conversation he didn't pay attention to everything around him. Something hit him on the head. He fell to the pavement, sprawling on his stomach. His hands and knees burned from the friction of the impact. His cell phone skidded across the pavement, stopping feet away by the front tire of his car. He could hear Ladon yelling, but he couldn't concentrate on that. Or alleviate Ladon's fear.

Instead, he turned onto his back just in time to see a woman standing over him with a knife in her hand. She had been in the bar, sitting with the rest of the white collars, sipping on a glass of what appeared to be wine. She had seemed like every other office worker until she didn't. Magnus had met assassins before, and she very much was one.

Her suit hiked up to mid-thigh as she straddled his waist.

He didn't care about anything but the knife making a fast track to his heart. By the time he grabbed her wrist, it was almost too late. The tip sank into his skin. He cried out at the pain.

It took everything in him to pull her away when he should have been able to overpower her easily. She smelled like a human, so her strength was extra.

He bent her wrist back. The knife slid across his skin, opening him up. He hissed at the burn.

His fangs dropped. He could suddenly see every vein underneath her skin. The one in her neck pumped faster when he vamped out.

She cried out when her wrist snapped. The knife left his skin, *clinking* to the pavement next to him.

He changed his focus, grabbing her throat. Letting out a roar, he pushed her off him. He expected her to come at him again, but she ran. He took off after her but couldn't keep up.

Given how much faster he was compared to a human, it should have been easy to catch her. She wore high-heeled shoes as well, so that alone should have slowed her down. Unfortunately, she kept one step ahead of him until she turned a corner where he lost her.

He stopped, catching his breath before he turned to make his way back to his car.

"What the hell, Magnus? Are you okay?" The fact that Ladon had remained on the phone was a small miracle.

Before answering Magnus had to control his breathing. "Just give me a second."

"Okay. Take your time. I'm here." The change in Ladon's tone was unmistakable, and it eased Magnus' nerves more than the words.

Pressing the lock on the car door was more of an afterthought than anything else. He should get his ass out of there, but he couldn't make himself move. He rested his head on the back of his seat as he closed his eyes, trying to calm his nerves.

He took a deep breath in through his nose and let it out through his mouth. His hand shook when he tried to put the key in the starter. He managed to insert it and turned it right away. "I gotta get outta here."

"Get to safety. And then you'll tell me what happened." That command calmed Magnus. It made him feel less alone and he needed that during the adrenaline crash. "Don't hang up."

"Yes, Alpha." Magnus knew damn well the teasing would irritate Ladon and he needed the normalcy of it. He pulled out and headed to his hotel. He needed time to process what just happened.

"Keep that up, and I'll paddle you when you get home."

"Ooh, promise?" Magnus sobered almost as soon as the joke left his tongue. Talking to Wesley might just have been a mistake. Wesley had been followed, and the woman had pegged him for a paranormal. He didn't know how she knew, but she obviously did. She might be able to track him. "I might need to change hotels."

"You think someone is following you?" If Ladon was upset by the thought, it didn't come through in his tone. He was nothing but calm.

"I don't think so. I know I wasn't a target before talking to Wesley Swenson, but I think I just made myself one."

"Are you hurt?" There was a hint of stress in his voice, although he did a good job trying to hide it. Magnus knew Ladon too well, though.

"Just a scratch. I'm fine now." The incident had shaken him up a bit but nothing more.

"Come home."

"I'd like to go to the senator's office first." Since he had Swenson's identification in his pocket, he might as well use it.

"If you're not back here in three days I'm coming after you."

Just the thought of Ladon getting hurt sent Magnus' heart into his throat. "No."

Ladon growled. "And now we're right back to where we started."

Magnus sighed. "I'm sorry. I'm worried about something happening to you."

"How the hell do you think I feel? Do you even have any concept of what it was like hearing you scream and not knowing what the hell happened?"

Yeah, Magnus hadn't thought about it. "That had to suck."

"Yes. It did. So we're done fighting. You understand that?"

"Yes, Alpha." The second time he called Ladon Alpha, it wasn't meant to tease. He used it like a curse word.

"And another thing. I am your mate. Not your Alpha. Stop calling me that."

"Then start acting like my mate instead of my Alpha." His patience wore thin each time Ladon made a demand.

"Someone has to keep you alive."

"I'm a lot older than you, Ladon. I've been doing just fine on my own."

Ladon sucked in a breath. It was the only thing he heard for so long he thought Ladon hung up. "You still there?"

"Yes." That one word held more emotion than Magnus expected.

"I didn't mean that the way it sounded."

"I have to go."

"Ladon."

The line went dead, and anything he wanted to say to clarify matters were hung up in the silence.

Chapter Seven

Wesley's hands shook when the senator's driver pulled into the parking lot of a warehouse. The building had metal panels painted brown. The metal siding made up the top half of the building. Thick red bricks made up the bottom story. It seemed as if the building had big machines that made things like car parts or metal tools. In his mind, he'd pictured Dr. Perkins' laboratory as more of a hospital than a factory.

The senator sat beside him in the back seat of the town car reading over some legislation about the national healthcare system, which was currently in a sad state and would probably stay that way for a while longer. If Wesley knew anything from working with the senator, it was that politicians couldn't decide on anything collectively. Teamwork wasn't a word they knew.

Mark, the senator's driver, pulled the car around the back of the building. He parked next to another car. The vehicle was occupied by a driver and someone in the back who had a cell phone in his pale hand. The screen would have lit up his face if not for the sun drowning the light source. His dark hair and pale skin made him seem like the Hollywood version of a vampire.

When their gazes met, the man smiled. His eyes narrowed just enough for the gesture to come off as sinister. Wesley shrank back into the seat's leather and averted his gaze.

Wesley focused on his hands in his lap until he heard a car door close. The man in the other car walked to the gray metal door and knocked twice, waiting.

The senator set the papers on the seat between them. "We'll be at least an hour, Mark."

"Yes, sir." Mark shut off the car and unclicked his seatbelt. He opened his car door and got out, making his way around the car to the senator's door.

"Are there paranormals inside, sir?" The very thought of encountering one left his stomach in knots.

"You'll be fine, Wesley."

"Yes. Yes, of course." He needed to prepare himself for seeing them. If he didn't, he might freak in front of the senator. Showing him any more weakness than he already had wasn't a good idea. The senator was very good at exploiting someone's weaknesses when needed. He hadn't ever turned on Wesley, and he didn't expect it from the senator, but it was still a possibility Wesley would have been stupid to ignore.

Wesley breathed through the churning in his gut when the senator moved to exit the vehicle. The leather of the seat made a creaking noise as he stepped out. Wesley hesitated with his hand on the handle. He'd give himself away if he stalled much longer.

He didn't ride in the senator's car very often, but when he did, he never let Mark get the door for him. Wesley thought it was unnecessary for even the senator to make Mark cater to him like that, so he wasn't about to entertain the behavior.

He took a deep breath and stepped out at about the same time someone let the stranger inside.

The senator followed him inside, waiting for Wesley expectantly.

Wesley made his way to the senator as slowly as possible. He refused to make eye contact.

Whatever happened inside the lab involved paranormals, and they were dangerous creatures. Dr. Perkins also was a crazy man who did things without asking whether he should, not that Wesley fully understood what exactly Dr. Perkins did inside the building. They were there to find out, after all. But Dr. Perkins lacked ethics. Not that Wesley minded so much because he focused on helping them fight against the paranormals taking over the country.

Wesley walked behind the senator. The room was white and sterile. It was anything but a warehouse on the inside. The floors were a hospital-type tile, and almost every door had a glass front with silver handles and numbered keypads that added to the sterile feeling.

Wesley focused on the door nearest him and saw a hallway with white walls and closed doors.

Wesley had never seen Dr. Perkins in a lab coat. He never came to the office with one. He had one on when he came through a door at the building's far end. He smiled when he saw the three of them standing there, but the smile didn't quite reach his eyes.

"To what do I owe your presence, Delano?" Dr. Perkins diverted his gaze to the senator. His Adam's apple bobbed when he swallowed. "I'll be right with you senator."

Wesley knew that name. The senator had dealings with him, although Wesley hadn't figured out how. He had just seen his name on a sticky note once and had written it down.

Delano turned to look at them when Dr. Perkins spoke. He kept his hands folded together behind him. "We may want privacy for the discussion, Jeffrey."

"I owe the senator a tour so whatever you have to say, make it quick."

"The shifter and vampire councils have merged. They protect the shifters. I no longer can protect you, should they find out about your little project here."

Wesley's heart pounded against his chest bone so hard the sound climbed into his head. He grew light-headed, grabbing onto the senator's arm to steady himself. The senator pulled his arm free, and Wesley stumbled. He righted himself quickly, though. "Sorry, sir."

The senator turned and whispered, "Don't make a scene, Wesley."

He would have pointed out that Delano was a paranormal of some sort, but it wouldn't make a difference to the senator. He wasn't the kind to coddle his employees. Wesley nodded and stuffed his hands into his pockets, so no one would see him shake.

Both Dr. Perkins and Delano watched them during the whole ordeal, but they turned back to the conversation when Wesley finally righted himself.

Dr. Perkins cocked his head to the side. "I don't need your protection anyway. Your little council has no leverage."

Delano chuckled. "Right. Well, I thought I'd do you the favor of a warning. Considering all you've done for my coven, I thought I owed you that much. Your funding is no longer needed, Doctor." Delano turned and had a hand on the door when Dr. Perkins grabbed his arm.

Wesley had never seen Dr. Perkins pissed before, but the anger showed in every taut muscle.

When Delano turned to face Dr. Perkins, his eyes glowed red. He hissed and bared long, pointy fangs.

Wesley jumped and backed away, screaming. No one paid him any attention, including the senator who ran across the room, as far from the threat as he could get.

Delano's gaze went from Dr. Perkins' hand on his arm up to his face. The doctor removed his hand and took a step back.

Delano let go of the door handle. He cocked his head to the side like a curious dog. "Perhaps money isn't everything." Delano bent down, getting within inches of Dr. Perkins face. "Humans are weak. It's why you have this lab, correct? Because you recognize the need for improvement."

Dr. Perkins swallowed. His Adam's apple bobbed up and down.

Delano smiled. He straightened and chuckled, meeting the senator's gaze. "His capabilities are lacking, senator. Surely you're smart enough to recognize that."

Wesley wasn't sure what Delano meant by that, and he wasn't brave enough to ask. So far, the attention was off him, and he would've liked for it to stay that way.

Delano walked out of the lab as if he hadn't a care in the world.

The senator ran a hand down his jacket as if the whole ordeal had left him rumpled. Wesley understood the feeling.

Dr. Perkins didn't speak. He stood there staring at the door for the longest time. "I can fix this, senator."

"Paranormals outnumber humans. We need some of them on our side if we're going to win against them." The senator gave Dr. Perkins a pointed stare. "I don't lose, Jeff. I suggest you either make nice with him or find another set of paranormals to manipulate."

"There is no one else. Not if the council is united."

For the first time in Wesley's entire career, the senator seemed angry. "Divide them, idiot."

Dr. Perkins cleared his throat. "Perhaps we should postpone the tour."

"We'll conduct it now."

"I have a lot of work to do, senator."

The senator cleared his throat and smiled at Dr. Perkins. "Don't try to outwit me, Jeff. You won't win."

Dr. Perkins seemed at the end of his rope. That made him more dangerous, not less. Wesley just wished the senator would see that.

Chapter Eight

Magnus replayed the phone conversation as he cupped the stolen identification card in his hand. The hard plastic bit into his palm and the fleshy part of his fingers. He held it with the width cutting across his hand, so there wasn't much give. If he held it vertically, the thing would bend.

Ladon had abandonment issues. There wasn't any doubt about that. It was something they had talked about on one of their nights together. Hell, they talked about everything just like best friends did.

Maybe Magnus had friend-zoned Ladon out of necessity. They both had. Magnus had gotten used to it until bonding had taken a backseat to keeping Ladon healthy. And it always fucking would. He didn't care if Ladon liked it or not. Ladon's safety and health came first.

No matter what he found in the senator's office, he would go home and make shit right.

He walked in plain sight, bold down the sidewalk as if he were out for a late-night stroll around the city.

He pulled his sweater's hood up over his head and slid on the leather gloves.

Focus on the task.

He needed confirmation the senator knew about paranormals. Nothing more. He needed to get it and get the hell out of there.

Magnus held his breath as he slid the card into the government building's front door. There were cameras everywhere, which he couldn't do anything about except to keep his face out of their line of sight.

A red light beside the card panel turned green. Magnus sighed in relief as he pulled the door open.

He would have scoped the building out some, but the attack last night had made him realize trying to get into the building a different way was pointless. They'd read Swenson's identification card and connect the dots.

Most likely they'd trace him back to Saint Lakes, or at the very least they'd trace him to Nicolono Stavros. He wasn't sure what he'd do about it yet.

With the way that female human had acted, finding out a reason for her superhuman strength and speed seemed more important than anything else.

One problem at a time.

Senator Fowler's office proved to be easy to find. Beside a closed door to the right hung a wall plaque with Fowler's name etched on it.

Magnus turned the knob, holding his breath and waiting. When the knob only turned a centimeter in either direction, he cursed under his breath. A key hung from the ring attached to one corner of the identification card, so he used it in the lock.

He was in the office with little fanfare.

As breaking and entering went, the government building was easy. Most of the time investigating meant spending time on the computer. Not that he was a genius when it came to that particular tool. He was mediocre at best, but he knew how to find a person through their digital imprint. It all came down to nosing around in someone's business.

Magnus had lived before computers were a blip on anyone's radar.

Magnus moved to the only desk in the room. There was a row of floor cabinets covering the back wall. The desk sat right in front of them and formed an L-shape. He'd bet money the desk was Wesley's.

Good ole Wesley Swenson. Prejudiced prick that he was, he didn't seem all that dangerous to anyone, including paranormals. So he was paranoid, maybe. Just enough that he'd created a website to find other paranoid, prejudiced pricks out there in the world.

Well, maybe they weren't all paranoid. They weren't wrong, after all.

What bothered Magnus was the Wesley from the bar and the website owner didn't mesh. At the bar, Wesley seemed stressed about his job but otherwise seemed like a nice guy. The website had been made by an idiot so maybe Magnus' first impressions were off.

He'd been wrong before, but it didn't happen very often.

Magnus sat in Wesley's office chair and leafed through his drawers. He didn't expect to find much and, after only about five minutes he discovered he was right.

If Wesley had anything to hide it would be on his computer.

Magnus eyed the technology sitting in the middle of the desk with the lid open. The laptop remained as lifeless and as dark as the surrounding office. It would stay that way for the time being. He'd take the thing with him when he left.

Magnus stood and made his way across the room to a closed door.

His hand was on the knob when his whole body stiffened.

The door to the outer hallway burst open, hitting the wall with a bang.

Magnus turned to find the woman from last night and two men in white lab coats. The second Magnus saw the gun in the woman's hand he cursed himself for not bringing a weapon of his own. Instead, he hissed, showing his fangs

The woman didn't respond. One of the men in lab coats smiled, though. "Hello, vampire."

Shit. Humans in lab coats calling him *vampire* didn't bode well for a safe exit. He'd make a run for it as soon as they moved away from the door.

He also knew what would happen to him next because Fane had spent some unwanted time in a lab. Magnus was about to suffer the same fate.

"Anna." The same smiling human spoke that one word, which was all it took for the woman to shoot.

Magnus ran, veering to the left as soon as the gun went off. A dart missed him by inches. He didn't take the time to see what it struck. He ran toward them, so fast he was probably just a blur, plowing into two of the humans. They stumbled as he ran past them, one falling to the carpeted floor.

Magnus was almost to the end of the hall when he felt a sharp pain in his back. He kept running, but the faster he went, the faster his blood pumped through his body, which let the drugs seep in that much quicker.

If he stopped, they'd catch him. If he didn't, they'd catch him. Either way, he was fucked.

The hallway swam in front of him.

The human kept calling him a *vampire* and told the woman to pick him up. He didn't even know he had fallen. Cold hands on his arms, lifting him. The woman had super-strength. His vision cut off and his limbs felt heavy when he tried to pull away.

He landed with a thud on something metal before the metal started moving.

Shit.

Magnus knew the safety protocols. He knew he should never let them take him to a second location.

Chapter Nine

- -

Ladon rolled down the window in the truck a crack, taking in the warmer air. The winter had lasted longer than was reasonable. Even the day before, a chill had frozen everything in its path. One day made a difference, and it finally felt as if spring might force winter behind the battle line. Ladon took advantage and let the spring in, even though he didn't much feel the renewal that came with the warmer weather.

His wrist lay on the steering wheel until he came to the four-way stop in town. There wasn't a stoplight in Saint Lakes, just the four-way, with a gas station on one corner and the small shopping complex kitty-corner to it. The shopping complex consisted of a grocery store, an ice cream parlor, the Saint Lakes Diner, Garridan's shop, and the accounting place that only opened in April when the government made everyone pay taxes. For most of the rest of the year, the place stayed dark.

Ladon's destination was Garridan's shop. Before the battle with Stavros' coven, he had an excuse to still live at home. Usually, shifters didn't leave the familial home until after they shifted for the first time, so Ladon wasn't beyond the norm. He didn't want to move out, but with the battle over and shifting on a regular basis, he was out of reasons to mooch, which was why he needed to talk to Garridan.

He parked in the back of the lot, giving those who might have difficulties walking an opportunity to park in some of the closer spots. Most everyone in town was a paranormal, so they didn't have health issues that restricted them. Ladon's concern was for those few human clan members who had old-age ailments.

Ladon shut off the engine of his truck and stepped out. He bounced his keys on the palm of his hand, liking the *clinking* sound. It was like white noise and relieved his need to fidget.

That restlessness was new, and he fully blamed Magnus, not that he wanted to think about him. And since he didn't want to, he wouldn't.

Not one thought thrown that way.

Magnus who?

Success wouldn't last long, so he focused on a woman who had a young boy by his arm, pulling him across the parking lot. The boy reached out behind him with his free hand, screaming.

Ladon stopped between two rows. He waited for the lady and her crying kid to draw near.

The closer she came the more Ladon recognized her as a clan member. She was a wolf shifter who'd graduated high school a few years before Ladon. Ladon remembered her because she had been pregnant in high school. *Some summer fun had turned into an oops. Her youngness had been the talk of the town.* "Did you hear about Miri Shea? Good thing she shifted already. And the boy was a tourist. She'll be raising that baby by herself, see if she won't." As disgusting as the gossipmongers had been, they had been right about the father.

She was a single parent at the end of her rope if the desperation in her gaze was any indication.

Despite the stress she was clearly under, she stopped and bowed her head. "Alpha." She tried to hold the boy to her side, but he continued to pull, screaming about ice cream. "Be respectful to the Alpha, Alfie Shea."

Alfie didn't hear a word she said. He kept on with his fit.

A blush grew from Miri's neck to her face. It seemed as if she were about to apologize.

Before she got the chance, Ladon waved her off. "I'm not much on formalities, and besides, I'm not the Alpha yet."

She kept her gaze averted.

Instead of embarrassing her further, Ladon crouched down. Alfie stopped struggling, the excellent fit-throwing forgotten for the moment. Ladon reached into his jacket pocket and pulled out a wadded-up napkin he had put in there from a recent diner visit.

When Ladon reached out to touch the boy, he fully expected the fit to begin playing again. Instead, the boy held still as Ladon dried the tears staining his cheeks.

When he finished, he stuck the napkin back into his pocket, making a mental note to throw it away after he went into Garridan's shop. "My mama always tells me to take three deep breaths when I'm angry." It didn't work anymore, but the kid didn't need to know that. "You wanna try it?"

The kid nodded and looked at Ladon as if he were some hero to be worshiped.

Ladon just smiled and tried to forget his discomfort. "Ready?"

Again, the boy nodded.

"On the count of three." Ladon counted and then took a deep breath in through his nose, letting it out through his mouth.

Alfie didn't follow suit. He took three quick breaths and then let out one frustrated sigh. Ladon wanted to laugh because it was cute, but he didn't want to make the kid think he was laughing at him. So instead, Ladon went on to the next breath. Alfie finally mimicked him.

When they finished, Ladon smiled. "Did that help?"

The kid shook his head.

"Why not?"

Alfie's little shoulders came up to his ears. "No ice cream still."

Ladon couldn't hold the chuckle back. "That's fair." Ladon stood and met Miri's gaze.

The embarrassment crept back up her neck, but she didn't cower under the feeling the second time. Instead, her chin came up. "He knows he needs to eat dinner first."

In other words, she couldn't afford it. Dinnertime for most everyone was still a couple of hours out.

Ladon nodded. "Your mama said no ice cream until after dinner. Sorry, little dude."

She seemed surprised as if she fully expected Ladon to go against her wishes or call her out on the lie.

Alfie just nodded. "I should listen to Mama?"

"Yep. We all have to listen to our mamas. They know best."

"Even you?"

"Yes, sir." Ladon crouched down again. "Maybe she'll let you meet me back here for ice cream after dinner." Ladon's discussion with Garridan wouldn't take very long, but he hoped Garridan would put him to work for a few hours. Even if he didn't, Ladon would come back.

"But I have to be good, huh?" His little eyebrows drew together as if he wasn't sure if being good was worth it.

Ladon chuckled. "Yeah, little dude, you'll have to be good."

Alfie bit his lip, meeting his mother's gaze.

Miri laughed for the first time, the stress completely leaving her face. "Sheesh, Alfie. It can't be that hard of a decision."

"I can go?"

"Yes." She met Ladon's gaze. "Thank you, Alpha."

"Please, call me Ladon."

Alfie stuck his thumb into his mouth and leaned against her leg.

"Well, I better get Alfie down for a nap."

Ladon nodded. "See ya later, Alfie."

Alfie waved with his free hand as his mother went toward their car.

It was when she turned her back that Ladon had a sudden thought. "Hey, Miri."

She met his gaze.

"Do you happen to know anything about computers and answering phones? Shi—" Ladon stopped himself at the last minute, wincing as he looked at Alfie. "Stuff like that."

"Yeah."

"Well, Maxine just found her mate and joined his clan over in Wingspan, so Dr. Tucker is looking for someone who could do that sort of thing. You can tell him the Alpha sent you if you want."

Miri's smile reached her eyes, and her shoulders lost some of the tension. "Oh gods, thank you."

Ladon nodded, trying to ignore how tears gathered in her eyes.

Ladon almost expected Jules' presence in the store. He stopped right inside the door and blinked at the counter Jules normally sat behind. Sage sat there instead. Ladon stared at him for longer than he cared to admit before reality came into focus.

Jules' mates had him tucked away in the cabin in the woods. Everyone called the cabin Magnus' because that was where he had stayed whenever he was in town.

Since Ladon had shifted, he'd gotten more possessive of Magnus, as if he were a thing instead of a human being. Ladon wasn't an asshole. Or at least, he didn't want to act like one, but his dragon had a primitive need to bond, and it felt like possession in a weird way.

They were mates, but if Magnus didn't want that, then there wasn't much Ladon could do about it. Hell, there wasn't much he would do about it. He wasn't chasing Magnus all over the country. He knew that much.

And there he went, thinking about Magnus again.

Ladon leaned against the counter, getting into Sage's space. He reached out a finger, intending to touch Sage, which would irritate him and that was fun. Immature. But fun.

Before he could do anything, Sage closed the book he was reading and sat up on the stool. He folded his arms at his chest and narrowed his eyes. "Don't even think about it."

Ladon chuckled. "How'd you know I was gonna do anything?"

"You and Vaughan are a lot alike."

Ladon moved off the counter and made a sound of false outrage. "I take offense." Of course, he didn't actually and knew Sage spoke the truth. Even though Vaughan could be a pain in the ass, he teased when he thought someone needed to stop taking themselves so seriously. Sage was one who needed lighter moments.

Sage lifted his eyebrows and gave Ladon a bored look. He turned the corners of his mouth up into a smile, but it was so quick Ladon almost missed it.

"So where can I find the daddy of all Somersets and everyone's favorite grouch?"

Sage snorted out a laugh and pointed to the closed door behind and to the left of him. "He's in the back."

"You not working at the diner today?"

"No. It's my day off. Thought I'd take over the front and the website. Garridan can't work a computer to save himself." It made sense that he wasn't able. Before Stavros had imprisoned Garridan, computers hadn't existed in homes. He'd never encountered one before getting rescued. "You can go on back if you want."

It was Ladon's turn to narrow his eyes. "Hell no. I go back there, and he's in the middle of something he gets growly. You go first." Garridan wouldn't have the same reaction if Sage went back there. Sage was Garridan's favorite person.

Sage chuckled and shook his head. "He won't have a problem with you interrupting him."

Ladon crossed his arms over his chest and locked his feet in place. "He will."

Sage sighed. "Fine."

Ladon followed Sage, who opened the door but stopped before entering. He turned and met Ladon's gaze. Sage drew his eyebrows together. His dark eyes seemed to probe through to Ladon's soul.

"What?"

"You seem mad."

Those three words put Ladon on the defensive for about a second before he remembered he couldn't show Sage even a little bit of anger, even if Ladon directed his anger at Magnus and it had nothing to do with Sage. It would scare him enough that his post-traumatic stress disorder would take hold. Sage had worked too hard to get to where he was for Ladon to set him back, even if it was just a little bit.

It took trust for Sage to say something so direct, and for that reason, Ladon took the time to process, moving the words around in his brain until they sank into his gut, churning around until they settled at the bottom of his stomach. Each word held a heaviness he didn't want to deal with, but Sage put them out there, laying them like bricks one on top of the other. Ladon had to either acknowledge them or knock them loose.

By the gods, he didn't want to talk about Magnus. "Had a fight with Magnus a couple of days ago and I haven't heard from him since."

"Is he okay?"

Ladon hoped so. "I haven't tried to call him."

"Well don't you think you should? Just to check."

Ladon nodded. "I'll have Ramsey do it." No way would he give in to the temptation. Not when Magnus said he didn't want Ladon around.

"Get in here already." Garridan's voice echoed across the big workroom.

Sage grinned. "Told ya."

Ladon rolled his eyes and grinned.

Sage opened the door all the way and walked through. Garridan laid sandpaper on a bare wooden table and straightened from his bent-over position.

Sage went right over to Garridan and wrapped an arm around his waist. Garridan returned the gesture.

Ladon had Garridan's full attention, which surprised him. "You okay, boy?"

Garridan's use of the word *boy* made him smile. Garridan called Bennett that as well which was why Ladon liked the term in relation to himself. Bennett and Garridan had a history that went way back. That history made them as much father and son as being blood-related. That one word gave him as much a sense of belonging as Ladon's last name, and he needed the reminder from time to time.

"Came to ask you something."

Garridan nodded. "Ask."

"Will you teach me carpentry?"

Garridan smiled about twice a year, and the appearance was random. It wasn't as if he reserved a smile for him and Sage's anniversary and then one for Yule. No, they were very unpredictable, and it was usually Sage that made them come out. But Ladon managed to get one.

Ladon knew he resembled like a fish out of water, all gaping mouth and wide eyes. He met Sage's gaze, pointing to Garridan. "I did that."

"Told you so."

Garridan shook his head. His arm left Sage's waist, and he patted him on the ass. "Ladon and I have work to do."

"What if I want to learn carpentry, too?"

"You don't but if you did it would require payment." The smile might have left Garridan's face, but there was mischief in his eyes.

Sage giggled like a high school girl. "What would be the price?"

Garridan growled and pulled Sage to him. "I think you know," he whispered right before they started making out.

Ladon screwed up his nose and waited for them to stop. When Sage's leg went up around Garridan's thigh in an attempt to climb him like a tree, Ladon knew he had to say something. "Still here."

Nothing.

He probably should get used to it if he were going to hang around the shop all day. "I have an ice cream date I gotta keep so could you get done with that by dinner time?"

Still nothing.

Chapter Ten

A guard walked the length of the hall with a gun in his hands and a stony look on his face. He stared at either the wall or the door, depending on his direction. He dressed all in black with a T-shirt and cargo pants.

Paranormals on one side of the cell block and humans on the other had become clear the second they'd brought Magnus in. Two days and three hours since they'd held him captive. Magnus didn't count the minutes or seconds, although he probably could as he knew the exact hour they'd kidnapped him.

In those two days, they hadn't given Magnus blood once. Thankfully, Magnus had a stash of bagged blood back at his hotel and had drunk some before he'd left to search the senator's office.

They hadn't given Fane blood for months, and it had driven him feral. Magnus had no reason to think they wouldn't do the same to him. The lack of blood was a concern but not an immediate one.

As yet, they hadn't done anything besides meet his basic needs.

No one talked, not even his cellmate, who was a shifter. Either he preferred his animal form, or he couldn't shift back. His bobcat form didn't take up much room, and he didn't seem to mind Magnus' presence.

He slept at the end of Magnus' cot every night. Magnus had a feeling the guy hadn't had contact with a kind touch in a long time, which was why he preferred the physical closeness.

The human was another issue altogether. Whatever they were doing to the poor guy left him ill. The guy shivered on his cot as if it were freezing in the lab. The air was cooler than someone would keep their home but not so cold he should be freezing nearly to death. Sweat covered his back even as he lay in a fetal position on his cot. Skin stretched over his bones, but little muscle remained.

The human's whole body shook with each breath and his spine curved into an *s*. The only thing the man wore were dirty sweatpants with stains all over them.

"What did they do to you?" If the human heard him, he didn't turn from his position. Perhaps it took to much energy.

His cellmate wasn't any help answering the question either, so Magnus took a chance and asked the guard. "Hey, do you know what this place is?"

The guys in white coats who had brought him there gave away the fact it was some lab but that didn't tell Magnus what their goal was. Magnus would've very much liked to know what they had planned for him. Information was power.

Magnus sat on the cot next to his cellmate when the guard didn't even blink his way.

"They don't just want information about paranormals anymore, do they? Not with them keeping the human." He kept his voice at a whisper so only the bobcat could hear. "It's the human and the woman who brought me in. She's…enhanced, I guess. As strong as any vampire for sure." Not as strong as most shifters, though.

The human took another heavy breath, straining under the weight of it.

Magnus sighed. "They studied Fane. Asked him questions. Took samples of his blood and stopped feeding him to see what would happen." Maybe they had learned all they needed to move the science forward.

Something had gone wrong with the man across the hall, though.

The door at one end of the hallway opened, and a man with dark hair came through. He had on white scrubs. He'd even covered his feet.

His face was as stony as the guards'. The two men didn't speak or even give as much as a twitch of the lips.

The bobcat beside him shifted before Magnus even registered the difference between fur and skin against his hand. Naked flesh was something a shifter was very used to, but Magnus was a vampire. The nakedness left Magnus uncomfortable enough that he removed his hand.

At least he knew the shifter had a choice and wasn't feral.

He had dark blond hair and hazel eyes the same color as his bobcat.

Magnus had so many questions that they all ran through his brain at once. He opened his mouth to speak, but nothing came out, his thoughts jumbling his words up too much.

The man in white came close enough for Magnus to see he carried something. The dark red liquid encased in plastic was unmistakable against the paleness of the man's hand and the white backdrop of his pants.

Magnus let out a breath he didn't even know he held and bent at the waist. He didn't know how scared he was that they'd starve him until he knew they wouldn't. He wasn't even worried about his own wellbeing, but rather about Ladon having to take care of him. Taking care of a feral mate wasn't an easy task but Ladon would do it. He did not doubt that, but what price would he have to pay?

The bobcat shifter shook his head. "Don't drink the blood." He shifted back before Magnus could ask any of the plethora of questions.

The man in white stopped at their cell. If they'd seen the bobcat shift, neither the guard nor the other free person said a word about it. Instead, he slid the bagged blood through the slit that appeared to be more of a mail slot than anything else. Half his hand was through as well.

Magnus sat on the cot, pretending he didn't know what the guy wanted. He ran his hand down the bobcat's soft fur as if he didn't have a care in the world.

The man jammed his hand farther into the slot and shook the bag at Magnus.

Magnus lifted his eyebrows and smiled. He let his fangs drop to see the guy's reaction.

Irritation came through in his expression before the bored expression crossed his face again. Not once was he scared of Magnus, which meant the guy had been around paranormals enough not to fear them. Either that or he trusted the glass cage.

Magnus focused on the ill person in the cell across from them. "The human is dying."

"Take it." He waggled the bagged blood at him again. Only he did it so vigorously Magnus could hear the liquid slosh against the plastic.

"What did you do to him?" Magnus didn't know why the answer mattered so much, but the need for it burned in his bones.

"Take the blood."

"And if I don't?"

"Then you starve. Nothing more."

"Will you keep trying or will this be the only time you offer?"

"If you don't take it, I won't offer anymore."

"*You* won't but will someone else?"

The guard didn't answer, although it was clear Magnus annoyed him.

He had nothing to lose by taking it. He didn't have to drink it. "Should I trust that it's safe to drink?"

"Yes."

It wasn't, or the bobcat wouldn't have told him not to drink it. "So it won't do to me what you're doing to the human?"

"We haven't perfected the formula for shifters yet." What the fuck did that mean? "The doctor will force you to drink." The man in white dropped the bag inside the cell and walked away. The door leading out of the cell block clicked shut behind him.

Magnus was left staring at the bag lying on the tile floor, with even more questions.

When he did finally pick it up, he immediately put it to his nose. The staleness of the blood came through, but he was used to that. He had drunk bagged blood for several years already. Underneath the staleness was a chemical smell.

He turned toward the bobcat. "Drugged?"

The bobcat nodded.

"Will the drug kill me?"

The bobcat shook his head, but the fear in his eyes said Magnus wouldn't like what was in the blood.

"What it will do is worse, huh?"

The bobcat nodded.

Shit. "Talk about a rock and hard place. Can't drink it but I can't *not* drink it. And those fuckers must know it." Must have done a lot of research on vampires versus shifters. Maybe they had access to vampires somehow, or a vampire was physiologically closer to a human than a shifter. Either way, it left Magnus vulnerable to the men in white.

Chapter Eleven

The light over the stove illuminated the landline phone. Ladon sat at the kitchen table drinking overly strong coffee and glaring into the dark.

Magnus hadn't called in almost a month.

A million reasons why Magnus hadn't returned ran through his mind, and none of them did anything to relieve the growing tension. If he gathered the speculations and put them into camps, he'd have two. One that suggested Magnus didn't want him anymore and the other implied someone had hurt Magnus. Even if the latter was the case, it didn't mean the former wasn't true also.

Either scenario left Ladon in a difficult spot, because his dragon wanted to fly straight to Magnus, but the human part of Ladon wanted to send someone else. Either way someone had to check on him.

Their argument seemed long ago but it still ran through his mind. Maybe the rejection wasn't true. Maybe Magnus hadn't meant it the way it sounded. And maybe he did.

He ran a hand through his hair.

The door between the kitchen and the living room swung open, and Vaughan walked through.

The night crept into every crevice of the room, concealing Ladon. All their mingling, familiar scents kept him hidden as well.

Vaughan opened the refrigerator door. The light made the entire area glow around him. Bending down, he perused the inside of the fridge looking for treasure. He wore pajama pants and nothing else. The pajama pants had hot peppers in sombreros holding colorful maracas. The words *hot stuff* was as plentiful as the peppers. He reached in and pulled out a plate of fried chicken Mom had made for dinner yesterday and shut the door, darkening the room again.

Vaughan put the plate on the center island and lifted the plastic. His back was to Ladon.

If Ladon had been in a different mood, he might've scared Vaughan. If anyone deserved it, it was him. But Ladon wasn't, so he just watched from the shadows, taking a sip of his coffee and not saying a word.

He needed Vaughan's serious side. Thankfully, that was one of the two sides he had.

It wasn't until Vaughan saw the green light on the coffee pot and the fact that it was most of the way full that he was alerted to Ladon's presence.

He turned with a cold chicken leg in his mouth and leaned against the counter, chewing as he regarded Ladon. At one point, Ladon focused on the phone again.

Vaughan had half the leg eaten before he spoke. "You going after him?"

"Someone is." Ladon knew that much.

"Why not you?"

"I don't know."

Vaughan gave him a knowing look. "You do too."

Ladon sighed and averted his gaze. "I don't know why he's MIA. I mean we fought the last time we talked and what if he decided I wasn't worth the hassle."

"The what-if game. Okay, let's play, since you want to do that instead of take action."

Ladon rolled his eyes even though he knew Vaughan was right.

"What if the fight was just a fight?" Vaughan raised his eyebrows.

"Then Magnus would be in trouble right now. Probably. Or he could be in trouble and still not want me."

"Or he could be in trouble and want the hell out of you." Vaughan took another bite of the chicken leg. Between the way he ate and the fact that he was half-clothed, Vaughan appeared barely evolved. At least he stood upright.

"You look like a caveman."

Vaughan turned and grabbed the roll of paper towel that sat on one edge of the counter. He wiped his mouth. "And you look like an idiot."

Ladon sighed and stood. "I know that."

"Then you probably also know that it won't matter what you do to protect yourself against the hurt. If it's even coming and I doubt it is. You're already too far over the edge for Magnus."

Magnus was the person Ladon told everything to. So yeah, Vaughan was right about saving himself any hurt.

Ladon needed to think, so he headed for the door. "I know that too."

Ladon had his hand on the door handle when Vaughan spoke next. "You know what pisses me off about your whole attitude."

Ladon turned toward Vaughan. He held his breath, waiting for Vaughan to say whatever he was going to. Vaughan was the one that would tell it to him straight whether he wanted to hear it or not.

"Only two people left you your whole life. And you probably barely remember it—"

"You're wrong about that." Ladon remembered his mother's hair and the way she'd cried when she'd left him with the neighbor lady. He remembered the way her hands had shaken as she'd touched his cheek.

"Okay. But you know your parents probably didn't leave you on purpose. It's irrational to think they did."

His fingers hurt as his grip on the door handle tightened. He nodded and turned his head slightly, wanting Vaughan to get to his point soon.

"You think everyone's ready to walk away from you. You used to think that about us and now you're putting that shit on Magnus."

"You don't know shit about what I think." Ladon took a deep breath, willing himself to calm down.

When Vaughan walked toward him, Ladon turned. "I don't see how it's not true."

Vaughan held his shoulders back, and his hands balled into fists at his sides.

Ladon's fangs dropped, and his eyes turned, his dragon interpreting Vaughan's stance as a threat. Ladon took a step toward Vaughan, growling to get the wolf shifter to back down.

Vaughan looked at Ladon as if he'd slapped him and then his expression hardened. His spine snapped into place.

The wolf shifter wouldn't win in a fight against the dragon. The dragon knew it and rolled around in the victory even before there was one. The wolf must have known it as well because he retreated.

The defeat had Ladon's dragon backing down. The dragon fell into the back of his mind, slowly, and as he did Ladon came back to himself.

He backed up until he felt the door at his back, and bent at the waist. He closed his eyes and ran a hand down his face. His palm touched his fangs when he passed them.

"Sorry."

"That's what I'm talking about." Vaughan's harsh tone threatened to make Ladon shift partially again. He spoke as if trying to calm a dangerous animal. "You're apologizing for being an Alpha. You needed to back me down. I get that. And the apology means you don't believe we have unconditional love for you."

Ladon put his hand down and opened his eyes. Ladon's fangs receded. "The apology means I don't know what I'm doing."

Vaughan's shoulders slumped. "Then why are you acting weird around all of us lately. Since right after you shifted. And don't tell me you haven't been, because that's crap."

"It's not easy for me right now."

"I understand that."

Ladon straightened and stepped away from the door again. His eyes shifted for the second time. Only he didn't try to fight it the second time around. "You don't know shit, Vaughan. None of you do."

"That's bullshit."

"It's not. You think my problem is about some childhood psychobabble crap and maybe that's part of it, but it's not all of it like you and the rest of the family think."

"If I'm wrong, tell me how." His tone turned complacent.

"I've known my mate for a long time, and I haven't been able to bond with him. We have successfully put each other in the friend zone and getting out isn't fucking easy, man. And I just shifted for the first time a few weeks ago. Do you even remember what it was like after your first shift? It's confusing as fuck because I have a...a nature, I guess, that I have to fight against. And I don't know if I can—"

"Woah. Just hold it right there." Vaughan held up a hand like a traffic cop. "Why do you think you need to fight against it?"

"Because I'm not a bossy dick, Vaughan. It'll get annoying after a while."

Vaughan's laugh was so loud Ladon thought he'd wake everyone else. Ladon opened his mouth to tell him to fuck off but nothing came out, and the more he stood there, the more Vaughan's laughter became annoying.

He ran his own words back through his mind, letting it cook. It didn't take him very long. His face heated up, which just made Vaughan laugh even harder.

Ladon shook his head and smiled. The smile turned into a chuckle.

Ramsey came through the kitchen door with a scowl on his face, scratching his belly. Fane followed right behind him. They both stood in the middle of the room, glaring at Ladon and Vaughan.

Ramsey was the one who spoke. "What the fuck, man? People are trying to sleep."

The door to the kitchen swung open again, and Bennett came through, followed by Garridan. Garridan had Sage tucked into his side. "Do you two have any idea what time it is?" Garridan's fatherly tone came through loud and clear. Ladon felt more like a kid than an adult.

Ladon took a step, standing beside Vaughan, letting the older, more experienced brother field the questions. Ladon might've been an Alpha and would soon take over the clan, but he still held the little brother card. He'd play it as much as possible.

Vaughan grinned like a lunatic before he turned back to their audience. "Ladon's worried he'll get annoying. You know, now that he's an Alpha and all."

Ladon elbowed Vaughan in the ribs, making him grunt and chuckle. "Asshole."

"That's what you said."

Yeah, he knew that, but Vaughan didn't have to repeat it. He made it sound even stupider than when Ladon had rambled it out.

Bennett crossed his arms over his chest. "You've been annoying since day one, so it's a little fucking late to stress over it."

"Thank you." Vaughan tilted his head to Bennett. And then gave Ladon a smug grin. "My point exactly."

Garridan's expression held concern, so Ladon felt compelled to explain. "All I was saying, is I'm just trying to get used to the changes. And then with being the next Alpha and Magnus not being here. I got a lot of shit on my mind." Ladon averted his gaze. He fought the urge to fidget like a child under Garridan's gaze.

Ladon could still feel Garridan probing for a better answer and he buckled under the pressure. "Maybe I'm not ready for all this...Alpha stuff. Or shifting. Or letting Magnus out of the friend zone. Maybe he's not ready either, and that's why he's staying away." His dragon roared with just how wrong he was about being ready. "I'm barely twenty years' old. I mean, I bet none of you even remember what being twenty was like."

Vaughan snorted. "I think you just called all of us old."

"I'm not gonna magically mature overnight because I shifted for the first time. My mind and my body aren't on the same page."

Garridan whispered something to Sage and then kissed his cheek right before Sage pulled out of his arms and went behind the center island. He dumped the coffee Ladon had made down the sink and rinsed the pot out before filling it again.

Ladon watched Garridan sit at the table. He pulled out a chair and gestured to it. "Magnus hasn't called?"

"No. Not in a month."

"We need to have a meeting." Garridan looked at Ramsey, who also sat with Fane on his lap.

Chapter Twelve

- -

L adon didn't think he had any right to plan a rescue because he didn't know the first thing about anything. He couldn't rescue a rabbit from a snare. For that reason, he stayed quiet as Garridan and Ramsey talked about what to do and where to go, listening to the experts talk.

He kept his hands around the coffee mug and his head down. The coffee was much better since Sage had remade it. Ladon wasn't sure how he'd managed to fuck it up, but the difference was remarkable.

Everyone else had gone to bed. Fane snored in Ramsey's arms. He even managed to make snoring sound cute, although Ladon wasn't sure how.

The three of them sat around the kitchen table, and Ladon looked out of the window over the sink, watching the sun rising over the tree line. The pink hues lit the sky, contrasting with the bare bones of the trees. It would contrast more when spring set in and the leaves grew back again. The hues would change to more of an orange color by then as well. Ladon knew because he had spent the better part of a year going to bed when the sun came up.

"What are your thoughts Ladon?" A hint of worry laced through Ramsey's question.

"I don't have any." Ladon tightened his grip on the coffee mug and tried to keep his expression blank. Ramsey would know Ladon lied if he gave him even a hint.

The truth was Ladon did have thoughts. Lots of them. But he didn't have enough experience to give his opinion.

"Are you paying attention?"

"Yes." The sunrise reminded him of Magnus' smile. He always had one whenever they parted at the end of their stolen moments. That was when color came back into the world.

The chair scraped against the floor when Ladon stood. He left his mug abandoned on the table and walked to the sliding glass door. Leaning against it.

"This is your mate we're talking about, Ladon." The accusation that Ladon didn't care was there, squeezing his patience.

"I care about him." By the gods, Magnus filled his every thought. "Don't suggest otherwise."

"I wasn't." Ramsey was a damned liar, but Ladon let it go.

"Whatever you guys think will get him back, I'm firmly behind that."

"Who do you want to go with you on the rescue mission?"

"I think Bandos or Sully is a good choice. Maybe Damian. And one of you." Ladon's heart rate picked up as his choices solidified into a decision. He tensed as his dragon roared with anger. "I'm not going."

Garridan growled at the same time Ramsey sucked in a breath.

"What?" Ramsey asked as if he heard Ladon wrong.

Instead of answering, Ladon turned just enough to meet Ramsey's gaze. Ladon laid it all out in that one look.

Ramsey's expression softened. "I think you're making a mistake, but I'll respect your decision."

Ladon turned back to the sun, which had crept up a bit farther above the trees. He gripped the handle of the door. "For the record, I'm thinking of Magnus above anyone else."

"How do you figure?" And there it was, the accusation again.

"If Magnus is staying away because of me then it'll give him the out he wants."

"And if he's not?"

Ladon pulled open the door and stepped out. The morning air washed over him. He could smell the humidity, promising the plants a little bit of moisture before the sun heated everything, although the sun could only do so much with the cold still hanging on with both fists most days.

His breath fanned out in front of him.

"I don't know." Ladon closed the door behind himself and stepped farther onto the patio, passed a lounge chair Kristin and Josh always commandeered whenever their family gathered.

The sliding glass door opened again. "Ladon."

Ladon stopped and turned. His eyes changed to his dragon's, and his fangs dropped as his dragon fought him for dominance. "I don't know." He couldn't keep the growl from his tone.

Ramsey stepped out onto the patio, shutting the door behind him. He must have laid Fane down somewhere because he didn't carry him out. "You don't trust your dragon and you should."

Ladon hadn't thought about it like that before. "Maybe."

Ramsey studied him as if he were a wild animal in the zoo. Ladon stuffed his hands into the pockets of his jeans and averted his gaze, afraid of what Ramsey would see. "Your dragon wants Magnus. So much I doubt you'll be able to stay away from him."

Yeah, Ladon hoped for more control than that.

"I understand you more than you think." Ramsey's voice went low, barely carrying above a whisper.

Ladon's gaze snapped to Ramsey.

"I've fought against my nature for a long time. I'm too aggressive to be an Alpha. It took me a long time to admit that to myself and even longer to say it to others, you included." Knowing Ramsey's admittance held weight made Ladon absorb the words, washing them through his brain. "Betas are aggressive. I'm nothing more than that, Ladon."

"So, what are Alphas?"

"Dominant. The clan needs dominance, not aggression."

"Can someone have both?" Because wouldn't that make them dangerous.

"Not our kind, Ladon. Humans. Vampires maybe. But shifters are simpler. We've adapted so we can protect each other."

Ladon liked the way Ramsey looked at being a shifter and his own natural tendencies. He smiled. "So, evolution."

Ramsey shrugged. "You can call it whatever you want. It just means we like living in groups. Even bear shifters who think they're loners. They keep coming back to their home clan for a reason. The need to protect each other is everything because there's safety in numbers and always has been. We've learned to value each other." Ramsey met his gaze with a pointed stare. "You need us to have your back, and we need you to make decisions. None of it works if you don't trust."

Shit. Ladon pulled his sweater over his head and laid on the lounger.

"Garridan, Bandos, and Damian will leave in an hour. You know, if you change your mind about going." Ramsey thought he would. It was there in his tone.

Ladon nodded and took off his pants. "I won't."

"Right." Was Ramsey smiling, because if he was then that just made Ladon want to smack him.

Ladon shook his head. "I won't."

Ramsey grinned. "Right."

Damn it.

He took off his pants and threw them beside his shirt. "I guess it would be completely normal for me to assert my dominance and tell you to knock it the fuck off."

Ramsey chuckled. "It would. I'm still technically Alpha, though."

Ladon met his gaze. "Technically."

The sun had risen high enough that Ladon could tell an hour had passed. He lay on the shore of North Lake in a secluded area with the forest at his back. His nose was so close to the water the surface rippled when he breathed.

Flying wasn't as easy as Bennett and Garridan made it look, which was why he decided to give himself a break and had found a nice spot where he could think things through.

The logical part of Ladon's brain told him to stay next to the lake until the rescue team left. The primitive part needed to protect.

He was done fighting with himself.

He stood from his prone position, letting his big, clawed foot touch the water's edge, feeling the wet sand give way beneath the weight of his dragon.

He lacked sleep, and that killed a lot of his willpower. He did what came naturally and took to the sky, water dripping from his toes.

He tilted to the left and then overcorrected, nearly sending himself into the water. It took him a bit to stabilize, but he did, making a beeline for home.

The distance when flying was nothing, and he arrived in no time at all.

His dragon chuffed in happiness when he saw Garridan standing with Sage outside his truck. Bandos sat in the passenger's seat with the window rolled down. A computer screen illuminated his face a bit, and he seemed engrossed in whatever was on the screen. Damian sat in the back staring out of the car window at the house. Owen stood in the front door, glaring with his arms folded at his chest.

Ladon had everyone's attention when he flew overhead. Garridan was the first to look away, focusing on Sage. He cupped Sage's cheek, getting his attention. Sage raised on his tiptoes and kissed Garridan.

Ladon intended to land in the yard, but he ended up on the road, skidding across the gravel as he came in too fast. He shifted halfway through, which ended up being a stupid move because he scraped the shit out of his hands.

He heard Sage giggle and Garridan told him to hush, although the rebuke held no weight.

"Ow, shit." Ladon picked himself up out of the dirt. "Thank the gods I caught myself on my hands and knees, or I'd have road rash on my balls."

Sage laughed even harder, which made Ladon laugh. He had been in a shitty mood before landing. All he needed to improve it was to embarrass himself enough to hear Sage's cute giggle.

He brushed the dirt off his knees, trying to be careful of the bloody scrapes.

He straightened when Garridan came around the front. Garridan took his hand, turning his palm up. He brushed the dirt off, huffing at the chewed-up skin. "Let me see the other one."

Ladon held out his other hand, and Garridan took it.

It was weird standing naked on the road in front of their house with Garridan holding his hands. He'd seen lots of naked bodies. It wasn't a big deal. Or it hadn't been until it was him with his bits all out and exposed.

"Okay. We're done now." He pulled his hands out of Garridan's grasp and turned to the house. "I'm going with you, so don't leave without me."

"Yes, Alpha." Shit. He didn't even know how demanding he'd sounded until Garridan spoke.

Ladon stopped, his body stiffening. "Sorry."

"Don't apologize." Garridan was back in Dad mode. His next comment confirmed it. "Clean up your wounds while you're in there."

Ladon sighed, the tension leaving his limbs.

He went around the back of the house. His clothes sat on the lounger where he had left them. He put his underwear and pants on first. It was as he lifted his shirt over his head that he bothered to look into the house through the sliding glass door.

Ramsey and Vaughan both sat at the table drinking coffee and watching him as if viewing their favorite movie. Mom stood at the stove flipping pancakes.

Ladon pulled his shirt over his head before entering the house.

Ramsey immediately started in on him. "You going with?"

"Yes." Ladon rolled his eyes, heading for the sink. "Need to clean the dirt off my hands and then I'm heading right back outside."

Mom turned with a scowl on her face. "Why are you dirty?"

"I fell coming in for a landing." Ladon held up his hands to show her before walking over to the sink.

Mom sucked in a breath. "Ladon Somerset, you need to be more careful."

"I'm fine, Mom. Almost healed already." And that was true. The raw skin had already started to repair itself.

Vaughan laughed. "Remember when Bennett first shifted. He landed on the roof and couldn't figure out how to get back down."

Ramsey chuckled. "Owen and Kristin shifting for the first time was funnier. They could see something on the ground from high up, and when they went in for the attack, they ended up crashing every time."

Mom tsked. "Nearly broke their necks."

He expected way more teasing from Vaughan. He washed his hands and wondered what was wrong with his brother. When he finished, he turned and met his gaze.

Vaughan's eyebrows drew together. "What?"

"What's wrong with you?"

"Nothing." Vaughan gave him a confused look. "What's wrong with you?"

"You're not teasing me about landing on my ass."

"Money in the jar." Mom pointed to the curse jar with the pancake flipper as if it hadn't been in the same spot his entire Somerset life.

He fished around in his pocket for a dollar, coming up empty. He pulled the wallet from his back pocket and put a five-dollar bill inside because that was all he had. He took three out, leaving two in because he was pretty sure Vaughan would make him curse at least one more time.

"You're Alpha now. Gotta keep it toned down."

"So that's all I have to do. Become head of an entire clan. And do you even know how to 'tone down'?"

Vaughan smirked. "I know how."

"Don't worry about it until I do. That's an order from your Alpha." Ladon smirked right back at him.

Ramsey's nod of approval laid a brick in Ladon's foundation.

"Oh, a license to pick on you." Vaughan chuckled and stood, starting across the room to Ladon.

Ladon saw him coming and nearly ran for the door. "Sorry. Don't have time for your shit. I gotta rescue Magnus." Even if it meant rescuing him from himself.

Vaughan laughed and gave up when Ladon went out of the door. Ladon was just about to round the corner of the house when Vaughan called after him. "Hey."

Ladon turned, meeting his gaze.

"I think you're making the right decision by going."

Ladon smiled. "Thank you. I think I needed to hear that."

Vaughan nodded. "Be safe, little brother."

Ladon closed the distance between them and hugged him. Vaughan returned it but let him go just as quickly. "Go. Before you piss Garridan off."

"Not as concerned about that as I am getting to Magnus." Since he'd made up his mind to go along, an urgency crept in by slow degrees. Just one small rain cloud at a time until they filled his entire body. The storm would come soon.

Chapter Thirteen

L *adon. Saint Lakes. My name is Magnus. I'm a vampire.*

Magnus' cellmate, Joey, sat on the cot, naked as the day he was born, gripping the edge of the thin mattress tight enough his knuckles turned white. He watched Magnus with wide eyes, and a crinkle in his forehead right above his eyebrows.

Magnus picked up the latest bag of blood just as Scrubs, the vampire feeder, left their section of the laboratory. He dropped it in the corner with the others. Magnus barely heard the outer door click shut after him.

When he had first arrived, he had heard the air displace around the door. He couldn't anymore. Just the *click*. He couldn't hear the human's heavy breathing anymore either, although he knew he took in air because his back moved. And he couldn't smell Joey's bobcat scent.

A stack of empty plastic lay in the corner along with the filled bags of blood he hadn't drank. The blood was spoiled since he didn't drink it, which was fine with Magnus. The craving for blood was nearly nonexistent, and it wasn't because he drank blood on a regular basis either. He only took what his body needed, but he hadn't needed any for a while.

Whatever was in the blood took something he didn't know he could lose. Little balloons of information that made him who he was whizzed away as if the blood worked as a pinprick.

Magnus stared at the blood in his hand, watching it slosh around inside its plastic container. "The blood is spoiled in all of them."

Ladon. Saint Lakes. My name is Magnus. I'm a vampire. He recited those simple facts because those balloons hadn't popped yet. If he lost those four things about himself, he'd be nothing.

He threw it into the corner with the rest of the bags and sat on the cot.

"They put something in it." He'd gotten used to the way Joey looked out for Magnus as if they were brothers. "I told you not to drink it. It's poison for a vampire."

"I know. I used to be able to smell the chemicals." His body betrayed him, forcing him to drink but he regretted every damn drop.

Joey hung his head. "They'll take you away soon. I won't be able to stop them."

There wasn't much Magnus could do about his future at the laboratory. The monsters who ran the place had the upper hand. Instead, he focused on the human across the hall. He counted how many breaths the human took, and it wasn't very many. "He'll die soon."

Joey's chin lay on his chest. "He used to talk about ways to get out of here. He fought them every time they took him out. Once he nearly got away. And now he lies there."

"Where did they take him?"

"They do tests and take his blood for studying. Inject him. Whatever they gave him made him like that, so they gave up." By the gods, everyone had written the poor human off.

Magnus stood, walking the few steps it took to get to the glass, separating them from the human. "I'm not giving up on you. You fight. Do you hear me?"

The human's breathing seemed to stop and for a second Magnus thought maybe that was it, but then the human rolled over, grunting and groaning with each inch of a turn. His cheeks were hollow, and he had a gray complexion. He had eyes that didn't seem to know if they wanted to be brown or green. Half of his pupil was either one color or the other.

"The whitecoats, they made you into something." That theory made sense considering Magnus felt less like a vampire with every sip of blood. Given the guy was human, they might have tried to make him superhuman like the woman, Anna. She had been fast. Strong, as well, but it was her speed that was abnormal for all other beings except vampires. "Joey?"

"Yeah."

"The other human, the one who died. Did they inject him with stuff?"

"They took him to another part of the lab."

Magnus turned. "What did he say about it?"

"Nothing."

Yeah, that might have been too broad of a question. He tried again. "Did he say he was in pain? Or anything like that?"

Joey bit his lip and looked down for a moment before answering. "He said it felt like something tried to claw its way out of him but couldn't."

Magnus thought about that for a moment. "And what have they done to you so far?"

"Taken blood. Injected me. But that's it."

"Were you in your human form or your bobcat?"

Joey snorted. "Bobcat. Those assholes kept trying to make me shift. I'm not giving them what they want."

"Maybe they have something that would make you stay in your human form."

Joey hung his head. "Yeah. Maybe. It would kill me if they made me stay in one form or another."

Yes. Magnus figured that out already. Feral was feral, stuck in the human form or not. Magnus didn't know that much about shifters. He'd grown up in a vampire village, so the knowledge he'd gained was from being around the Saint Lakes clan. Being stuck in a human form hadn't ever come up as a problem, so Magnus didn't have a clue what that would do to a shifter. Its likely shifters didn't know either, but still, he had to ask. "Is the animal form stronger?"

Joey raised a hand and waved it back and forth. "Kind of. I mean, I guess that's one way to look at it. It's more like my bobcat is more...present."

Magnus turned back to the human, who held an undercurrent of inner strength. The scientist hadn't gotten to that part of him yet. He covered the entire length of the cot. His feet would have hung off if not for the bend of his knees. His hair was greasy and stuck up on his head at odd angles, but if he were clean, Magnus would bet he kept his hair cut short. Military cut, maybe? Picturing him fit and healthy was near impossible, but the shell lay there on the cot like an outline of his former self. "Were you a soldier?"

The human blinked once, trying to nod but it was so slight Magnus barely recognized it as such.

"Did you volunteer to be here?"

The human's eyebrows drew together, and his lips thinned right before he flipped Magnus off. His hand still lay against his chest, and he drew in on himself, but the meaning came through loud and clear.

Magnus grinned. The fact that the human could feel something besides pain meant he wasn't as far gone as everyone thought. "I deserved that."

The human smiled. It was slight, and the pain still laced every line on the human's face.

Magnus smiled back. "I have people who will miss me. They'll come for me soon. You hang in there until then. Got it."

The human's smile fell, and he closed his eyes as he nodded. He wouldn't be able to hang on much longer.

Scrubs came in with three guards. Each guard had a cattle prod. Just seeing those things pissed him off. They weren't fucking animals.

He was pissed off enough for his fangs to drop, but nothing happened.

He closed his eyes and shook his head as he tried to come off as threatening again.

I'm a vampire. Vampire. Not a human.

He focused on his gums and fangs, willing them to drop. The need for it built up in his gut.

He screamed when it happened. Blood spurted in his mouth. Some of it dripped down his chin and even farther, landing on his shirt.

He pounded his fists against the glass when Scrubs drew closer. "What the fuck did you do to me?"

Scrubs grinned. "Did that hurt, vampire?"

Yes. And it never had before, not even when it had first happened as a child.

When Joey had shifted, Magnus didn't know, but he came up to the glass beside Magnus, snarling and hissing. It was the first time Joey had shown aggression.

"We're making you human." Scrubs pressed some numbers on a keypad. Each cell had one. Magnus looked at the keypad across the hall because he couldn't see his. They had situated the panel like a calculator.

Magnus concentrated, trying to remember where Scrubs had pressed. Seven numbers altogether. The first two were the same and were either a two or a three. Definitely too far over to Scrub's right to be a one. And they were on that row. The next was five.

Two-two-five. Or three-three-five.

The next came from the last row. Nine, probably. Maybe an eight but Magnus thought Scrubs fingers were over too far for it to be the latter. Back to the middle next. Six. Definitely a six.

Two-two-five, or three-three-five-nine-six.

Magnus never lost focus as they pulled him out of the cell. They were unnecessarily rough, gripping his arm. He didn't fight them. Wherever they took him would lead to different information.

Joey lunged at the guard who'd grabbed Magnus. His mouth opened ready to take a bite. The guard zapped him. Joey screeched at the pain and then hissed even as he backed away from the long stick.

"Where are you taking me?" He recited the number code in his mind even as he asked the question.

"You're ready for the next phase."

What the fuck did that mean?

"I didn't know I was in a phase."

Scrubs made a sound in the back of his throat. "Dr. Perkins requires all vampires who come under our care—"

"Don't make it sound like you people have my best interest at heart." Magnus recited the number sequence again, committing it to a memory he didn't quite trust. Not after the whitecoats got done with him.

Scrubs smirked. "Dr. Perkins requires all vampires to go through a set of tests. You just completed the first one."

"Which is?"

They led Magnus down the hall out of the door at the end. The area was just a big room. At the far wall was a counter with various machines along it with papers scattered about. A woman focused on a microscope. She didn't avert his gaze from her task or acknowledge they had entered the room at all. She was a whitecoat and donned the offending garment.

"Introducing a suppressant into your system."

"Suppressant."

"Yes. It's designed to alleviate your need for blood."

Magnus could guess that, and it did a lot more than make him not want blood. "How many stages are there?"

"Three." Good to know he was a third of the way done.

"Is there a reason you don't put the bobcat shifter through these phases?"

"They fail on a shifter."

"Meaning you've murdered a bunch of shifters and keep the poor bobcat hostage for, what...fun?"

They led Magnus down another hallway with closed doors spaced a few yards apart. Someone screamed, and that was the thing that finally made Magnus resist, although resisting consisted of stopping in his tracks. They just dragged him after that. He tried to pull out of their hold, but the chemicals had made him weak.

"'Murder' is a strong word, considering."

Magnus disagreed. "Considering what?"

"Considering all the shifters will be dead soon. You vampires will be next, just as soon as we build an army strong enough to kill your kind off."

"Well, now I know you're a prejudiced dick." As if that was in question. Some prejudiced dicks had redeeming qualities, but Scrubs didn't. Magnus could tell by the smug look on his face.

"You don't count, vampire."

Magnus snorted but otherwise didn't comment. There wasn't any point with someone like Scrubs. Nothing Magnus said would change his mind about anything.

They came to a door that had a small wooden plaque on the front identifying the room inside as *Laboratory Nine*.

When they opened the door, Magnus didn't give them any leverage to pull him anywhere near the upright table. Brown straps with buckles hung down the sides of the table, and a set pooled onto the floor.

He pulled as hard as he could, mustering every ounce of strength he had left. Fingers dug into the flesh on his arms, scraping the first layer of skin off. He hissed and focused on the vein pulsing in his captors' throats.

His captor released the hold he had on his arm, and he tasted his first drops of freedom.

He didn't stop to analyze how many days they'd held him captive. Days had meshed together until a few hours felt like weeks. He didn't bother attacking them either. Instead, he turned and ran for the door. He reached out for the knob but didn't get his hand around it. A shock of pain zapped him in the back. It brought him to his knees, paralyzing him.

That was all they needed to regain the advantage.

They lifted him to his feet and brought him over to the table, strapping his hands in first. He fought against the restraints, hissing at them as they drew near. Since they treated him like an animal, he decided to act like one. He bit at one of the guards when he got close enough. His teeth closed around the human's arm. He ripped at the flesh, pulling it from the bone with everything he had.

The human screamed and backed away, which helped Magnus' cause. He spit the human's tissue and blood at the guard closest to him.

Magnus growled when a whitecoat came in, baring his teeth.

"Get him out of here." The whitecoat gestured to the bloody human.

Magnus could have been wallpaper for all the attention the whitecoat gave him. Everyone else in the room stopped what they were doing, even the injured man, who held his arm to his chest and had a sheen of sweat covering his face. They acted as if royalty had entered the room. The king gracing them with his presence.

Magnus saw him as a murderer. A threat to everyone, paranormal and human alike.

Scrubs gestured to a healthy guard, and the one led the other out of the room. The door clicked shut.

The whitecoat picked up a needle and a vial of some clear liquid. He filled the syringe, turning the vial upside down, draining it. He thumped the needle, getting the air bubbles out.

Magnus met Scrubs' gaze. "I'll take one more of you out before he sticks me with that thing."

"Now, now. It's only a little prick." The whitecoat was the one who answered, and without stopping what he was doing. He continued to thump away at the syringe.

"You're a little prick. Get near me and I'll take flesh."

The whitecoat turned to him. "You may call me Dr. Perkins." When the doctor smiled, he turned into more of a predator than anyone Magnus had ever met, and he knew Nicolono Stravros, so that was a hard-won spot on that particular crazy train. "Genetically, not much separates humans from vampires. Did you know that?"

Magnus knew the doctor was about to do shit to him that may cause permanent damage.

An image of Ladon popped into his head. Ladon had always looked at Magnus as if he was the most special being on the entire planet. It was that image he kept in his mind.

"Shifters aren't so simple. Their human and shifter genes are harder to isolate." The doctor focused on the only guard left in the room. "Strap his feet, please."

When the guard drew close enough, Magnus kicked out, connecting with the guard's stomach. He doubled over.

Magnus was so focused on the attack he didn't notice the doctor closing in until he felt the pinprick on his shoulder.

Magnus turned, hissing.

"The first stage has isolated the genes that make you a vampire. This stage will separate them and help us study the genes by attacking them. It'll be painful but not fatal."

"If it's not fatal, how come others have died?" Magnus' skin itched at the injection spot. It seemed to spread out like a group of bugs eating at his flesh. He wiggled, trying to stop them, but the table and the straps kept him in place.

"Shall I say, it's not fatal to you yet. The third stage is fatal. I haven't figured out why."

Magnus shut his eyes and tried to ignore the burning that had started from the inside out.

His fangs receded, and he lost the red haze. "Ladon. Saint Lakes. My name is Magnus." The flames burned the last one right out of his mind.

Chapter Fourteen

L adon peered out of the truck window at the tall buildings and dark, shiny glass. His legs hurt from being in the same cramped position for so long.

"I think I outgrew your truck." Ladon's knee went into the back of Bando's seat when he tried to stretch out. "Sorry."

Poor Bandos probably felt as though he was on a stationary amusement ride. "You wanna switch?"

"No. It's fine. I'm just saying the manufacturer of this truck didn't take into account that six-foot-four dragon shifters might want a comfortable ride."

Bandos chuckled.

Ladon knew cities had tall buildings. He watched television, for the love of the gods. But seeing it inside of a box and with his own eyes were two very different experiences.

The government building wasn't all that remarkable compared to the others surrounding it. Silver skyscrapers rose up into the sky to flirt with airplanes. Gazing up at them made his stomach churn, even from inside the truck. People crawled around like bugs on the sidewalk. So many Ladon couldn't even wrap his head around everyone. It reminded him of his mother's yard during the battle.

"Way too many people," he mumbled.

"Ignore them. Focus on the task." Garridan made it sound like a demand, which Ladon took as disrespect.

The growl came out before he could stop himself. "Sorry."

Garridan held up his hand halfway through Ladon's apology. "No. It's me who should apologize. You're strung tight because of the situation, so your dragon feels challenged even by me."

"Strung tight is...accurate." Way too accurate. He could shoot an arrow with his body.

"Once we see this Wesley Swenson guy, we'll have a bead on Magnus."

"How would Swenson know where Magnus is? We should go by his hotel first."

Bandos shook his head. "Magnus is smart enough to pay cash and use a fake name. No way would he do anything else. Not with the investigation being dangerous. We'd never find which hotel he's in."

Ladon growled again over the words *dangerous* and *investigation*. If Magnus wanted to bond, than they would have a long talk about that *dangerous* part. Not that Magnus had mentioned bonding. In fact, he'd done everything possible to ignore the subject when they had last talked.

"After we make contact with Swenson, how do you want to proceed, Alpha?" Bandos, Rocky, and Sully were very good at their job. They were arguably the best private investigators in the country. Bandos deferring to Ladon, who lacked any experience at all, didn't make sense, but whatever.

"Grab him."

Damian sat in the backseat with him. "I think we should kill the prejudiced prick. After we get what we need from him, of course." It was the first thing he'd said in hours.

Garridan gave him a narrow-eyed stare but averted his gaze a second later. "Can you control yourself around the human?"

"Meaning will I kill him?" Ladon couldn't say. "That depends on the circumstance. I won't let him hurt any of you. Or Magnus."

Ladon thought for sure Garridan would put his dad hat back on and argue with him about not killing the fragile human. All he did was nod and turn back around.

Garridan and Bandos looked at each other. Ladon wasn't privy to whatever passed between them.

Ladon didn't care if Magnus wanted him romantically or not. He'd get Ladon's protection because he was part of the clan.

Ladon ran a hand down his face. Who the fuck did he think he was fooling? He was in love with Magnus and always had been. It didn't matter that Magnus had friend-zoned him in that little cabin he claimed as his own. That was so long ago. When Magnus had still worked for Stavros, and he hadn't figured out how young Ladon was.

He'd die for Magnus. It was as simple as that.

To change the subject, Ladon said, "Stakeouts are boring."

Bandos chuckled. "Just wait until you have to piss."

"You do this all the time, I take it." If Ladon had been by himself, he'd have gone stir crazy. *By himself* wasn't something he did well. He talked too damn much for that to be comfortable.

"It's part of the job."

"Yeah, I think Magnus mentioned it once, but I didn't understand what he went through until now." Ladon loved listening to Magnus talk about his adventures. He just never thought he would go on one of his own. He wasn't sure if he liked it.

And wasn't that one more thing that lay between Magnus and himself. Magnus' sense of adventure and Ladon needing the comforts of home.

He had Saint Lakes in his blood. At no time was that more apparent than when he was sitting in the truck in the middle of a city that left him nauseous, at best.

Ladon hadn't been out of Saint Lakes his entire Somerset life except to go to one of those big box stores with his mom two towns over once a month. His Somerset years had reduced his world to three lakes and a very small paranormal town. Even the tourists, who came every summer and had Ramsey's permission to come back as often as they like, were repeat vacationers, so there had to be something about Saint Lakes that appealed.

Bandos nodded to a car that had pulled into a parking space three spots ahead of them. "That license plate is government-issued."

Ladon didn't understand. "So?"

"Why isn't the driver parking in there?" Bandos pointed to the four-story garage next to them. The garage had a sign on the gate system that read *government employees only*. Ladon had noticed because he had never seen exclusive parking before. Hell, he'd never really seen a parking garage except in passing. The human hospital had one and they passed it whenever they went to the big box store.

"Maybe the garage is full."

"The gate guard would put a sign up." Bandos nodded again as a woman got out of the car. She had long hair and sunglasses almost as big as her face. She had on a navy-colored business suit that seemed about as government-issued as her car. "She looks like a cop on one of those CSI shows."

"She's not a cop. Look at her badge." Bandos had eyes like a damn eagle.

She had the thing held loosely in her hand. The identification part faced them, but Ladon could only make out her picture, although just barely. He shifted his eyes to his dragon to make the words visible. He didn't know what he was reading, though. All he saw was the word *special operations* under the name Anna Boyle. She walked too fast for Ladon to make out anything else. "Is she a soldier?"

Bandos shook his head. "I don't know."

"She's an assassin." Everyone in the car turned to Damian when he spoke. He shrugged, his expression bored but alert. "Takes one to know one."

"Like those Bourne movies? Serious." Ladon's heart beat a fast rhythm against his chest.

"Never saw the movie."

"Magnus was attacked by a woman. I was on the phone with him when it happened. Managed to get away all in one piece."

Bandos turned in his seat with his eyes wide and exasperation on his face. "You didn't think to tell us that before we left the house?"

Ladon narrowed his eyes at the same time he changed his eyes to human again. "I told Ramsey after it happened."

"You didn't have a protective instinct to go after him at that point?"

"My dragon went fucking nuts." It roared to get out even as he sat there trying to stay as calm as he could.

"So why didn't we leave the day that happened?"

Why, indeed. And wasn't that a loaded question that hit way to close too personal. Still, he might as well get it said. "Because Magnus rejected me."

He sat back, folding his arms over his chest. He met Garridan's gaze through the rearview mirror. "Did he say that or is that just what you heard?"

"What's the fucking difference?" Ladon averted his gaze back to the building. They were less than extraordinary since he had put a voice to his relationship issues.

"You know what the difference is, Ladon."

Yeah, well he didn't want to talk about it. Not when his heart knotted so tightly it hurt. His skin itched all over with the need to shift and find Magnus. His dragon blew fire in his mind. The smoke from it rolled out of his nose. "Something's wrong."

"Don't change the subject, boy." Nothing else mattered but Magnus' life, which was on the line. His safety sat between them all.

Ladon let his fangs drop, and his eyes shift again. He unfolded his arms and leaned forward. "There are more important things than the state of my mental health. Something is wrong with my mate. I can feel it. We need to find him sooner rather than later."

Ladon could practically feel Magnus' pain.

Garridan bowed his head the way a dragon shifter would defer to another. "Yes, Alpha."

It was the first time Garridan had completely surrendered to him. Garridan's dragon was almost as strong as Ladon's, and he certainly knew how to fight better. But it was the *almost* part of that they both had ignored, preferring the parental relationship they had cultivated. Apparently, they weren't ignoring it anymore.

Ladon reached over and touched the back of his neck as was the proper way for an Alpha to release one of his clan members. "I don't like the hierarchy. You know that."

"In this circumstance it's necessary."

Ladon nodded. His eyes and fangs stayed, and smoke rolled out of his nose every time he breathed. "He's hurt. I can feel it...just under my skin. It's making me panic."

"We'll do our best to speed things up, Alpha." Bandos pounded away at his computer keys.

"We need to stay safe. We can't help Magnus otherwise." He said the last part more to himself than the rest of them.

"Of course." Bandos didn't take his eyes off the computer or lose his sudden focus.

He tried to shift his eyes back to human just as an experiment to see if they would, but nothing happened. The way his dragon demanded to take over was a new experience. A part of him wanted to let it all happen the way his dragon insisted, but he'd be a breaking news story if he did. "The rest of me wants to shift too, but I keep holding it off."

"We'll get Swenson first. Talk to him. Find out what he knows. After that, we'll figure out where Magnus is and rescue him. We'll use Swenson how ever we have to." Garridan's eyes shifted when he looked at Ladon. "We stick to the plan."

Stick to the plan. "Yes."

As plans went it seemed simple enough, but there were a lot of little elements in between those bigger ones that Ladon didn't have enough experience to factor in, so a part of him was in the dark and he didn't like it.

One element at a time and the first one was to get Wesley Swenson.

Chapter Fifteen

Wesley sat at his desk with his heart beating a wild rhythm. He eyed the senator's closed office door, which hadn't opened all day. Not even for coffee and lunch.

Wesley had made mistakes before. Once he'd accidentally talked to a reporter about legislation the senator should have signed but didn't. And then there was the time he almost outed the senator's mistress to his wife. He didn't know what he'd done, but the senator wasn't happy with him. That much came through with one scathing glance that morning and Wesley hadn't been able to keep the stress at bay since. He searched his brain to figure out a reason why but came up empty.

He wanted to go to the senator and ask if he intended to fire him. Because if he was and the senator made him sit around all day, well, that made Wesley a little mad because it was unnecessary stress. He'd rather go home, wallow in self-pity for a week and then search the help wanted ads. Not that he knew what he'd do after the senator did finally fire him. He'd never work for another politician again. The senator would see to that.

Wesley put his forehead down on the desk and closed his eyes.

His life was over. As soon as he got off work, he was jobless. He'd lose everything he'd worked so hard for his whole life. It wasn't like he could rely on his parents for help again either. His dad might have gotten him the job with the senator, but that had been before he'd come out to them. They had successfully written him off. It had been years since he'd talked to them.

When the door to the outer office opened, he snapped his head up. Embarrassment burned up his neck at getting caught wallowing in self-pity when he should've been doing his job, even if there were only a few minutes left.

The embarrassment turned to fear as soon as he saw who it was.

Always before he turned a blind eye to the woman's purpose. He knew why she came. He wasn't stupid. He connected the dots. Over the years, Wesley had gotten very good at reading the senator's moods. Sometimes, but not always, those he had a problem with would go missing. Wesley had even seen news stories, especially if they were high profile.

The woman who walked in didn't bother to even glance his way. She could have been a robot for all the emotion she showed. If giant birds and other monsters existed then robots who appeared human could too, and she was one of them. He certainly wasn't ruling anything out.

She didn't bother knocking on the senator's office door but just went right on through as if she owned the place. But then that was the way she did things whenever she came, not that it was very often.

Wesley's hands shook when he opened his desk drawer and drew out his car keys. His day wasn't officially over, but it didn't matter.

He needed to get out before she came back. He swallowed around the sudden dryness in his throat and shut the drawer.

He stood just as the woman came out with a file folder in her hand. He sat again as if she'd caught him sneaking around. She was only in there long enough to get the file. It was likely her and the senator hadn't even spoken to each other.

She didn't give Wesley a passing glance when she left.

Might as well wait the fifteen minutes. If she followed him home, then he knew he was in trouble.

God, what would he do if his information was in that file folder?

Chapter Sixteen

"Looks like we're not the only ones waiting for someone." Bandos nodded at the woman's car.

Ladon didn't care about Anna, the assassin. He just wanted to get to Magnus as soon as possible. "She's only important if she gets in my way."

"She could be useful. Especially if your hunch is right and she's the one who attacked Magnus." Damian was the one who spoke. He could've been talking about something as mundane as the weather.

"If that's the case, why are we sitting here looking at her damn bumper?" Ladon balled his fists. He rode the edge of anger like a barely controlled beast. He wanted off the anger train but couldn't figure out how to dismount. He'd stay on as long as he could feel Magnus. "Maybe we should take her instead of Wesley."

"It's too big an assumption." Bandos was nothing if not the perfect picture of calm in the face of a hell of a lot of stress. Well, Ladon had stress. Maybe Bandos didn't have a vested interest in the situation, other than he'd pledged his allegiance to the Saint Lakes clan. Ladon could see where even that wouldn't make the situation with Magnus as personal as being his mate.

Ladon didn't fault him for the lack. Someone needed to stay stable because the gods knew Ladon wasn't capable. "All I know is Magnus said it was a woman who attacked him. It's too much of a coincidence to think it was someone else. And now he's in pain. A lot of it."

"But she's sitting in her car at the moment, which means she's not the one hurting Magnus." Bandos could've given a class on basic logic.

Ladon rolled his eyes. "Doesn't mean she's not the one who put him in the wrong place."

"True." Well, thank fuck for small miracles. "And I think we should question her if we get her in a place that's not so public. But we shouldn't lose sight of Swenson either. Both are potential leads."

Ladon's leg bounced as if he had a spring in his shoes and his leg had a mind of its own. He couldn't sit still even if he tried. He nodded and looked out of the window, away from Anna the Assassin because Garridan, Damian and Bandos had that covered. Instead, he watched a man jaywalk across the road toward the government build-ing. His coat was one of those long tan ones that floated around his calf muscles when the air took it. He had a button-down shirt on that seemed dressier than the overall ensemble warranted. He was basically a cowboy without the hat. A very out-of-place politician, although the politician part came through in the way he styled his hair and the keycard in his hand.

Ladon returned his gaze to the woman's car. He could see the back of her head through the rearview mirror. She sat staring at the govern-ment building's front doors. "She could be waiting for Swenson or the senator."

"Could be anyone." Damian didn't take his eyes off the building. Ladon had never met someone so ready to kill.

Ladon smiled. "The fact that the Fates paired you with Owen is fucking hilarious."

The first real emotion Damian had shown was in the form of a lifted eyebrow. Just one. Single. Eyebrow. "Why is that?"

For a moment, Ladon forgot about his stress and focused on Damian's ignorance. "Dude, he's the most emotional shifter I know."

And then miracles of all miracles, the independent eyebrow aligned with the other one and the corners of Damian's mouth turned up for one millisecond before his expression went to steel again. "I don't need you to tell me that."

"I think you do. I think you need a fucking handbook."

Damian snorted. "Probably."

Ha, Ladon might have cracked through that cold shell.

"Stop poking at Damian and pay attention." Garridan's reprimand was like a bucket of ice water dumped over him. His good mood from moments ago disappeared and the urgency of the moment returned full force. "Swenson just walked out."

Ladon's gaze snapped to the front of the government building, and he eyed the enemy. As diabolical conspiracy theorists went, Ladon had an image in his head of a man who didn't remember to groom on a regular basis and had trouble leaving his house.

Swenson seemed like every other white-collar worker with his business suit and perfectly styled hair. Ladon would consider him average build by human standards.

He had a pretty face and appeared young. Naïve.

He clutched keys in his fist and stopped on the sidewalk's edge as if he were waiting for a taxi. He didn't scan up and down the road, though. Crossing the street didn't seem to be on his agenda either. No, studying each vehicle, even the truck. Their gazes met before Swenson moved up the row of vehicles. As soon as he saw Anna, his eyes widened. His face turned white, and he scurried off the sidewalk, crossing the road like a scared mouse.

"Swenson must know what she is," Damian whispered.

"It's not good news for us. It means we'll have to get to him before she does." Bandos followed Swenson with his gaze until he disappeared into the parking garage.

"As long as we get the information we need before she kills him," Damian said.

"We're not letting her kill him." No way would Ladon entertain Damian's attitude. That might have worked well for Stavros because he was a psychopathic criminal but Ladon wouldn't run the clan that way.

"And if he did something to Magnus, are you going to be able to restrain yourself?" Everyone was capable of killing given the right circumstances. Sometimes it was a kill-or-be-killed situation. But Ladon wasn't a murderer.

"You saw Swenson as clearly as I did." Wesley's website was formed by someone who ran on fear and nothing else, not even curiosity.

"I saw a human. Nothing more."

"A scared one."

"Fear makes humans dangerous."

Swenson all by himself wasn't a problem for them, but the senator had people in his pocket. All politicians did. "The senator is more of a threat then Swenson. That much I know."

Bandos turned in his seat and nodded approvingly. "That's right. We're going after a small player in a sea of much bigger threats."

Ladon's gaze met Damian's. "So we're all going to save our energy for the bigger threat. Swenson won't die today. Not by our hands and not by hers."

Before Damian could comment—because he had to have the last word on everything—Ladon realized the truck had moved. Garridan pulled out onto the road, following the woman. "Swenson's on the move."

"He knows she's following," Rocky explained.

"Does she know we are?" Ladon didn't think it mattered if Swenson knew about them or not. He'd find out soon enough.

"I think so, yeah."

Questioning Swenson had just gotten a whole lot harder.

Anna followed Swenson to his house. She parked on the street behind a family-type sedan and was out of her vehicle before Swenson had even unlocked the door to his house. Ladon wasn't even positive she'd shut off the car's engine.

Swenson fumbled with his house keys and began crying before she made it across the road. Her strides were long and sure, eating up the distance.

Garridan parked so close behind her car there was no way she could get out of the spot when the time came. All four of them were out of the truck and following her.

"Let me take care of her," Damian whispered as they crossed the road.

"Just don't kill her. She might have information we'll need."

Damian nodded, but the disappointment rolled over him clear as day.

They stood back, letting Damian take the lead. Ladon couldn't see Damian vamp out but he knew the exact moment he did because Swenson lost all color from his face. He even swayed on his feet to the point he had to lean against his closed front door for stability.

As soon as Damian grabbed the woman's wrist, she turned and kicked him across the cheek.

Ladon's mouth fell open, and his eyes widened as he watched Damian get his ass kicked on Swenson's front lawn. "By the gods, Damian, restrain her already."

"I'm trying. She's not entirely human." What the fuck did that mean? Not human.

And then he remembered something Magnus had said about how strong the woman had been who attacked him.

Damian finally had a hold of her around the middle. She tried to struggle out of his hold and even used her foot to kick him in the shin. He hissed and must have loosened his hold just enough that she was able to break free.

She went right for Swenson, pulling a knife from the inside of her blazer.

Ladon acted on instinct when he partially shifted. He was only about a foot away when he blew fire at her feet.

She managed to turn onto her back, holding the knife blade up as Ladon drew closer. Ladon grabbed it, the blade slicing through his palm even as he ripped the thing from her grasp.

He shifted everything back to his human form except his eyes as he met her gaze. For the first time, she looked truly scared. "You know where my mate is."

It wasn't a question. He knew she knew. But she shook her head anyway.

Ladon handed the knife to whoever had come up beside him and knelt. Blood dripped down onto the grass from his palm. The wound stung, but he ignored it.

Garridan and Bandos went to Swenson. Garridan took the keys from him and opened the door. They disappeared inside with Swenson without a word.

"You do, and you'll tell me where he is before morning."

"I'll get the information out of her." Damian played along with him, soaking in just the thought of torturing her.

Ladon grabbed the woman by her shirt, lifting her from the ground. She tried to kick him, but he anticipated it. All she kicked was air. He turned her and held her arm behind her back, wrenching it up whenever she tried to fight him.

"Do you have the ability to heal like a vampire?"

"Fuck you."

"It wasn't a threat. I'm curious."

"Yes."

"Good to know." He pushed her across the lawn and up to the house. She tried to stop him from taking her inside by bracing herself with a hand on the doorjamb, but Damian brought his arm down on her hard enough to get his message across.

Garridan and Bandos already had Swenson sitting on the couch. Swenson's face was still so white Ladon was surprised he hadn't passed out yet.

"Find something to restrain her." Ladon held her captive for the moment, but that wouldn't last forever. Anna would eventually get the jump on him. She was too smart and way too good at fighting not to.

Damian walked past him over to Wesley. "Do you have a rope?"

"Na-no."

Damian walked out of the room without a word.

Ladon met Garridan's gaze, needing the reassurance that he was about to do the right thing. Garridan nodded. "You're doing well, boy."

That gave Ladon just enough momentum to continue. "Now, one of you knows where my mate is, and one of you will tell me."

Swenson was the first to speak. His whole body shook. "I don't know anything. I'd tell you, I swear."

For the first time, Anna spoke. "Shut your mouth." She gritted her teeth and even leaned toward Swenson as if just that inch or two threatened his existence enough to satisfy.

Swenson moved away from her, scooting down the length of the couch.

Ladon lifted her arm a bit more, causing her to hiss at the pain. "Dark-haired vampire. Has a trimmed beard and dark eyes. Ring any bells?"

"By now, he's probably a babbling idiot." She laughed.

Ladon lifted her arm even more and felt something give, either bone or muscle, Ladon wasn't sure. He must have either dislocated her shoulder or broken her arm.

He let her go, holding his hands up. He searched for Garridan's reassurance once again. Garridan's expression hardened, and for a moment Ladon thought he was the cause, but then he turned to the woman before returning his gaze to Ladon again.

She cried out, holding her arm to her chest. When she met his gaze, she narrowed her eyes. "What is it with you people and breaking limbs? Fuck!"

Damian came through with a couple of neckties in his hand. He stopped just inside the door, taking in the scene. "Looks like he didn't need the restraints."

Ladon swallowed the bile rising in his throat. He stepped away from her, and that was when he felt Magnus in pain again. He could practically hear him screaming.

Ladon bent at the waist. "Where is he?"

Her face hardened. "Strapped to one of Dr. Perkins' tables."

"Dr. Perkins?" Who the fuck was that?

Ladon sniffed the air, trying to capture her scent. He partially shifted. "You smell weird. Like stale blood and pine. Human and vampire all mixed together. Doesn't quite make you as good as paranormals, but almost."

"They made me less human." She meant it as an insult, implying paranormals were incapable of feeling anything beyond what was instinctive. The fact that she thought that, made her more vulnerable, not less.

Ladon chuckled. "Your people don't know as much as they think. That's the thing that gives us the advantage, although we don't know what to do with it yet. Your kind has us there. When we figure it out, your side will lose." He hoped he could back that last claim up. It was a loose threat, but he tried to sound as confident as he could.

She didn't speak for the longest time. "Your mate? As in life partner?"

"Yes. You took him. And now I've come to get him back." Smoke rolled out his nose and mouth. "And I'll do anything. Understand?"

"I'll take you to the laboratory if you promise not to give me to Dr. Perkins." She wasn't in a position to make demands. She had to know that.

Damian walked over with the ties and began binding her without a single word. She screamed when he wrenched her injured arm behind her back but didn't pay it any mind.

"You'll take me to my mate because it's what's going to keep you alive." Ladon nodded to Wesley. "I can use his fear to get the information, and you know it."

"He doesn't know anything." Ladon couldn't tell if she gave that information to protect Wesley or because it was the truth. The latter seemed more likely. "Perkins' lab is in the warehouse district."

Chapter Seventeen

"It's there." Anna nodded to a building on the right. They had her hands tied behind her back, so she couldn't point. She sat at an awkward, forward angle. Ladon almost felt sorry for her but then he remembered she had brought Magnus to a laboratory which had held him captive and caused him pain.

Magnus hadn't screamed in several minutes. The quiet caused an urgency to swim through Ladon's blood, making his heart beat heavy.

How Ladon knew what Magnus felt was anyone's guess but he was glad for it. It meant they had developed a connection whether Magnus wanted one or not.

Garridan drove past the building.

Ladon didn't take his eyes off the place as they made their way to the next building over.

The lab was similar to every other warehouse in the area, and they were plentiful. It was a big, square box with a flat roof. The other buildings around seemed to manufacture medical equipment. The sign in front of the boxy building read *Perkins Laboratory*. The letters were blue and thin like small snakes all wrapped around each other for one common purpose.

Perkins Laboratory. Ladon wanted to vomit at the sight of the pretty font. All that deception turned his stomach.

Ladon turned toward Anna. "You better not be lying."

She rolled her eyes.

She sat beside Damian. The two could've been twins. Anna would kill any one of them if she got the chance and Damian would kill anyone Ladon told him to without a single thought. Not because Ladon was Alpha, but because Ladon was Owen's Alpha. Whatever trouble his brother had with Damian, loyalty wasn't it.

"I have more reason to tell you the truth than to lie."

Wesley sat between him and Damian. With Anna's injury and her hands tied behind her back, she was the least likely to escape, so putting her by the door wasn't as risky.

Swenson practically sat on Ladon's lap. Four bodies in the back seat was a bit too much, especially with Ladon and Damian being as big as they were. Ladon wanted nothing more than to shove Wesley off but he resisted the urge.

"If you are, I'll kill you." Damian flashed his fangs and red eyes at her.

Wesley's face went white as if Damian had intended to harm him. He looked at Ladon as if asking him for help. Smart man. Ladon was the lesser of the two evils.

If he didn't get to Magnus by the time the sun declared morning, Ladon would unleash Damian.

Ladon shrugged and turned back to the scenery outside the window.

He didn't have a choice but to trust. If Magnus wasn't there, he would kidnap the senator. He'd get serious jail time and end up on every news station in the country but at least he'd find Magnus.

Garridan turned at the next right just past the lab. No one spoke as he parked in an empty parking lot. Trees shadowed the area.

Bandos tapped away on his laptop keyboard. The screen lit up the cab, glowing around him.

"So, Perkins does own that laboratory." Bandos' voice broke through the silence. "The place is supposed to do specialized testing. Like for rare diseases and stuff."

Anna snorted out a laugh but then groaned in pain a second later. She must have moved against her injury or something.

Swenson shook his head. "Dr. Perkins does experiments on humans and paranormals." He cleared his throat and eyed Anna. "Most don't volunteer, even the humans." It was the first time Wesley had spoken. Ladon wasn't sure why he'd given the information, but it was useful.

Damian met Ladon's gaze. "Seriously. She volunteered for guinea pig duty, and you won't let me kill her?"

Swenson held up a finger. "Umm...actually, the senator lied to the volunteers." Swenson dropped his hands back into his lap after he finished making his point.

"You talk too fucking much." Anna gave Wesley a hard stare. It was the first time she had shown emotion beyond the occasional eye-roll.

Swenson's shoulders came up to his ears as he folded in on himself.

Bandos leaned forward into his computer a bit. "I think I can hack their security system, but I need to get a remote device in the building first."

"Are workers in the building twenty-four-seven?" Ladon asked the question to whoever would answer.

To his surprise, it was Anna who spoke. "Yes. There will be a shift change in about an hour when the night crew starts."

Ladon smiled to himself before opening the door, sliding out of the truck. The overhead light turned on, but Garridan's nimble fingers clicked it off. Ladon tapped on the front passenger's window.

Bandos rolled it down and handed Ladon a small, black box. "Make sure he puts it next to a computer. Any computer will do."

Ladon nodded and put the device into his pocket before grabbing Wesley's arm.

Wesley went into panic mode when Ladon pulled him from the vehicle. "What? No. I can't go in there."

Anna smirked. "Better hope Dr. Perkins isn't staying overnight." She looked at Ladon, growing serious again. "He sometimes sleeps in his office. Especially when he has an experiment going on. If he's here, we're all screwed. Especially me."

"Why?" Garridan pulled the keys out of his ignition and handed them to Bandos, who took them with barely a thought. Garridan exited the truck but stood in the open driver's side door.

"Why what?"

"Why is Perkins dangerous to all of us, especially you?"

"Perkins is smart. Calculating. His mind is always working. The rest of us are his goons. Only the senator isn't scared of him, and that's because they both need each other."

"How do they need each other?"

"One needs money and the other needs silence. What would happen if the world learned about what Dr. Perkins was doing in that building? And what would happen to Perkins' little secret if the senator didn't get reelected every year?"

Ladon met Bandos' gaze. "What do you think about making that information public?"

Anna shook her head. "If you do, you're making yourselves a big target."

"I'm already a big target." He shifted his eyes and let smoke roll out of his nose. "I shift into a dragon."

She struggled against her bindings, grunting when her injury became too much. "Send me in. I have clearance. It'll be a clean entry."

Ladon narrowed his eyes. She'd brought him to Magnus. He probably shouldn't, but his gut told him to trust her. She had held up her end of the bargain, so Ladon would hold up his and protect her. He couldn't do that if he sent her into that building. "No."

She leaned forward. "Look, I might not like it but I'm on your side now. The senator will have me killed once he learns you got the better of me. And he will learn that, won't he, Wesley?"

Wesley shook his head. "He would have you kill me."

Anna smiled. "Not killed. Just handed over to Dr. Perkins."

"Same thing." Wesley turned enough to meet his gaze. "You can't trust her. She'll sabotage the whole mission."

He closed the door to the truck when Garridan did. He took a step to the right, Wesley in tow, until he could meet Garridan's gaze. "If Bandos can get through their security system then I'll send Wesley inside."

"Yes. He's the one we can't trust. We'll make sure he gets the device in the building. If he gives us away after, it won't matter by then. We don't need the element of surprise anyway. We need inside."

It didn't escape Ladon's notice that Wesley had paled as they spoke. He tensed, and he tried to pull his arm free. Ladon tightened his grip.

Garridan came around the vehicle and grabbed Wesley by his free arm. Ladon let him go. Swenson whimpered when Ladon took his coat off. Ladon ignored him and looked around the parking lot.

"Calm yourself. He's not going to touch you."

Ladon rolled his eyes. "You must think we're all savage beasts."
Ladon laid his coat on the hood of the truck and pulled his shirt over
his head, laying it on top. "All paranormals have a mate. We recognize
them by smell. Once we find them, we're faithful. Not like you humans who have a history of cheating. Magnus is my mate, not that I
would touch you even if he weren't. I'm not a rapist. Or a monster.
Or whatever the fuck you think, you prejudiced prick." He kicked off
his shoes.

"Th-then why?"

Ladon had his hands on the button of his jeans. "I'm going to
shift."

"Why?"

Ladon got right in Wesley's face. "Because it's easier to kill you when
you fuck me over, so don't if you want to live."

Wesley shook as if he were cold.

Ladon finished stripping, pulling the device out of his pocket and
handed it to Wesley.

"Go in there, find a computer to stick that next to. If you don't, I'll
track you down and kill you with one single bite. Understand?"

Wesley nodded.

"I'll escort you over."

"Naked?" That was the thing Wesley was worried about. Really?

Ladon shook his head. "Only humans have a problem with nakedness."

"Not only humans," Damian shouted.

"Fine." Ladon rolled his eyes and shifted.

Wesley screamed the second he saw Ladon and ran across the parking lot, toward the lab as if Ladon were chasing him.

Escorting. Chasing. Whatever. It got him moving.

As soon as Swenson's hand touched the button on the speaker, Ladon shifted back. He closed the couple of yards separating them. Ladon eyed the camera at the top of the building and tried to stay where he wouldn't be visible. He hoped he succeeded. One way or another he'd get Magnus out of there. "Remember, don't fuck it up."

Swenson whimpered when he heard Ladon's voice but nodded. He pressed the button. Crackling came through the small speaker before someone spoke. "Yes?"

"Senator Fowler sent me to pick up a file on one of your patients." Wesley met Ladon's gaze. He either wanted Ladon's approval or he made sure Ladon wouldn't come after him. Ladon wasn't sure which.

"Yes, sir."

There was a buzzing noise before the door clicked. Wesley pulled it open, looking back at him one last time before going inside.

Ladon held up all five of his fingers. "Five minutes and then I'm burning the fucking building to the ground with you in it."

Chapter Eighteen

----

*L*adon. *Saint Lakes. My name is Magnus.*

He used to have four things to remember but the last one had slipped from his memory.

Ladon. Saint Lakes. His head lolled. His neck couldn't hold it on his shoulders anymore. A fine sheen of sweat had long since turned sticky. The sweat trapped the cold under his skin until it had nowhere to move except inward. The chill wrapped around his bones until it stole his focus.

"I'm Magnus," he whispered to himself again. The medication fucked with his body on a soul-deep level.

He took a deep breath and let it out, closing his eyes. He needed rest while he could get it, but the thought of shutting his brain off in order to sleep scared him.

"Ladon. Saint Lakes."

What if he didn't wake up? Or remember who he was? Or worse? What if he forgot who Ladon was?

The door opened, and two men in lab coats walked in. One man had an auburn beard. The hair on his head was more blond than red, though. He had freckles everywhere, even on the part of his arms Magnus saw. The other man had slicked-back dark hair and eyes that looked about as wasted as Magnus felt. Something about the second man put Magnus on alert even though he couldn't do anything about it.

The door clicked shut behind them, and then their sneakers squeaked on the industrial tiles.

Each one began undoing the buckle restraints on his ankles without a word. It didn't take them very long to move to his wrists. His left wrist was free before the right one. He hissed at the pain in his muscles. Holding them in the same position for hours hurt. He could tick that one off his list of things he never wanted to find out but did anyway.

The second the whitecoats freed his right wrist, they grabbed him around his arms.

He tried to stand, wanting to escape. Going passively into captivity wasn't exactly Magnus' style. His legs gave out, and that was all that came of it.

The whitecoats half-dragged, half-carried him through the building until they came to the closed door that would lead him back to his cell.

Tears gathered in his eyes at just the thought of getting a reprieve from the shots and whatever else they did to him. The shit they pumped through him ripped his body in half.

Logically, he knew the prison cell wasn't safe, but the illusion was enough. None of it mattered the second the whitecoat pulled open the door. All his mind and body knew was that no one would cause him pain inside that small glass box.

He almost cried when the whitecoats stopped halfway inside the door with him dangling between them. They all turned at the same time as if they were one unit.

Wesley stood next to an oval-shaped counter. The top of a computer screen peeked above it. One of Wesley's arms disappeared but only for a second.

"The lab is closed for the night." The whitecoat's tone remained neutral.

"Yes. S-sorry." Wesley met Magnus' gaze. His brows drew together, wrinkling his forehead further. He opened his mouth to say something but shut it just as quickly, averting his gaze to the top of the desk. His arm came back around, and Magnus immediately noticed his hand was empty. "The-the senator asked me to pick up something from Dr. Perkins."

"Dr. Perkins didn't say anything about that."

Wesley took a step away from the counter. His hands shook but then he clasped his fingers together, so it wasn't as noticeable. "Yes, well." He seemed to contemplate something or perhaps he was searching for a good lie. He shuffled from one foot to another.

He met Magnus' gaze again but turned away quickly. His hands unclasped, and he took a step toward one of the whitecoats. "I've been kid—"

Metal banged against wood right before the most menacing roar Magnus had ever heard echoed throughout the building. The whitecoats dropped Magnus right where they stood. He fell to the floor in a heap, his legs folding underneath him.

The door leading to the prison room rested against his left side, pressing against him, demanding he move so it could return home.

The whitecoats ran toward the sound, leaving him with Wesley, who stared at him as if he were the undead.

"What did they do to you?" Wesley whispered the question, so Magnus didn't know if he should answer or not. He didn't have the energy anyway.

Fighting.

He recognized the scuffling and grunts even without the screams.

Wesley's eyes widened. He searched around for an exit right before he took off in the opposite direction of the ruckus.

Another scream and then a roar that shook the building. Pain laced through the next roar. Something about it called to Magnus until he had an overwhelming urge to protect whatever beast had created the sound.

"Stick him with that needle, and they'll be cleaning up pieces of you." Damian? No way.

By the gods, why would his mind manufacture someone like Damian? If he were going to hallucinate anyone, it should have been Ladon.

Magnus leaned his head against the door and closed his eyes. He just needed rest. Just a few minutes.

Even when someone else screamed and bones crunched, he couldn't bring himself to care enough to move.

"Ladon. Saint Lakes. I'm Magnus." There used to be a fourth one, but he had lost it. Searching in the dark proved pointless.

A sudden gust of wind blew at him, moving the strands of his hair. They lay back in place at the same time something rubbed against his cheek, nudging him. He still didn't open his eyes, fearing that what he suspected was all a manifestation of his mind.

"Ladon. Saint Lakes. I'm Magnus." He slipped into a tight space in his mind. Survive.

"Shh, I'm here." Ladon. And then someone brushed his hair off his face, soothing. He moved into the touch, wanting more even if it was something his mind made up to cope. "I'm gonna take you home."

Magnus shook his head. Home meant Saint Lakes, and that was too much hope. His emotions cracked open and leaked down his face. Even his closed eyes couldn't hold them back.

"Might want to get him moving before the second wave gets sent in, Alpha." Damian again.

Magnus reached up and wiped at the wetness on his chin. By the gods, Damian was the least comforting person Magnus could think of.

"I don't even know if he can move. He's-he's bad off."

"Might want to carry him then." A gun going off took Magnus by surprise, and he jumped. "Too late."

The hand left his hair, but it was the air displacing around him that had him cracking an eye open. The first thing he saw was a green, scaly tail. Magnus had seen dragon shifters before. Saint Lakes had dragons, although he'd never seen that particular one. Still, his whole body relaxed even as he kept his eyes open enough to take in the scene around him.

The dragon kept himself between the whitecoats and Magnus. Biting when they got too close. One whitecoat had a gun pointed at the dragon. The dragon blew fire from his mouth in a steady stream until the whitecoat lit up in flames. The gun clattered to the floor as the whitecoat ran around, looking for a way to cope with the pain and put out the flames.

The man on fire grabbed another whitecoat, holding on as if his life depended on it. He succeeded in nothing more than catching his co-worker on fire.

Magnus didn't know where Garridan had come from, but he stood in front of him, blocking the fight. Magnus wanted to touch him, to see if he were real but he feared his fingers would go right through Garridan's ghost.

Garridan's lips spoke, but Magnus wasn't focused enough to hear anything. It wasn't until Garridan's big hand closed around his shoulder and lifted him off the door and into his arms that Magnus paid attention. "...more inside?"

"Ladon. Saint Lakes." He floated as Garridan ran across the tiles. And he could smell the laundry soap all the Somersets used. Mother Estelle's homemade soap. Everyone in the Somerset house used it, including Ladon.

"Are there more inside?"

More what?

He couldn't ask the question because the outside air touched his cheek, which was the first thing that gave him an indication it all might be real.

"Can you stand?" Garridan put him on his feet before Magnus had a chance to answer. His legs buckled, and he would have fallen if not for Garridan bracing him against the wall. Garridan bent down enough to get right in Magnus' face. "Are there more victims inside?"

"Two. A human, and bobcat shifter." He wanted to say more but his brain throbbed against his skull. He put a hand to his forehead, attempting to relieve the pain before continuing. "Human is bad off. Might be dead by now." He rattled off the codes for both cell doors.

How long had he been away? He wasn't sure. If felt like days but it could have been minutes for all Magnus knew.

Garridan nodded and pulled something out of his back pocket. He handed it to Magnus and before he knew it, cold metal pressed against his palm. He looked at the handgun and then up at Garridan again. "Shoot the orderlies if they come out."

Magnus floated the word orderlies around in his mind, finding a meaning for it past the pain in his head. "Whitecoats."

"Whatever. Just shoot them." Authority dripped from every word.

Magnus nodded. "What about the green dragon?"

Garridan's eyebrows drew together, and he studied Magnus as if they just met. He sniffed around Magnus. "By the gods, what did they do to you?"

"I don't know." None of what he had experienced made sense. He struggled to comprehend even the smallest thing.

"The green dragon is your mate."

"'Mate'?"

Garridan moved out of his personal space, although he didn't go far because he still held Magnus up with help from the building. Garridan shook his head at the same time he closed his eyes. When Garridan met his gaze again, he asked, "Did you smell Ladon?"

Magnus nodded to Garridan's clothing. "The laundry-soap."

"But you didn't smell his unique scent? At all?"

"I can't." Not anymore. That had been the first things to go. "I didn't even know what I had until it wasn't there anymore." And fuck, he was tired.

Garridan patted his shoulder. "You'll get better."

Was that a command? It sounded like one. He intended to ask but then the door opened, the fight spilling into the parking lot.

The green dragon's head came out, biting around the shoulder of a whitecoat. The whitecoat fell to the ground, landing on his ass when the dragon let him go.

The dragon's big body couldn't make it out of the doorway, and he tried, which would have been comical under different circumstances.

Magnus blinked when the dragon turned into a very naked Ladon. His back was to Magnus, but he still saw the blood splattered across Ladon's pale skin.

Hope bubbled up, spilling out his mouth in a desperate laugh. He tried to move away from the wall, but Garridan pushed him back. "Stay here."

"I just...I need..." By the gods, he didn't know what he needed. He only knew if he could touch Ladon and he turned out to be real, then he'd trust it enough to hope.

Ladon shifted into a green dragon again.

Garridan let Magnus go, turning to join the fight. He shifted into a dragon as well. Only he was brick-red instead of the shiny green.

Magnus slid down the wall to the pavement. His legs were gelatin and wouldn't hold him upright.

His Ladon. That made sense.

Damian came spilling out of the door. Five whitecoats running after him. Magnus raised the gun and shot one of them before turning the gun on another. Both fell to the ground like trash. They lay there next to him, one dead and the other struggling for life. The dead one had a needle in his open hand.

Damian punched a whitecoat in the face with the butt end of his gun before turning the barrel up and shooting him in the center of his forehead, execution style, as he fell to the pavement. The other two whitecoats took off across the parking lot, not staying to fight.

Sure enough, Damian lifted the gun, shooting one before pointing to the other. Both fell to the ground, but one managed to take a few steps before dropping to his knees. He swayed for a few seconds before landing on face.

Damian met Magnus' gaze. "No way would you be part of my comfort hallucination."

Damian chuckled. "But fighting is, huh?"

"I find it more comforting than I do you." The fight was another thing that seemed off, though.

Damian turned when another whitecoat came out. He lifted the gun and took the shot. "No one ever said you were stupid."

"But you're here, which confuses me." The last time Magnus had seen Damian was at Stavros' mansion. That had been years ago.

"Long story short. My mate is Ladon's brother, Owen. Found him injured during the Battle of Saint Lakes."

Ladon. Saint Lakes. Both words were a part of him. Tears clogged in his throat again until he couldn't speak for fear of choking.

"You need help getting to the car?"

He nodded. Damian took a step in his direction at the same time Magnus felt a prick in his leg. He looked down to see an injured whitecoat's hand around a needle.

Magnus didn't react fast enough, so the liquid filled his system. Magnus met the whitecoat's gaze. The whitecoat had blood around his lips and teeth when he smiled. "Phase two."

He couldn't breathe past the panic.

Damian shot the man in the head. A red hole formed, and his hair dampened with blood. The needle slid from the whitecoat's hand, lying next to Magnus' leg.

Damian pulled the needle out of his leg and threw it yards away next to the building. That was all the time it took for the pain to start.

Magnus screamed as the medication shredded his body.

Chapter Nineteen

Everything stopped, including Ladon's breathing when he heard Magnus scream. He turned, taking in the scene. Damian pressed the barrel of his gun against the forehead of an orderly. The orderly shook visibly. If piss had run down his pant legs in the next few minutes, it wouldn't have surprised Ladon.

Magnus lay on the ground clutching his chest. He tore at his shirt collar as if the material choked him.

Ladon couldn't move. The horror of the scene cemented him to the pavement.

"What's in the syringes?" Damian pressed the gun to the man's forehead even harder.

Either the orderly couldn't get the words past the fear, or he didn't know because he shook his head and stood there as though he was waiting to die.

"You'll tell me, or you'll die." Ladon strongly suspected Damian would kill him whether he gave him the information or not.

Magnus' shirt tore until he exposed his chest. He clawed at his skin, creating ugly, bloody scratches. An urgency slammed into Ladon like getting hit by a bus. Everything in him roared to life until the sound leaked out of his mouth.

He stalked across the parking lot, shifting halfway.

As soon as he closed the distance, he grabbed Magnus' wrists, pulling his hands away. Magnus fought against Ladon. Ladon tightened his hold until he thought he might leave bruises.

His stomach rolled, the bile rising into his throat. He fought against nausea and let instinct take over.

He pulled Magnus to him, pressing their chests together. Ladon held him around the waist, blocking him from touching his wound. Instead, Magnus dug his fingernails into Ladon's back as if he knew he had to get through Ladon to get to himself.

Ladon stood and pressed Magnus against the wall while Garridan finished off the last of the orderlies and Damian demanded answers.

"Explain. Now!" Damian lifted the gun, pulling the trigger before returning the barrel to the guy's head. The orderly cried out when the hot metal burned into his skin. "Don't worry. You won't feel the barrel burn after I shoot you."

Ladon's ears rang at the blast, but Magnus didn't stop screaming.

The orderly held up his hands when Damian cocked the gun again. "Oh god. Okay. I-I think it might be phase two."

Damian sighed and rolled his eyes. "What the hell is phase two?"

Ladon hissed when Magnus' nails dug in a bit too much. "Just bite me if you have to, Magnus."

Magnus didn't give any indication he'd heard Ladon. Hell, Ladon couldn't even hear his own voice past the screams.

The orderly looked like a sweating statue. The only thing that moved was his mouth. "It's a drug."

Damian's eyes turned red, and his fangs dropped. He hissed and said, "I care about one fucking person in this whole world, and he cares about them." Damian pointed to Magnus and Ladon. "So you better start talking."

"Um...I-I don't know. I swear. It just takes away the paranormal part of you guys."

What the fuck did that mean? And did Ladon want to know?

Probably not.

Damian hissed again and pulled the trigger. "By the fucking gods, that was pointless."

"Just go check to see if there are other prisoners."

Garridan came up behind them. He must have grabbed Magnus' wrists because the digging stopped, and Magnus fought against the hold again.

"Magnus told me there are two others. A bobcat shifter and a human." Garridan had to yell so others heard him over the screams.

"Go get them." It was the first real command Ladon had ever given without feeling like he shouldn't demand anything of anyone. He thought it would feel unnatural, but it was the exact opposite, even when he directed the command at Garridan.

"If I let go, he'll keep scratching."

"It's fine. Just go."

"Yes, Alpha." Garridan let Magnus' hands go, and he followed behind Damian.

He had just stepped through the door, his hand about to let it close, when Ladon said, "When you get them out, burn the place down."

Garridan nodded and looked at Magnus. "Giving him your blood might help heal him faster. Can't hurt, at any rate."

Ladon cupped the back of Magnus' neck and put a hand under his ass, lifting him up and off the wall. He made his way back to the truck.

Magnus was heavier than Ladon had expected. Ladon might've been taller, and he had gained muscle mass over the last few months, but Magnus was no little man. His wide shoulders and heavy muscles were never more apparent than when carrying him through the trees. And then he wiggled around, clawing Ladon and screaming the entire way.

"Bite me, Magnus. Just do it already." Ladon had a bad feeling about why he wasn't.

When Ladon came out of the forested area, Bandos hurried out of the truck. "Shit. What the hell happened to him?"

Ladon couldn't answer. He had one goal, and that was to take away the pain. "Get the back door."

Bandos obeyed the order and Ladon set Magnus inside, pulling away to sit next to him. Magnus immediately began clawing at his chest again.

"By the gods, your back looks…" Bandos must not have had the heart to finish the sentence and Ladon didn't care to hear it anyway.

"Help me hold him down."

Ladon grabbed Magnus' wrists, and they struggled. Magnus opened his eyes. They were glassy with pain. He pushed Magnus down until he lay across the backseat next to Anna, who scooted across the seat, as far away as she could get. Ladon lay over him.

The other backdoor opened, and Bandos moved Anna out of the way before taking hold of Magnus' hands. Anna stood just to Bandos left, looking in on them.

Ladon let his fangs drop and bit into his wrist before pressing the blood to Magnus' lips. Magnus turned his head away from the blood as if he didn't like it.

Ladon fought to ignore the lump lodged in his throat even as his eyes swam with tears.

Sweat broke out on Magnus' brow.

"Look at me." Ladon took his chin in his other hand, holding him still. "Magnus!"

Magnus' gaze snapped in place.

"Drink. Now."

Magnus opened his mouth, wrapping his lips around Ladon's wound.

Ladon's tear dripped onto Magnus' face, sliding across his cheek until Magnus' hair absorbed it. A tear trickled down to the end of his nose. He turned his head to wipe it against his shoulder before focusing on Magnus again.

Magnus never took his eyes off Ladon. He also never sucked down the blood as a hungry mate would. Instead, he let the blood drip onto his tongue and swallowed when it collected at the back of his throat.

The glassiness of his eyes slowly left, and finally, Magnus truly saw him.

Ladon smiled. "That's right. Just keep drinking."

Magnus swallowed another mouthful of blood.

"He's not fighting the hold anymore." Bandos kept his voice at a whisper and his gaze down as if he felt he was intruding on a private moment. Maybe he was. Ladon didn't know.

"You can let him go." Ladon didn't take his eyes off Magnus. He wouldn't look away as long as Magnus needed him.

Bandos released Magnus. He cleared his throat. "You need me to hang out here or…"

"No." Another tear dropped.

Bandos shut the truck door softly.

Magnus cupped Ladon's cheek at the same time he swallowed.

Ladon's blood had slowed, coagulating, so he moved his wrist away from Magnus' mouth and bit into it again.

"Ladon," Magnus croaked his name. He blinked, and his eyes stayed closed for long seconds. His hand slid across Ladon's cheek to the nape of his neck.

Ladon returned his wrist to Magnus' mouth. "I'm going to lift off you."

Magnus' eyes widened, and he shook his head at the same time he swallowed again. He tightened his hold on Ladon.

Ladon wrapped his arms around Magnus' waist and lifted him at the same time as he sat up. "By the gods, you're heavy." Ladon's muscles strained. Magnus didn't help things when he held on as if his life depended on it.

Ladon pressed his wrist to Magnus' mouth, though. It wasn't easy moving around with only one free hand.

When they finally settled on the seat, Magnus sat on his lap, holding him tight. Through the whole process, Magnus never once broke eye contact.

"I need to know what they pumped into him." Ladon smiled at Magnus even as he spoke to Bandos. "They called it Phase Two, I think. Can you find out more about it?"

Bandos clicked away at his computer before answering. "On it, Alpha."

Magnus drew back until Ladon's wrist wasn't at his mouth anymore. Ladon licked across the wound, sealing it.

"Your teeth didn't drop down." And his eyes hadn't changed the entire time. Ladon cupped Magnus' cheek and wiped the blood off his bottom lip.

Instead of answering, Magnus laid his head on Ladon's shoulder. His face turned into Ladon's neck. It didn't even take a full minute for Magnus' breath to even out.

Whatever those fuckers had done to Magnus, they'd pay.

Anna opened the door and got in opposite them. Her hands were free, and she never said a word.

Magnus mumbled something against his neck, but Ladon couldn't make it out.

"What?"

"Ladon. Saint Lakes."

Ladon had heard him say that once before but didn't have time to reflect on it. "I'm here and we're going home."

"I'm Magnus."

"Yes." Damn.

When Bandos turned his head, Ladon tightened his hold. The need to protect came over him like a wave. Ladon's fangs dropped, and his eyes changed. He growled.

"Woah." Bandos' eyes widened. "I'm not a threat."

"I know." And he did. It was a primitive reaction he couldn't control.

"I hacked into Perkins' computer. He has a bunch of crap about that drug you mentioned. Has a fancy name I can't pronounce, so we'll keep calling it Phase Two. All the information on it is way over my head. Someone more knowledgeable may have to look at this stuff. But from what I can tell it's a psychotic medication designed to trick the brain."

Ladon nodded. "Trick it into doing what?"

"I have no idea, honestly, but my guess, just based on what this place is and the fact that Fane went feral in a similar lab, possibly even this one. I'm still digging around their files searching for info on Fane, by the way. But, anyway, I think the drugs make a paranormal feel human."

"But it doesn't change anything?"

"Change as in making a paranormal human?"

"Yeah."

"No." Brandos shook his head. "I'm no scientist, but there's no way they can figure that out. That would be like changing someone's eye or hair color. It's all just DNA. Science hasn't gotten that far yet. At least not to my knowledge."

Brandos might not have been a scientist, but he was smart. If anyone could learn more, it was Bandos.

And maybe one other.

Henri Carpentier might know about genetics. Hell, he probably had thirty books on the subject and was more of an expert than the bastard who ran the lab. And Henri was also Rocky's mate. The two hadn't connected for some reason, although Ladon knew Rocky wanted to. Maybe having Henri around the house would help.

Ladon tightened his arms around Magnus. He could feel Magnus' breath against his skin, steady and content.

If he could've snapped his fingers and make all the bad shit go away, he would've in a heartbeat, but whatever Magnus had gone through, it wouldn't be that simple. Not even Lucas could fix the memories of it.

The crackle of flames met his ears even before he saw them glowing through the trees. He smiled when he realized Garridan had just set the lab on fire.

The truck door opened, and Damian practically threw someone on the seat next to Anna. A bobcat hopped in next, lying on the seat next to the human. The man dug his fingers into the bobcat's coat immediately as if that gave him some comfort. The poor guy looked emaciated. His flesh hung on his bones as if he hadn't eaten in months and he stank from lack of washing. Damian got in next to the bobcat at the same time Garridan pulled the driver's side door open. The truck bounced as they all piled in.

"Hang on everyone." Garridan wasted no time in starting the truck and backing it out of the parking spot.

"What happened?" There was an urgency in everyone, including Damian, who didn't have a worrying bone in his body. He never let it show anyway. That was the only reason Ladon even asked.

"Someone called in the cavalry. Cops are everywhere," Damian answered.

"Probably Wesley." Anna sat next to Ladon.

Ladon shook his head. "He's scared."

"I could kill him for you." Anna's suggestion didn't come without a cost, and they both knew it.

"I'll deal with Wesley myself." That comment put an end to the conversation.

Chapter Twenty

Magnus' head would detonate in the next few seconds. The way it pounded left no doubt. He groaned and turned into the one thing that made his world right again, only to get thrown out. The vehicle turned a corner at too fast a speed.

A hand cupped the back of his head, and someone cursed.

"Ladon." His voice sounded more like a croak, even to his own ears.

"Shh, we'll be out of trouble soon." Trouble?

It all came flooding back to Magnus. The whitecoats and the big green dragon. "You shifted." He pressed his nose against Ladon's neck. He liked the way Ladon smelled.

"What?" His head would have fallen away again if not for the hand holding him in place. "How the hell did they find us?"

It took Magnus a moment to figure out that Ladon wasn't talking to him. "What's going on?"

Ladon's lips brushed against Magnus' ear. "The police are pulling us over."

"Why?" One thing Magnus had learned in all his years of investigating was that cops were just like everyone else. Some of them did their job well, protecting everyone, including the bad guys. Others were out for themselves. Weeding through the slush pile was the trick and that required trust in his instincts. Over the years, he had gotten it wrong, trusting the wrong cop to give him the answers he needed, but there were more times that his instincts were correct.

"Someone called them after the laboratory went up in flames."

It took Magnus a moment to work through Ladon's sentence and all that it meant. His mind didn't work as fast as it had before Perkins had had his wicked way with him. The violation left him addle-brained and a little bit dirty on the inside as if some pervert had touched him in unwanted ways.

"We set the building on fire?"

"Yeah."

"Whose idea was that?" Magnus stiffened. He had a clear picture of his bobcat friend's charred body left in the ruined remains. No one would recognize the black, ashy shell and they'd discard him like trash. His memory scattered like ash. Magnus couldn't let that happen.

"Mine." Ladon growled the word. "Why?"

"Did you get the human and the bobcat out first?"

"Of course, I did. By the gods, Magnus."

Ladon spoke of the offense before Magnus even knew he had said one. Maybe if his brain wasn't throbbing, he could have thought before he spoke. "Sorry."

"Just relax and trust me to protect you."

"I do."

"Do you, though?"

Magnus didn't know what to make of that comment. He couldn't process it all the way through. He just knew the question held a hint of hurt and he didn't know why. "I can't think."

The car rolled to a stop. "Okay. The bobcat needs to stay hidden or shift." Garridan's fatherly voice rolled through Magnus. He wasn't Magnus' father, but he made him miss his.

Magnus hadn't had the best parents. His mother abandoned him twice. Once when she'd left him and his dad, and once again when Magnus had found her at Stavros' mansion selling her body to his coven members. She had refused to come home with him then. In all her drunken wisdom, she had told him he had to pay for her time just like every other male who came into the place. He had left her to the next paying customer, preferring to mourn her against the mansion's brick.

He had been a teenager at the time. But his father had never gotten over her loss, and Magnus had never forgiven him for it. Or rather he had never forgiven him the neglect he had shown Magnus in the face of his grief. Garridan reminded Magnus that after all those years and all their imperfections he still mourned the loss of both his parents.

"Get on the floor. I'll block you with my legs." Ladon had gotten more demanding since the last time Magnus saw him.

The seat bounced a bit.

The night air tickled his nose, so he tilted his face farther into Ladon's neck.

"What seems to be the problem officer?" Garridan asked in a smooth voice as if they had just come from a party and were all tired, wanting to go home.

"Can you step out of the vehicle please?"

Ladon stiffened underneath him and loosened his hold on Magnus as if getting ready to protect Garridan.

"On what grounds, officer?" Again, with the calm tone. Only Magnus recognized something else in Garridan's voice. He had heard it one other time when Magnus had kidnapped Sage. Garridan's tone had been smooth but held a hint of a threat all at the same time. He remembered it because shortly after that Garridan had nearly choked him to death. They had since mended things between them, and Garridan had never talked to him in any other way but kindness.

Still, he committed the crime, and he couldn't take it back the way he wanted too.

And why the hell was he remembering old shit?

Magnus moved even though it was the last thing he wanted to do. He groaned when his brain protested, holding it on his neck with both hands. Ladon pulled his hands down, holding onto his wrists. He brought their joined hands to Magnus' mouth and put a finger over his lips, silently telling him to be quiet.

What Ladon thought he would say, Magnus didn't know. Magnus just nodded and waited for the shit to hit the fan.

"Thank the gods," Ladon whispered.

Magnus' confusion must have been written on his face because Ladon just smiled. "You feel better, don't you?"

Before he could answer, the cop said, "Get out of the truck, sir."

Magnus turned toward the window trying to get a glimpse of the guy.

"Am I under arrest?"

"Your vehicle matches the description of one seen at the scene of a fire."

"I wasn't anywhere near a fire."

"Get out of the vehicle. Now."

Garridan sighed and opened the driver's door. The cop immediately told him to turn around. "Put your hands on your head." Garridan complied, letting the cop pat him down as if he were a common criminal. He could have fought and was probably strong enough to take on the cop.

It was when the cop pressed Garridan against the truck hood and tried to cuff him that everyone in the car mobilized.

Bandos began tapping on his keyboard. "Cop has a computer in his car I bet."

Damian looked right at Ladon and asked, "Want me to kill him?"

"No." Ladon's face hardened. "I'll protect Garridan." He leaned forward, holding onto Magnus to keep him in place with one hand and tapping Bandos on the shoulder with the other.

"I'll let you know what they have on us, Alpha." It was the first time he had heard anyone call Ladon an Alpha. He hadn't been coherent enough to pay attention if someone had called Ladon that before.

The list of things to mull over in his mind got a bit longer. All of it lay on his chest like stone slabs. What else would get etched onto it and when would his brain heal enough so he could start checking off boxes?

Metal clinked and then the familiar sound of handcuff tines clicking into place.

Ladon's face hardened right before he moved Magnus enough to open the door. He somehow slid out from under Magnus with little effort and left Magnus sitting by himself. Something felt wrong about that.

He grappled for any part of Ladon he could get. Ladon meant comfort, and he hadn't felt that in a long time. Even before Perkins had kidnapped him.

He ended up grabbing Ladon's arm. The bareness of his skin took hold of Magnus' brain, and it was then he realized Ladon was naked.

"Stay here. Need to protect him." Ladon mumbled the last part as if saying it to himself.

Magnus might have been addle-brained, but he could help with the situation.

He looked at the person next to him to get someone on his side. All thoughts fled when he saw the familiar face of the human. His face was gaunt, and he had a gray tint to his skin that wasn't healthy.

Magnus smiled at him. "Glad you made it out."

"Thanks..." he took a deep breath, his lungs working hard to get air in and out. "to...you." Each word proved to be laborious, so Magnus didn't make him speak again. He just patted the man on his skinny leg.

A roar so loud it shook the windows startled them both. The human focused on something out Magnus' window. His eyes widened.

Magnus turned in time to see Ladon half-shifted with his fangs and eyes flashing. He held the cop against the driver's side door with a clawed hand around his neck. "Take the cuffs off."

Magnus scrambled out of the truck, putting his headache on the back burner.

"He said to stay in." Damian sounded as if he were talking about the weather for all the excitement he showed. He also sounded like the good kid on the playground about ready to rat Magnus out for disobeying the teacher. Or in their case, the Alpha.

Magnus didn't respond. His main concern was defusing the situation before Ladon got himself on the ten most wanted list.

He shut the door, the sound grabbing Ladon's attention. Ladon gave him a narrow-eyed look, and suddenly stepping into the mix felt like a bad idea. "I told you to stay in the truck."

Magnus swallowed and wrapped his hand around Ladon's wrist. "We're out in the open."

Garridan lay handcuffed on the hood of his truck. "Listen to him, boy."

"Won't be a prisoner ever again. Get the cuffs off him, Magnus."

Magnus dug through the cop's pocket for the handcuff keys. He found them on the first go and pulled them out.

As soon as Garridan was free, he wasted no time. He put his hand over Ladon's. "I'm free, boy. You can let him go."

Ladon didn't move. Smoke curled out of his nose. "He won't take you to prison. He won't take Magnus either."

Damian rolled down the window. "Do you need help, Alpha?"

"He doesn't need to identify the rest of you." Ladon's protective nature hadn't ever been so strong. It must have come when the first shift had.

The driver's side window rolled down. "Grab his body camera. Should be on his chest somewhere." Bandos clicked away on the keys.

Ladon sighed. "Roll up the damn window." The windows were tinted, so it was hard to see inside. Ladon relied on that to conceal everyone in the car.

The window went up.

Garridan was the one who looked for a camera. It took him a few minutes to find it. Magnus completely understood why he had trouble. The last time he'd been arrested body cameras weren't a thing.

Garridan grabbed the cop's gun next. He handed it to Magnus. As soon as Magnus had it, he pulled the clip, checking to see if it was full before pushing it back. He took a step back and pointed the gun at the cop.

Garridan happened to be standing on the other side. "Don't shoot me by mistake."

"I don't make mistakes when it comes to guns." Magnus clicked the safety off. The sound might as well have been a bullet leaving the chamber for the reaction the cop gave. Ladon took his hand off the cop's throat and stood in front of Magnus, although not in the line of fire.

The cop held up his hands as if he were under arrest. At about the same time, they heard sirens in the distance.

Magnus' head swam as the adrenaline level ebbed. The cop became two people.

Ladon must have sensed it because he stood behind Magnus.

Magnus waved the gun, silently telling Garridan to move away.

Ladon watched Garridan get in the driver's side before addressing the cop. "Get in your car and drive off. Tell them you lost us, or I swear to the gods, there won't be anywhere you can hide."

The cop's face turned white, and he ran for his car.

Magnus didn't lower the gun until the car pulled away.

The window rolled down again, and Bandos said, "I deleted the information. At least from his computer. But I need to get into the mainframe to delete it for good. To do that, I'll need my bigger setup." In other words, Bandos needed to go back to Saint Lakes. Bandos cleared his throat. "Swenson called it in. Probably from somewhere inside. Not sure if he made it out of the building before we set it on fire or not."

"Little bastard was too afraid to be trusted," Anna smirked.

Bandos rolled his eyes. "Anyway, they're after Magnus. He's the only name they got, and they only have his first name. The rest of us 'aided him'. Their words, not mine. Magnus' description was even whacked, which means Swenson either forgot a lot of details or he gave a false report for some reason. Either way, he's gonna get himself killed."

Ladon's eyes stayed reptilian.

Magnus leaned into him, needing his support. "I can't go back to Saint Lakes. Not until I find a way to keep Perkins and the senator from coming after me. I can't stay off the grid enough to not leave a trail right back home."

Ladon took Magnus by the shoulders. "No way are you staying here."

"It's best for Saint Lakes and you if I do. I know how it all works, Ladon. If I go back, Dr. Perkins has a lot of paranormals to choose from. It's a damn buffet. I need to get dirt on Dr. Perkins and the senator. Find something I can use against him. It's the only way he'll leave you alone."

"Or we could just kill him," Anna spoke up.

"I hate to agree with the enemy, but she has a point. It's easier," Damian said from beside her.

"I'm not the enemy anymore, douchebag."

They both looked at Ladon, waiting for him to make a decision. The word Alpha hadn't fit with Magnus' image of Ladon until the rescue. He had always seen Ladon as too young for everything, especially finding a mate. Ladon was barely hatched compared to Magnus.

Ladon met Magnus' gaze. "If you stay here, I'm staying with you. Got it."

"No way. It's too dangerous." Oh yeah. There went his protective instincts kicking up. Perkins' Phase Two did nothing to stem it.

Ladon rolled his eyes. "Seriously. I just helped rescue you, and you're pulling that card." He sighed. "Whether you like it or not, you're stuck with me. At least for the time being. You need my blood."

"I just want you to stay safe."

"Because it has nothing to do with you pushing me away, right?"

Was that sarcasm? "You want to have this argument now? Right here?"

Ladon's jaw muscles jumped around as he clenched his teeth. "Let's go before more cops come."

The hotel was only a few miles away. "Don't know if I can walk very far. And you're naked."

"But you don't want me to come with." Ladon shook his head. He held out a hand toward the driver's side door and Garridan tossed him Ladon's coat which had his pants and shirt bundled inside.

"Shut up."

The sirens grew closer.

"Let's go, Magnus." Ladon wrapped an arm around Magnus' waist and picked him up, carrying him away. "Take off for home, Garridan. We'll call you as soon as possible."

"Stay safe. Both of you," Garridan said before taking off.

Ladon watched them even as he carried Magnus across an empty field.

"If we're going back to the last hotel I used, it's in the other direction."

Ladon gave him an annoyed look and before turning around.

Chapter
Twenty-One

M agnus nearly fell over with exhaustion by the time they arrived at the hotel. He leaned heavily on Ladon, who practically carried him the whole way.

"Let me do the talking." Magnus tried to move away so he wouldn't appear as if he were a drunk on a bender but Ladon held him to his side.

"You can barely stand up." Ladon was still in a growly mood, which Magnus had never experienced in person before. The argument they had while on the phone had been the only time they'd ever fought.

He still didn't have the thinking capacity to figure out why, so he just went with his instincts. "You still need to follow my lead. This is what I do."

"You're barely coherent enough to finesse yourself out of a paper sack."

"I'm good at getting information. And what they did with my stuff isn't that hard of a thing to figure out. It's probably in the back somewhere. I have to get them to give it to me."

Ladon sighed. "It's a small thing to let you do."

"Exactly. I could do it half-dead."

Ladon growled and pulled him closer. "Don't talk like that. It almost happened."

"Sorry. I didn't mean it literally."

"I know. It doesn't matter." *To his dragon* came through loud and clear. Magnus could see it in the way Ladon's eyes constantly shifted from human to reptilian.

"You might have to stay out here while I talk." A human couldn't see Ladon's eyes change. They had already exposed themselves to the cop. They couldn't keep doing that.

"I'll keep my head down."

"And what happens when the front desk person gets a glimpse."

Ladon met his gaze. "I don't know, but you're not leaving my sight."

Magnus sighed. "This is why you should have gone with Garridan and left me to my job."

Ladon stiffened beside him. He stopped just under the hotel's front door overhang. Lights illuminated Ladon's face. His jaw muscles jumped. With his reptilian eyes, Ladon looked more hardened than before he had shifted, more in control.

Wheels turned in Ladon's mind as he studied Magnus. And then a light dimmed. Magnus wasn't aware Ladon had a light until it wasn't there anymore. His whole demeanor changed as he took Magnus' arm. He pulled him inside the building. "We need to get a room."

"I need to start finding dirt on Perkins."

Ladon leaned into him, whispering in his ear. "Get a room."

"Yes, Alpha." Magnus had always thought it was cute the way Ladon didn't realize he made demands until after it was out there and then he got all sheepish. But there was a difference between before the shift and after.

"Don't call me that."

Magnus narrowed his eyes. "Stop treating me like any member of the clan."

Ladon tightened his hold but not enough to hurt. "I'm just giving you what you want."

"You don't know what I want, Ladon." Magnus pulled his arm free of Ladon's hold and nearly fell on his ass. Ladon grabbed him around the waist. His head swam as if he were under water. "Stop pushing me. It's making it worse. I can't even think properly."

"What do you mean you can't think?"

"I mean, I can't get my fucking brain to work enough to figure out your cryptic, emotional shit. I'm your best friend, Ladon. I know you better than you think, but right now I can't work out the harder stuff."

Ladon sighed but otherwise didn't make a sound because the door slid open. He walked them up to the counter. A man with a fake smile greeted them.

Magnus returned the smile. "I stayed here a couple of weeks ago. Unfortunately, I had an emergency and couldn't make it back before now. I was wondering if you still have my luggage."

"Your name, sir."

"John Smith."

Ladon gave a little growl for reasons Magnus didn't know.

The front desk clerk looked at him with concern but otherwise didn't comment.

Magnus elbowed Ladon with a smile still plastered on his face. He never averted his gaze from the clerk even when the guy began clicking away at his computer. It took no time at all for the clerk to meet his gaze again. "Yes, sir. Management requires us to keep all leftover luggage. Returning it requires identification."

Magnus gave the guy an exaggerated wince. "That's the thing. I left my driver's license with my luggage."

"Just a moment, sir." The clerk left the counter, going through a door on the opposite wall.

"Does your ID really say John Smith and is it really with your stuff?" Ladon tightened his hold as if afraid Magnus would fall over.

"Yes. I never take it when I break the law. Even the fake IDs." Magnus laid his head on Ladon, fatigue setting in even more.

"How often do you do something illegal?"

"Once or twice each time, depending on what I'm investigating."

Ladon growled. "You put yourself at risk far too often."

"Nah. I've only been caught a few times." Magnus closed his eyes.

"You were imprisoned and experimented on, Magnus. That's bad."

"I meant by the police."

Before Ladon could respond, the clerk came back through the door with his duffle bag. He'd have recognized the blue bag anywhere. Every fray in the handle's fabric was as familiar as his own body. The dark coffee stain on the top right panel held a story that was all his own. Years of his life were on the outside of that bag. On the inside were only things. They had changed over time, but that bag was like a third arm. "I left my wallet on the dresser near the television."

The clerk put the bag on the lower counter next to the computer.

"If I may open the bag, sir." The clerk waited for Magnus to consent and when he did, he slid the zipper open. Magnus had to peer over the top counter, but when he did, he saw his wallet nestled on top of his clothing. The clerk lifted it out of its little bed and opened it. Magnus' driver's license was on the inside flap behind clear plastic. The clerk assessed his photo before smiling. He put the wallet back in the bag, zipped it back up, and handed it to Magnus.

"Thank you for keeping it."

"It's our pleasure, sir. Can I help you with anything else?"

"Yes. We need a room for the night." Ladon was the one who answered him. With his free hand, he reached into the back pocket of his jeans and pulled out his wallet.

"Pay cash," Magnus whispered as he leaned against Ladon's chest.

"I know." Ladon rolled his eyes. "I watch television. Sheesh."

Magnus chuckled.

The clerk eyed him as if he had lost his mind but plastered a face smile on his face and said, "We have vacant rooms on the second and third floor."

"Either is fine." Ladon pulled out bills from his wallet and waited.

He didn't have to wait long. "What's your name, sir?" The clerk pulled open a drawer and grabbed an envelope. He had a pen with the hotel's logo held at the ready.

"Ladon Somerset." Magnus knew using his really name would bite them in the ass later, but he couldn't wrap his mind around the consequences.

He wrote the name on the envelope and put the money inside.

"Do I pay for the room now or what?" Ladon turned his head so the clerk wouldn't see his eyes.

"During check out, sir. I'll need a credit card for incidentals."

"I'll pay cash." He pulled more money out of his wallet and held it at the ready.

The clerk typed something into his computer and put the cash in a drawer before handing Ladon two key cards. "The elevator is right around the corner to the right. Get off on the second floor and go left. Your room will be on the left-hand side."

Ladon carried him to the elevator.

"I can walk."

There went the eye-rolling again, which Magnus found endearing. He should have found it annoying. Somehow, it only made Magnus curl into Ladon even more.

"We should only stay here a few hours." Magnus closed his eyes when he spoke.

"You need rest and maybe a shower. No offense, but you stink."

"Yeah well, I haven't had a shower in longer than I remember, and I sweated my ass off when they shot me full of that phase two shit."

Ladon pulled him in closer and kissed the top of his head, which was just about the only part of Magnus he could reach. "That will never happen again."

Ladon walked them into the elevator and pressed the number two button.

Magnus wanted to argue because how could Ladon know it would never happen again, but he didn't have enough energy to think past that one fact, and Magnus knew Ladon well enough to know he would win if that were Magnus' only point.

Sitting on the bed felt good. So good, Magnus lay down. Ladon knelt on the floor between Magnus' legs. It would have been the most erotic moment they'd ever had if not for all the clothes they had on and the fact that Magnus was half asleep already.

He felt Ladon fiddle with his shoes and then his feet were free. His socks came next and then Ladon was at the button on Magnus' jeans.

Magnus popped open one eye when Ladon pulled his zipper down. Ladon's eyes were reptilian, and his fangs had dropped. His hands were at Magnus' waist. His warm fingers brushed his bare skin, and Magnus shivered.

Ladon took Magnus' jeans off, growling again when Magnus' underwear came next, but he never made it about sex.

Ladon held him at the waist. Those full lips were inches from Magnus' dick. They were all he could thing about as he watched Ladon take care of him. "Sit up, baby." It was the first endearment Ladon had ever used. Something about it left Magnus feeling cared for.

Ladon lifted Magnus at the same time he sat up on his own. Magnus laid his head against Ladon's chest to get a nose full of laundry soap. Ladon took his coat off and then lifted the hem of his shirt, making Magnus move so he could get it off. But he put his head right back on Ladon's chest.

"Hey." Ladon tried to meet his gaze, but Magnus wrapped his arms around him, holding him in place. Magnus' chest tightened. "Can you stand up in the shower on your own?"

"Probably." He had no fucking idea if he could, and he didn't care. "I almost died in that place." The knowledge of it hit him all at once and his gut clenched.

"But you didn't." Ladon tightened his hold, giving Magnus comfort.

By the gods, Ladon was too young to deal with Magnus' lifestyle on a regular basis. "I kept thinking I'd forget things. Like my name and you. Saint Lakes. There were four things, and I forgot the last one. I still don't remember it."

"You're out of there now. Never going back."

"It might happen again. Maybe not that place but another."

"It won't."

"It will. It's inevitable."

Ladon took his face in both of his hands, cupping his cheeks. He met Magnus' gaze, refusing to look away. "Listen to me. You're only alone because you want to be. It doesn't have to be that way anymore."

"What are you gonna do? Come with me?"

"And what would be so wrong with that?"

"You're Alpha."

"I don't have to be. I can give it up."

Magnus smiled and rested his forehead against Ladon's. "We both know you don't want to do that."

"No, but I will. For you, Magnus."

Magnus closed his eyes and sighed. "I know." He couldn't ask that of Ladon. Ladon would make a fair, kind Alpha. He might've been a little young, but with guidance and time, he'd come into his own.

"Don't think about it right now. Just focus on getting better."

"What if I don't get better? The shit they pumped through me might be permanent."

"If that were the case, my blood wouldn't have helped so fast. Plus, you'll get better because I won't allow anything else." Ladon moved away, standing even as he lifted Magnus to his feet.

Magnus held on to Ladon, gripping his shoulders until the material of his T-shirt wrinkled around his fingers. Some manic, irrational part of his brain knew that if he let Ladon go, he'd never see him again. Maybe he would be in that cell with the bobcat, staring at the human through the thick glass. If it was all in his head, then he never wanted to experience reality again.

"That last statement is your age talking."

Ladon tightened his hold as he carried Magnus the few feet it took to get to the bathroom. "Maybe it's my Alpha talking. Ever think of that, Mr. I'm-older-than-the-gods."

Magnus smiled. "I never said I was older than the gods."

"You have a problem with my age. Always have. You used me not shifting as an excuse, and now that I have, you'll use my age. Bonding is gonna be an issue. My age is just one of the reasons. Being Alpha will be another."

Damn him for being right. "You don't know that."

"I know you better than anyone." Ladon sat him down on the closed toilet lid and tried to pull away, but Magnus tightened his hold, keeping him in place, so Ladon knelt in front of him and returned the hug. "See. You need me, but you don't want to admit it."

"Not true. I do need you, and I have no problems admitting it. I don't want you to get hurt. If I drag you into my lifestyle, than you will. It's inevitable."

Ladon sighed. "You're starting to feel better, I think. You're able to have a conversation now."

His brain didn't feel as if it were trying to leak out of his skull. It was down to a dull ache. "Don't change the subject. We have to talk about this."

"We agree on that much at least."

When had they become so disagreeable with each other? Whenever Magnus was in Saint Lakes, they had spent hours just sitting in the middle of a field talking. Never once had they argued. They'd had more reason to be at odds then. With Ladon's first shift not happening, it should have been frustrating, and it had been at first. But he had grown complacent.

Ladon pulled away, and Magnus let him. He watched as Ladon used his canine teeth to bite into his wrist. When he stopped biting two drops of blood slid down his wrist, gravity taking control until they dripped onto Magnus' leg.

His stomach turned when Ladon lifted those bloody trails on his wrist up to Magnus' lips.

"Drink." Ladon's jaw muscles ticked as he gripped the back of Magnus' neck. His gaze held no room for arguments.

Magnus had no choice but to wrap his lips around it. The second it touched the tastebuds he wanted more. It didn't taste like the bagged stuff the whitecoats had given him at all. Gone were the cold chemicals. Ladon's blood was warm and tasted sweet like liquid sugar.

He gripped Ladon's arm and held it firmly, latching on like a leech.

Ladon smiled. His eyes turned reptilian. They glowed a bright green that seemed otherworldly. There wasn't anything as paranormal or as sexy as Ladon with his eyes like that.

Magnus forgot about everything as his headache disappeared entirely. He sniffed the air when something good met his nose. Something more than laundry soap.

His cock grew hard, so he put a hand over it and moved closer to Ladon. Everything about him called to Magnus in a way he had forgotten. He vowed never to forget again.

"Your eyes turned blue." Ladon smiled.

Magnus sucked at his wrist harder, wanting more.

"You started the bonding process."

He certainly felt something on a deeper level. And his cock liked Ladon a lot.

"Can I touch you?" He knew what Ladon wanted. The anticipation ran through him, singing in his blood until his cock jumped.

Magnus nodded and opened to the possibility of Ladon's touch.

When Ladon wrapped his hand around his shaft, Magnus whimpered. It had been so long since someone else touched him and knowing it was Ladon only made the feeling better. So good he feared he'd come from that one touch. Ladon's gaze never left his as he moved his hand up, his fingers rolling over the head of Magnus' cock.

Magnus groaned, his mouth falling open. His blood intake forgotten. His eyes closed as if on their own.

"Look at me." Ladon's voice held a huskiness Magnus had never heard before.

He obeyed and opened his eyes, searching for Ladon's gaze. Those dragon eyes looked right into his soul. They told him exactly how Ladon felt, which was something he already knew, but the confirmation gave him more to think about. Later. After.

They needed lube, but even without it, Ladon's touch was the best thing he'd ever felt.

"Keep drinking my blood, baby." There went that endearment again, swelling Magnus' heart, unsettling every other organ in his body.

Magnus pulled Ladon's wrist to his lips, licking it before sucking.

Ladon pumped his cock in a steady rhythm, making it impossible to concentrate on anything else, including drinking. He couldn't care about that or anything else. The only thing that kept his lips on Ladon's wrist was the command. It was impossible to disobey.

Magnus moaned again. Blood smeared his mouth, the sweetness of it leaked onto his tongue. He wanted more so he licked his lips, and that was when his orgasm started as a tingle in his core.

Magnus whimpered, moving into Ladon's touch as the orgasm built. He whispered, "I'm gonna cum."

Ladon growled, and his fangs dropped. "Do it."

It was as much the command as Ladon's touch that allowed his body to give over to the pleasure. The pleasure was too much to contain. He cried out Ladon's name as cum dripped from his cock.

Ladon growled again. "We have a connection whether you want one or not. Understand?"

Magnus wrapped his lips around Ladon's wrist by way of an answer.

Chapter
Twenty-Two

The metal chair grew uncomfortable the longer Wesley sat in it. If he stood and walked around, he'd appear nervous. He didn't want the police pegging him as guilty. Of course, he hadn't set the fire but they seemed to suspect him. Maybe because he had called them when the dragon had blown flames at the building. He had never been more scared in his life.

A can of soda sat opened and untouched on the cold, gray table. Condensation had come and gone hours ago, so it sat at room temperature, dry and boring. He studied it, wanting it to tell him why the police refused to let him leave.

He sighed and rolled his head around on his neck, attempting to relieve some of the tension.

He looked at the mirror and wondered if someone was on the other side, watching him. He doubted it. Most likely, they stuffed him in the first available room to wait for the senator. He could manipulate the police into holding Wesley there.

The longer he waited, the more his legs shook and the sweatier he became. He pulled at his shirt collar and wanted to take off his sports coat but didn't. It created a barrier between himself and the people who held him captive. He needed the illusion that kept some part of his emotional distress hidden. The shield was all in his head. A part of him recognized the logic, but another part of him grappled for any form of comfort he could get.

If he had to pick between Dr. Perkins coming for him or the senator, he'd pick Dr. Perkins. Wesley knew the senator wanted him contained for some unknown reason. According to Anna Boyle, the senator had hired her to take him to Dr. Perkins, which meant he didn't want Wesley dead.

He wanted something far worse.

Making him into one of those monsters would allow the senator to keep Wesley under his thumb. Wesley had been there the entire time he'd worked for the senator. He hadn't minded so much when he wasn't the senator's target. The senator must have thought Wesley had turned on him. How or why, Wesley didn't know. There was nothing Wesley could say to change his mind. When the senator made up his mind, he stuck to it.

Wesley sighed and turned the can around until the logo faced him. He traced a finger around the edge of the two-toned circular logo and thought about a way out of the mess he found himself in.

Wesley jumped in his seat when the door opened.

The officer who shoved him in the room stood in the doorway and snapped his fingers at Wesley. "On your feet."

Wesley pushed his chair back from the table. The officer walked to him when he stood and grabbed his arm. He had a smirk on his face that seemed at odds with the moment.

"I can go home now?" Not that home was a smart place to go, but he didn't have anywhere else. The paranormals might still have Anna as a prisoner, or maybe she had joined them. She was more like them than not anyway, and she was right about the senator killing her if he found out she'd helped them. Even if they threatened her and did bodily harm, the senator still would consider her a traitor. They may have been waiting for him somewhere.

The cop didn't answer. His smirk became even more pronounced as he led Wesley down the hallway.

Almost every door was open and inviting. The exception was the one to the room he had just been in and the one beside it. They were also separated by the fact they were metal and not wooden.

Wesley expecting one to swallow him whole. Or maybe belch out a criminal.

They walked through to the end of the hall. The exit led to freedom. Wesley knew because the opposite side was the one that led to his brief incarceration in that sterile room with the one can of soda and a mirrored window.

As soon as they were on the other side and the door closed behind them, they were in the main part of the station, which consisted of several desks and a large counter. On the visitor's side of the counter stood two of the senator's men dressed all in black.

As soon as he saw them, his heart pounded against his chest bone hard enough he heard it in his brain. He tried to pull his arm out of the cop's hold when the lightheadedness took hold.

The senator's men must have noticed his reaction because they entered the cop's side of the room and grabbed at Wesley. He pulled away from them, backing up. "Don't touch me!"

They each gripped an arm, their fingers digging into his flesh. He tried to free himself, but their hold tightened. He couldn't hold the tears back as they dragged him outside.

He blinked when the sun hit his eyes. Before his vision could adjust, he was in the backseat of the senator's town car.

The senator sat beside him. "You gave them your identification."

Wesley swallowed down the bile that rose in his throat. "I didn't. I swear." He searched his mind for a plausible reason why his identification had gone missing. "It's probably at home. I'm sure I just misplaced it."

The senator turned toward him, and their gazes met. "I can't have them digging around. It'll be far too damaging."

Wesley shook his head. He tried to speak, but the tears welled up in his eyes. "Please, sir. You know I'm loyal."

"Your carelessness reflects poorly on me." The senator never looked his way as the vehicle rolled forward.

Chapter
Twenty-Three

Ladon stretched his hand across the bed without opening his eyes. The bed sheets were cold, and Magnus' warm body wasn't within reach. He popped one eye open, and sure enough, Magnus wasn't in sight.

Ladon rolled onto his back and tried to work up the energy to get out of bed. He'd worry about Magnus if it weren't for his scent all over the place. He sniffed the air and realized Magnus sat at the small table that sat in the room's corner. Paying attention to the sounds around him confirmed that he typed on a keyboard.

"Magnus."

"I'm here."

Ladon yawned and stretched. He had no idea what the time was, but it sounded like a good way to start the process of getting Magnus back into bed. He felt as if he had been trying to do that since the day they'd met. "What are you doing up so early?"

Ladon opened his eyes and turned in Magnus' direction. Sure enough, whatever was on his laptop screen held his attention. He had on orange boxer briefs and nothing else. His hair stuck up, each strand at odds with another.

Ladon got a good look at his strong thighs and weighty package. They had slept in their underwear last night, spooning with Magnus being the little spoon when they started. Ladon had woken at some point last night to discover Magnus snuggled behind him. Ladon hadn't ever slept in the same bed with anyone he wasn't related to and it was the first time he'd ever spent it snuggled up so close. It turned out he liked to cuddle. Especially with Magnus.

"It's not that early."

"Early enough that you should still be in bed."

Magnus met his gaze above the laptop and smiled. "It's nearly ten o'clock in the morning. We have a lead to follow, so whatever you're thinking, we don't have time."

"That's been the story of our relationship so far. And you have time to come over here and drink more blood, don't you?" At the forefront of Ladon's mind was Magnus' health. Even taking in Ladon's blood twice hadn't healed him completely and Ladon wondered if it ever would. Magnus' eyes changed once, turning blue almost as soon as Ladon touched him, but his fangs hadn't dropped.

Magnus sighed. "You're right." Halfway across the room, Magnus' eyes glowed for a second time.

Ladon's focus went straight to Magnus' cock, which gradually grew hard beneath the cloth of his underwear.

Magnus chuckled. "You're so obvious."

Ladon grinned. "Oh, so you think you know what I'm thinking, huh?"

Magnus sat next to him. He immediately touched Ladon's exposed chest. Magnus' rubbed circles between Ladon's pecs. "I know you."

"So you know I was thinking about your underwear."

"Taking them off, maybe." Magnus' eyes glowed blue but something bothered him, so Ladon decided to pull him out of his funk the only way he knew how.

"Nope. I was thinking you probably regretted wearing orange."

Magnus laughed for the first time since they'd reunited. The stress completely melted from his face. His whole body brightened in a way Ladon hadn't seen in a long time. "You did not."

"I did too. Who buys orange underwear?" Ladon couldn't keep up the teasing without chuckling. He ran his hand up Magnus' side, feeling his smooth skin.

"I do."

"You make them look good. Not the other way around." He did too. He had a great ass, muscular without being too much and a perfect handful, if Ladon ever got to touch it. He wasn't pressing the particular issue as it wasn't the right time, but he could think whatever he wanted.

It might never be the right time to take their relationship to the bonding stage.

Magnus brought his hand up Ladon's neck to his cheek. His smile turned to concern, and the lines returned to his forehead. "What put that look on your face just now?"

Magnus proved very good at reading Ladon. So much so that he couldn't keep much from him.

Ladon let his fangs drop and bit into his wrist. He held it up for Magnus, who took his arm in a firm grip as if he expected Ladon to pull away. Ladon let Magnus have control.

"I don't know what you're thinking about us bonding." Magnus tried to pull Ladon's wrist from his mouth but Ladon growled. "Don't talk. Listen."

Magnus nodded and sucked hard against Ladon's skin.

Magnus' eyes seemed to glow from a dull blue to a brighter shade. His nails grew long and pointy. The only time Ladon had ever seen a vampire's nails grow was during the battle.

Magnus' eyes turned red and then blue again. His body tried out all the things that made Magnus a vampire, testing each one as they returned, tuning each little piece of his engine until it was fine again.

Ladon knew his eyes had changed. He wished they wouldn't, but everything in him wanted Magnus. He wanted to mate, to bond so hard they'd both be exhausted for a week.

"I know you think I'm young. I agree with you on that." As soon as Ladon spoke the latter sentence, Magnus' gaze snapped heated as if he wanted to say something but didn't dare. "I'm not too young to understand you have an issue with bonding."

Magnus released Ladon's wrist, licking across the wound. That one lick was a very paranormal thing to do. It relieved some of Ladon's worry more than Magnus willingly drinking had.

Magnus moved just enough to straddle Ladon's lap, the bed sheet and their underwear an unwanted barrier. Magnus bent down until they were chest to chest. His face inches from Ladon's. His eyes turned from blue to red, glowing with anger. "Fuck you for thinking I don't want you."

Ladon wasn't about to let Magnus get away with that. "I don't want to fight with you. Not when you're finally feeling better."

Magnus growled. "You say you know me, but you don't know shit. If you did, you'd know how much I've wanted to bond from day one. You're the one who told me I had to wait."

"That's not fair and you know it." Okay, Ladon wasn't playing around anymore. He growled and gripped Magnus' waist. "Get off me."

"No." Magnus bent down. His eyes turned blue. "I've done nothing but protect you. Even going so far as to leave Saint Lakes when being around you became too much."

Ladon sighed and ran his hands up Magnus' sides. "Yeah. Okay. I know that."

"Then you know you're putting shit on me I don't deserve."

"My statement about my age still stands, Magnus. You and I both know that's an issue for you."

Magnus sat up. "It's not an issue for my dick."

Well, that was...unexpected. Maybe they had a few things left to learn about each other.

Magnus trailed his fingers from Ladon's neck to the center of his chest and the, over to one of Ladon's nipple before circling the other one.

Ladon grunted, arching into the touch. By the gods, who knew his nipples were so sensitive? Not him. It certainly didn't feel as if electricity zapped through at any other time. And it made his dick not only hard, but it jumped around, begging Magnus to give it attention.

So much for friend-zoning. That had gone out of the window yesterday when he'd jerked Magnus off. Maybe Magnus was right, and their issues didn't exist. He certainly didn't seem to have any problems with intimacy like he'd had before Ladon had had his first shift.

One second Magnus was in his face, with his pretty scowl and glowing eyes, and the next he'd moved Ladon's underwear, tucking the rim under his balls and had his cock in hand, pumping once.

"Big." Magnus licked his lips. Lust covered him like a blanket.

Ladon moaned when Magnus licked across his cock head, lapping up the pre-cum leaking out of the slit. Ladon couldn't take his eyes off the scene playing out. He'd never experienced something so erotic before.

As Magnus licked him again, he met Ladon's gaze, giving him a little smile.

Ladon closed his eyes, unable to watch anymore.

"What's wrong?" Magnus kissed around his slit.

"Nothing. It's just that I'm gonna come if I see you kiss me like that again."

"Really?" Another lick farther down the shaft.

Ladon could feel an orgasm already building in his core. His heart rate picked up, and he panted. He peeked at Magnus, who grinned. "Yes, really."

"That's hot, baby."

"It is?" Ladon thought it spoke too much of inexperience.

"Oh yeah." Magnus held his cock at the base, lifting it just enough to wrap his lips around it.

"Oh." The pleasure sang through his blood.

He needed the connection. Needed to know that it was Magnus between his legs, sucking his soul out through his cock, so he placed his hand on the back of Magnus' head, running his fingers through his hair.

And came. No warning at all. It hit him hard. He curled around Magnus, holding him in place as the pleasure worked through his body. Magnus coughed around his cock, sending waves of electricity through him. It also served to let him know he was choking the shit out of Magnus.

He released his hold, lifting his hand away. To his surprise, Magnus didn't pull all the way off. Instead, he held it in his mouth, relaxing his lips.

"I'm sorry." Ladon didn't know if he was apologizing for choking him, for coming without warning, or for coming too soon. All three?

Whatever. He needed to apologize.

Magnus hummed around his cock, caressing the underside with his tongue a few times before pulling off. "It's okay. I liked it."

"I came too soon." Heat worked itself up his neck. He had an overwhelming urge to push Magnus away and pull him closer all at the same time. Magnus lay his cheek against Ladon's abdomen, right above his softening cock.

"Just enjoy the moment."

"Come up here." Ladon uncurled, lying flat on his back again.

Magnus wiggled his way up Ladon's body until they were eye to eye. His hard length pressed against Ladon's softened cock. "It was good. You taste good."

Ladon ran his hand down Magnus' back to his ass. He could smell his cum on Magnus. It made his dick jump in excitement. "Can I try that with you sometime?"

"Yes. Please." Magnus moved off him, standing at the side of the bed with his hand held out. "Ever fooled around in the shower?"

Instead of taking his hand, Ladon sat up. He wrapped his arms around Magnus' waist, kissing him just below his belly button, on the happy trail of hair that led down to the thing Ladon wanted a taste of. "You know I haven't."

Magnus wiggled around until Ladon had to let him go or get pulled off the bed. He stood, taking Magnus' hand and let Magnus led him to the bathroom. "Come on, Youngster. I'll debauch you under the warm spray."

"'Debauch' is an old person word, Old Man."

Magnus chuckled. "Okay, jack each other off. Whatever. Guess what we're going to be doing later."

"Buying breakfast and lube, I hope."

"That too but I was talking about the investigation." Magnus paused. The anticipation built until Ladon was about ready to tickle the answer out of him. "We're going to go see a prostitute."

Ladon growled and grabbed Magnus around the waist and pinned him against the wall next to the bathroom door. His eyes shifted to his dragon's, and his fangs dropped. "That's not fucking funny."

Magnus exposed his neck. "If I would have known you'd react this way, I wouldn't have joked about it."

Ladon's dragon was too close to the surface, and it wouldn't back off until they properly bonded. He might not push the issue, but he wouldn't hold back his emotions when it came to Magnus either. Why the fuck should he? Magnus had to know what his expectations were. They'd been dancing around each other long enough.

Magnus parted his lips. They held Ladon's attention. "If you let someone else touch you, then everything you just said was a bunch of shit."

"I didn't mean it that way. It's just how you took it."

"What the fuck else do prostitutes do, Magnus?"

"Talk about their johns. Hopefully. We have an appointment in a couple of hours with the guy."

"You called a prostitute to talk?"

"Yes. About Perkins."

Ladon relaxed and moved away from the wall, pulling Magnus with him. "How did you find the guy?"

"I'm good at my job, Youngster." Those lips turned up into a smile. "How about you explain it to me after our shower, Old Man?"

Magnus licked his lips. "Fine. And if you're gonna kiss me, then do it already. The anticipation is killing me."

Ladon chuckled and brushed his lips across Magnus', settling into the familiarity of the one intimacy they let themselves have over the course of their long, platonic relationship.

It wasn't platonic anymore.

Chapter
Twenty-Four

L adon had never met a prostitute before. Or at least he didn't think he had. It wasn't as if they wore a sign, *I had sex today*. It was just a job. Something to bring in money just like every other job. Honestly, he didn't understand why it was illegal. If someone wanted to sell their body, it was their right. It was their body, after all.

Ordering a prostitute off the internet came as a surprise.

Ladon placed a hand on Magnus' lower back, needing the confidence when they walked into the brothel. It appeared to be an ordinary house from the outside. A red glow emanated through the open crack of the front window's curtains, and several cars lined the long driveway. Beyond that, it seemed normal.

The owner of the home left the light on at the front door even though it was mid-afternoon.

Magnus held Ladon's hand as they walked up the manicured sidewalk to the front door.

Bushes lay spread evenly apart up the walk. They looked like mini-pine trees but were probably called something else. Mom would've known their names.

And why the hell was he thinking of his mother?

Ladon hesitated when they came to the door, but Magnus went right up to it, oblivious to Ladon's nervousness. He wiped his free hand on his jeans and took a deep breath before grabbing the knob.

And then they were inside.

If ever there was a den of iniquity it was that place, and it wasn't just the mostly naked men flirting with the ones who were clothed. Almost everything was red and black, and reminded Ladon of a movie about vampires. Weren't they associated with red and black in almost every horror film?

Ladon leaned into Magnus. "You need red boy shorts." With Magnus' dark hair and his tan skin tone he would be sexy and very much like a vampire.

Magnus chuckled. "Like the color, huh?"

"I'll like you in red." He didn't know about liking the color itself, but just seeing Magnus in it.

Magnus met his gaze. "I think I might have some back at home. I've never worn them."

Ladon grinned. "Why not?"

"Saving them for you. I've collected others over the years."

Ladon's mouth dropped open and his eyes widened. He probably knew looked ridiculous, but he couldn't help it. News that Magnus had bought sexy clothing and saved it for when they bonded was unexpected.

A part of Ladon thought Magnus' little speech about wanting him was just something he'd said to stop the arguing. Maybe thinking that was Ladon's way of coping with the rejection when it came. Like a precaution.

It was a shitty thing to think about a vampire who'd done nothing but protect him since the day they'd met. Hell, Magnus had even protected Ladon from himself when he had to.

"I've been insecure and I'm sorry." They'd laugh at the fact Ladon had come to the realization in the entrance of a brothel. He hoped.

Magnus gave him a forgiving smile and kissed him. The kiss was quick, just a peck on the lips but it was what Ladon needed to redirect his focus.

"I keep thinking about sex. And this place isn't helping." Ladon pulled Magnus to his side, wanting him closer.

Magnus chuckled.

A red velvet bench lined three walls. The owner of the place had hung red and black curtains behind them. The black carpet and light also added a certain sexual feel to the room.

A slim male in white glowing thongs seemed as if he were gliding across the floor. confidence rolled off him. Whether he was or not was beside the point. The surroundings made it so, and that was all that counted. An older human sat in one of the corners. He wore a suit and probably came from some corner office in a high-rise downtown. The slim male straddled his lap. "Were you waiting for me?"

The human's hands instantly went to his exposed ass cheeks, kneading them like a cat. "You know it, sexy."

The music was loud enough for others not to hear their exchange. Whoever adjusted the volume had humans in mind, not paranormals. Even Magnus, who still struggled to get all his vampire qualities back couldn't hear their conversation.

Ladon slid behind Magnus until his chest touched his shoulder blade and arm. He leaned down. His lips touched the shell of Magnus' ear. "We just landed on another planet, right?"

Magnus grinned. "Not quite."

And he would never live that down when Ladon told the story of how Magnus had taken him to a whorehouse, and everything was sex red. "I'm very glad my dragon is green."

"Baby, you're green in more than just one way."

Ladon bit at Magnus' ear, making him gasp. He was just about to make a comment when a man came up to them. As soon as he closed the distance, Ladon could smell vampire. He dressed in just a silky bathrobe, and surprise, surprise, it was red, although it was as dark as the color of blood.

The vampire put his hands together, clapping a bit. "Ah, welcome to my den. Rules for paranormals are no biting any of my boys. They aren't blood whores. And no shifting."

"Understood."

The vampire smiled. "Now that we've covered the rules, how can we meet your needs?"

"We have an appointment with Keaton."

"Of course, let me check his schedule. I'll be a moment, but please make yourselves comfortable while you wait." The vampire gestured to the bench couches where the suit and Thong Boy made out.

Magnus nodded and pulled Ladon to one corner of the couch. He pushed Ladon on the shoulders, silently telling him to sit. The next thing Ladon knew he had a lap full of Magnus. Both of his hands laced through Ladon's hair. "Let's make out."

"Wha—" All he knew was Magnus' tongue licking across his lips.

The song changed to a slow grind. The bass bumped to a sensual rhythm. The song reminded Ladon of soft touches. Or maybe it wasn't the music that reminded Ladon of making love, but the way Magnus kissed.

Everything around them fled until they were the only two beings left on earth. Ladon knew Magnus' firm lips and that hint of a tongue always wanting a taste. He knew the cotton of Magnus' T-shirt and the muscles playing underneath.

He trailed his hand down Magnus' back to the swell of his ass. He was just like the lecherous human in the suit pawing at the young male. They were at opposite ends of the couch but Ladon imagined they looked similar. The only difference was Magnus covered his ass in denim. It wasn't bare for all to see.

Ladon growled at just the thought of someone leering at Magnus.

Magnus brought his hands around to Ladon's cheeks. A thumb rubbing across his stubble and the kiss-that beautiful kiss-ended. Magnus rested his forehead on Ladon's and closed his eyes. "This place makes me possessive."

Glad he wasn't the only one. "I understand the feeling." Ladon moved his hand up to Magnus' waist. He liked the spot because the curve proved the perfect resting place.

"The kid in the thong looked at you as he passed. It set me off."

Ladon hadn't noticed. "Barely saw him."

Magnus chuckled. He lifted away just enough to meet Ladon's gaze. "What held your attention?"

Ladon grinned. "Fishing for a compliment, Old Man?"

"Absolutely, Youngster."

Before Ladon could answer the question, a vampire walked up to them. He had black hair and almond-shaped eyes. His tight black bikini style underwear showed off pale skin and a slender body. "You started without me." He grinned as if he thought that was funny.

He touched Magnus' shoulder, so Ladon let his eyes change, growling low in his throat. The vampire, presumably Keaton, removed his hand with a smile. If the growl put him off, he didn't show it. "Right. Well, if you'd like to take the party somewhere more private, follow me."

Magnus moved off Ladon, grabbing his hand when he stood and pulled him up.

They followed Keaton behind a beaded curtain. The curtain hid a hallway with several closed doors with numbers on them like a hotel. Only the numbers were one digit instead of three. Keaton opened door number five and let Ladon and Magnus in first before following them inside.

The door clicked behind them, and then silence reigned except for the growl Ladon couldn't hide.

In the center of the room was a king-size bed. It took the stage simply because it was so devoid of blankets. Just a white fitted sheet and the matching top. Two pillows lay at the head of the bed. The bed was simplistic in that it was devoid of a head and foot board.

Nothing else was in the room. No artwork on the walls or anything personal that would indicate the room belonged to Keaton. There was a door on one side. Maybe a bathroom or a closet. And one plush chair in the corner. The chair was red and went with the rest of the décor.

Keaton kept the smile plastered on his face even when he hopped onto the bed. He stretched his legs out in front of him and braced himself on his arms. He seemed the picture of comfortable except for his shoulders coming up to his ears and the caution in his eyes.

"Have a seat anywhere you like." He made no move to invite them onto the bed.

Magnus pulled Ladon over to the chair and pushed him down again. Instead of sitting on his lap as he did before, Magnus stood next to the chair. "You've figured out we're not here to fuck."

"Yes." Keaton met Ladon's gaze but averted his gaze quickly. "You're very strong." Maybe the tension in Keaton had to do with Ladon's strength. The growling didn't help relax anyone, including Ladon. He wished he wasn't so growly, but his dragon didn't like the place.

Ladon didn't respond because he didn't know what to say, or if he should speak at all. The whole whorehouse parade was Magnus' show, not his. Ladon was just there to keep Magnus safe.

"He's my Alpha." Magnus seemed rebellious against Ladon's Alpha nature up to that point, so the statement surprised him.

Keaton's eyebrows drew together. "Alpha?"

"I'm the leader of my clan." Almost, but Keaton didn't need to know that. Ladon would bet humans raised Keaton. "Magnus is a part of that clan."

"You're not a vampire, right?" Keaton smelled the air.

"Nope. Dragon shifter." Ladon smiled. "Good call."

"Is that, like, a thing most paranormals do? Like have mixed clans?" Keaton held up his hand. "Not that I think there's anything wrong with that. I'm just curious."

"It's not common but not unheard of either. We're mates, so there's that also." Ladon thought that last part needed said just in case Keaton got ideas about fucking around with Magnus. If he wanted to live, he wouldn't touch either of them.

"I've lived with humans my whole life. Foster care." The way he said the last two words made them sound like curse words. "I mean I can guess what a mate is, but I don't know the details."

"Paranormals smell their mate first. Most of the time. It's an instinctive knowledge."

"So you two are like it for each other." The shield Keaton held in front of him with every fake smile disappeared. In its place was something genuine. "That's super sweet."

"Yes. After we bond, which consists of drinking each other's blood and making love, we'll be tied together for life." Magnus was the one who answered, and he called it *making love*. Not sex or fucking.

Keaton's smile fell. "Why are you here?"

Ladon let Magnus lead the conversation.

Magnus met his gaze and nodded before turning to Keaton. "We want to talk to you about one of your regulars."

That cautiousness in his eyes was back in full force. "Which one?"

"Jeffrey Perkins."

Keaton's eyes widened, and he shook his head. "I can't talk about him." He hopped off the bed and pointed to the door. "You should leave."

Keaton's reaction struck Ladon as overly dramatic. He must know about Perkins' laboratory and what he did there. And even knowing that, Keaton still took Perkins' money in exchange for sex. That meant Perkins either threatened him with the phasing drugs, or Keaton didn't care about the harm Perkins inflicted on others.

Keaton scrambled to the other side of the bed when Magnus took a step toward him. The bed sat between them, keeping Keaton isolated. Magnus appeared as if he'd run over the mattress to get to Keaton and that would scare him, so Ladon took his arm, pulling him back.

Magnus obeyed but his muscles stayed tense, and his eyes glowed red. Ladon wasn't sure if it was from Keaton's overly fearful response or if he was preparing to make Keaton cooperate.

The fact was they needed Keaton more than Keaton needed them. They'd get more flies with honey and all that crap.

Ladon softened his facial muscles and nodded to the bed. Maybe Keaton wasn't part of his clan, but he still might listen to Ladon's Alpha. For the first time since shifting, Ladon purposefully brought the nature out, trying to exude control and confidence. "Sit. Now."

Sure enough, Keaton sat on the edge of the bed with his hands between his knees. His shoulders curled in on themselves. His back and the entire width of the bed between them.

"Do you have a robe or some other clothing?"

Keaton nodded.

"Put it on and then sit here." Ladon point to a spot on the bed right in front of them.

Keaton stood and went over to the door across the room. It turned out to be a bathroom, but a black robe with big colorful flowers hung from a hook on the door. Keaton pulled it down and on before walking back across the room.

Ladon could almost smell the fear rolling off him, not that he needed to smell it. Keaton's body language showed nothing else. He shook the closer he got, and he stopped when his legs hit the edge of the bed. Again, he kept the expanse of it between them.

Instead of making demands on the poor guy again, Ladon waited him out.

Maybe the silent attention was too much. With that in mind, Ladon wrapped his arm around Magnus' waist and pulled him closer.

"What?"

Ladon pulled a little more, asking Magnus to sit on his lap.

Magnus didn't understand what he wanted if the confused look was any indication. To be fair, Magnus wasn't the type to sit on someone's lap despite the show earlier.

"Sit on my lap."

"Maybe I don't want to."

Ladon smiled. "I'd sit on yours, but I'm bigger than you. It would look weird."

"And we care how it looks...why?"

"I might crush you." Ladon grinned, knowing full well Magnus was strong enough to hold him. Even if the chemicals compromising Magnus' system affected his strength, he'd still be fine.

Magnus chuckled. "Just get up."

Ladon stood and moved to the side long enough for Magnus to plop into the chair. Once he did, Ladon sat. He didn't put all his weight on Magnus on purpose just to tease.

Magnus laughed even harder. "You're not funny."

Ladon wrapped one arm around Magnus' shoulders and leaned into him, kissing Magnus on his temple. "I made you laugh."

Magnus gripped Ladon's waist, pulling him closer. "You always make me laugh."

"That's because I'm so funny."

"With so much modesty." Magnus ran his hand up Ladon's side and then back down again.

Keaton came around the bed and sat, the fear gone. He even smiled and watched them as if they were the evening's entertainment. His eyes still held some felt trouble Ladon wasn't privy too, but his body lost some of the tension.

Ladon rested his forehead against Magnus' temple. "You take over. I'm too comfortable now." He closed his eyes and breathed in Magnus' scent. His fangs dropped, and he knew his eyes had shifted.

Nothing mattered. Not the investigation or the reason why they were in a whorehouse. Not even the whorehouse itself. Ladon had gone so long without Magnus. He appreciated Magnus' physical presence. Every second together became a blessing.

"Tell me about Jeff Perkins."

Ladon opened his eyes and turned just enough to see Keaton's expression.

Keaton shuttered and shook his head.

"What if I told you I know why you won't talk? That I have firsthand knowledge of what *Doctor* Perkins has in store for a vampire who crosses him."

Keaton swallowed and lifted his body off his hands. He sat up, rubbing the silk of his robe as if the softness gave him courage. "Why are you here then?"

"I need dirt on him. Real evidence that will do damage if it got out, and it can't have anything to do with paranormals. It's the only way he'll leave my clan alone." Magnus got down to the truth faster than Ladon thought he should. But then Magnus was good at reading people, so maybe he figured Keaton wouldn't buy the bullshit. Magnus smiled. His thumb rubbed a circle on Ladon's waist through his T-shirt. "We can promise protection."

"Um...Protection for good?" Something in Keaton's eyes shifted from weariness to hope.

Ladon nodded. "You come with us and pay allegiance to me. I'll make sure you have everything you need."

"How can I trust you?" Keaton didn't trust him, but he would find out the truth of it soon enough.

"How do I know you won't lead Perkins right to us?" It could happen. Perkins seemed like a smart enough guy to have gotten to Keaton first. If that were the case it was up to Keaton to choose a side. Ladon just hoped he chose right.

"You don't." Keaton sat up straight. Ladon noticed Keaton's hands shook, but then he folded them between his legs. He averted his gaze.

"Exactly. We both have things to lose."

Keaton bit his bottom lip and peeked at them. "What if...what if Jeffrey hurts you guys?"

It was an odd question, considering there were so many other important questions he should have asked.

"We'll do everything we can not to let that happen." Ladon sat up so he'd seem more authoritative. "Either trust me and pack your shit or stay here. It's up to you."

Keaton's spine straightened. "Wait. You mean right this second?"

Magnus smiled. "No more of this life if you don't want it."

Keaton stood and ran to the bathroom. He stopped in the doorway. His eyebrows drew together. "You're serious, right?"

"You have my word and my protection." Ladon let the truth sit between them until they both soaked in it. Even if Perkins had gotten to Keaton, something about the hope in his words let Ladon know Keaton needed help. Sometimes all it took was one act of kindness to change someone's life.

Keaton nodded.

Ladon turned back to Magnus, leaning on him again. He kissed him on his cheek before whispering, "The kid doesn't trust."

"The *kid* is older than you are I bet. By at least ten years." It was hard to tell most paranormals age, especially most shifters and vampires. The aging process wasn't like with other beings, because they stopped physically aging at a certain point in their life and that point was different for everyone. Magnus appeared as if he were in his thirties when he was closer to the one-hundred-year mark. Ladon looked his actual age, but that was because he was young.

"I bet he's no younger than twenty-seven." Oh, Ladon could work a real bet out of Magnus. He held out his hand.

Magnus smirked and took Ladon's hand. "If I win, you owe me a back rub."

A chance to touch Magnus on a continuous basis. Not a hardship. "Done. And if I win, you have to...do a striptease in those underwear we talked about earlier."

"Absolutely not. Pick something else."

"What! Why not?"

"I can't dance."

"Really?"

"Really. It wouldn't be pretty."

Ladon shook his head. "Anything you do naked would be pretty. Trust me."

Magnus chuckled. "Just pick something else."

Ladon wanted to say Magnus had to bond with him, but that was a shitty thing to bet. It wasn't fair to make light of bonding when it was such a sacred thing. "I still think it's unfair that I don't get a dance, but I'll change it. Just for you."

Keaton piped in just then. "I can teach you to dance. I do that on the daily. Seriously. It's the best way to get a john."

He was crouched in front of a small closet with a pink bag in front of him, stuffing clothing inside. His robe was open, concealing his body as it fell forward. He didn't stop packing as he continued to speak. "I could teach anyone to striptease. Even if you don't have rhythm. No problem."

Magnus scowled. "I suppose you'll think I'm a coward if I don't learn."

Ladon grinned. "Absolutely. The biggest scaredy vampire ever."

They shook hands again and then Magnus focused on Keaton. "How old are you?"

"Twenty-three." Keaton chuckled when Magnus cursed. "Sorry."

Ladon just kissed Magnus on the temple. "I can't wait to watch you shake your ass just for me."

Magnus shook his head and sighed. He grew serious. He cupped Ladon's cheeks. "That was the fourth thing. Being a vampire. I forgot it."

Ladon leaned in and kissed Magnus. He didn't know what to say. Maybe words weren't necessary. The only thing he knew how to do was remain as supportive as possible and stick close, so Magnus stayed safe.

Chapter Twenty-Five

Perkins had covered every dirty thing he'd ever done, except hire a prostitute every so often, and even then, he only ever hired Keaton. Maybe if it were the senator hiring prostitutes it might have made the news, but no one would care about a nobody like Perkins.

He left no computer trail that Magnus could find, although Magnus wasn't Bandos. He might have better luck. Magnus typed a message, asking for his help.

"The last time you saw Perkins, what did you talk about?" Magnus didn't stop tapping when he asked Keaton the question. He needed to find a paper trail.

He peeked over the laptop at Ladon, who watched some movie on one of the hotel's cable channels. The movie was a comedy, so Ladon had a smile on his face that would kick up a notch during a funny part. He lay on the bed with his ankles crossed and his head resting on two stacked pillows.

He watched too much television. Magnus would have to do something about Ladon's consumption when they got home. Maybe encourage a hobby. Too much television would rot his brain.

"How much I wanted his dick?" Keaton continued with the eye pencil. He leaned into it, so close Magnus couldn't see half the pencil from his vantage point. "Total lie. That man isn't that big, not that I'm a size queen. I'll take a small dick if the male using it knows how to fuck. Jeffrey doesn't."

Magnus shook his head. "I can't use that information." And he certainly didn't care about Perkins' prick. He wouldn't even if he held the record for the biggest one in the world.

"After that, we didn't talk."

Okay, Magnus would have to take a different approach. "Any conversation you might remember."

"He asked me about my family once. Not that there's much to tell. I mean it's not like I have one. Human foster care until I turned eighteen and figured out I wasn't human. Nearly went feral before a vampire client told me what I was and that I needed blood. I lied to Jeffrey because I thought he wanted to use me for one of his experiments. Told him I had family down south."

"Anything else?"

"He said he contributed to a senator's campaigns once. Paid him to keep his mouth shut about his lab."

Magnus stopped typing and looked at Keaton. His mind moved in a thousand different direction all at once only to come back to the same thing. "When did he start talking about his experiments?"

Keaton shrugged and put down the eyeliner pencil. He turned to meet Magnus' gaze. "I don't know. Over a year at least."

Ladon yawned. "Where'd Perkins get the idea to experiment in the first place? Was it even his idea?"

Magnus had the same questions.

Keaton sucked in a breath and then came over to the bed Ladon lay on. He bounced onto the end, sitting on his knees. "Jeffrey came from money. I guess his parents knew about paranormals and did things to get rid of us. Like pay other important rich people."

"Being an asshole must run in their family." Ladon never took his eyes off the television.

Keaton smiled and then continued, "He also told me about a guy once. I can't remember his name, but he said they had an affair. He stole some papers from him."

"Did he say anything else about the human?"

"Only that he wasn't a human. He was a shifter. A turtle. I remember because I thought how cool it was that someone could shift into something like that and swim underwater. Like there's a whole world under there that most of us don't get to see, but that guy does."

"You watch documentaries about sharks and shit, don't you?" Ladon nudged Keaton with his foot and grinned.

"All animals, not just fish." Keaton stuck out his tongue at Ladon and pushed his foot away. Ladon had a way of making even a stranger comfortable around him. He brought others into his world, blanketing them with just enough teasing to make them feel like family in under five minutes.

Magnus smiled as the conversation continued.

"Did you have animals growing up?"

"No. I've just always liked them. *Big Cat Week* is my favorite show."

"You want to work with animals?" Of course, Ladon would think of that. He was a good Alpha, despite his young age.

"I'd love it."

Ladon nodded. "I might know someone." He turned back to the television screen, closing the conversation.

"Wait. You'll get me a job?" Keaton bounced on the bed again. He grabbed Ladon's leg and held on as if he needed something tangible to ground him, as if he'd soar into space otherwise.

"Maybe. I'll have to ask when we get home."

Keaton smiled, turning his gaze to Magnus as if to include him. Magnus winked and returned the smile before focusing on the task at hand.

"Is Bandos still at Mother Estelle's house?"

"Should still be there. Last time I heard they hadn't closed the sale on their cabin yet." Ladon yawned. His eyes drooped a bit.

Magnus picked up his phone and dialed the landline number. It was late, but it was Magnus' experience that someone was always awake, and Bandos wasn't answering his computer message.

"Do you know what time it is?" That was Hacen's idea of a hello because of course, it was. Hacen, Thomas, and Jules must have mended things if he was the one answering the phone. Hacen had needed to lose his prejudice toward shifters if he wanted to mate with Jules. He must have succeeded.

"Late. I need to talk to Bandos if he's around." Magnus typed with his free hand and pulled up a data bank site that would tell him where Perkins kept his money. From there he could find his purchase information, including what bills he paid. It might tell him how much money was going to the senator and when. The senator was the key. If Magnus could get the financial records and get dirt on the senator, he'd keep Perkins on a leash.

"Who's on the phone?" Jules' voice was muffled but close enough Magnus didn't have to strain to hear it.

"Magnus. He needs to talk to Bandos."

"I'll go get him." That was Thomas. Some lip-smacking and what sounded like a lot of tongue right before Thomas said, "Don't go anywhere. Either one of you."

"Not planning on it." Hacen's tone held a softness Magnus hadn't heard from him before. That more than anything told Magnus, Hacen had cultivated a good relationship with his mates.

Silence reigned after that as if someone had put him on hold, and then fumbling before Bandos spoke. "Bandos here." Someone else spoke in the background. A male voice but Magnus couldn't figure out who.

"Can you hack Perkins' computer system?"

"Yeah probably. Just need him to be online. What am I looking for?"

"Anything that looks scientific. I'm looking for the idiot who supplied Perkins with knowledge. Perkins got the idea to genetically alter paranormals, and humans too for that matter, from someone else. I need that guy's name. He's a turtle shifter. Not sure where from."

"Got it. Anything else?"

"Yeah, be available when I break into the senator's office again. You can hack that if I create a door for you, right?"

"Yeah, the security system is top notch but it's doable from here."

"You got it."

Ladon shot up off the bed and stalked to Magnus. His eyes burned into Magnus' soul. His lips thinned out, and jaw muscles ticked out an irritable rhythm. He leaned on the table, over the computer. "Like hell."

"Pissed-off mate, you have to deal with alone. Call me back when you need me." Bandos hung up the phone.

Magnus put his cellphone down beside the laptop and met Ladon's gaze. "I have to do this, or Perkins will be Saint Lakes' next battle."

"No fucking way." Ladon moved closer, looming over the top of Magnus' computer until their faces were inches apart.

Magnus pushed on Ladon's chest, moving him out so he could stand, as the chair was against the wall, and with the way Ladon was leaning so far over, he had Magnus pinned. Ladon straightened, giving Magnus the room he requested. He was at a disadvantage with Ladon's Alpha nature so strong and in his face. That was never more apparent than with Ladon so large and in charge. "This is my job."

"Your job is not to put yourself in harm's way." Ladon came around the table. He pinned Magnus again. Only it was worse because he pressed up against Magnus.

"Back off, Ladon." Magnus pushed at Ladon again. He didn't budge.

Ladon got right in Magnus' face. "They kidnapped you from that place once already. You seriously want a repeat?"

"I want to do what's best for Saint Lakes. This is it. You should want that too."

"I do, but I don't want it at the expense of you. We can find another way." Ladon's shoulders slumped, and he braced himself with his forearms on the wall beside Magnus' head.

Magnus placed a hand on Ladon's chest. "I'd feel the same way if you went."

"And if you get recaptured. Then what?"

"It's a risk I have to take. It all comes down to Perkins paying off the senator. Nothing else will matter to the senator, and he's the one who will keep Perkins quiet. I need information that will threaten his political career."

"What about the guy Perkins used?"

"That proves paranormals exist. It's good to have. We need to know the circumstances behind that and the shifter who figured it out because we need to stop the experiments. It won't help Saint Lakes, though. It would do more damage by exposing us. Not less."

He could see the resignation in Ladon's eyes.

Magnus sucked in a breath. Had he seriously won the argument?

Nope. Ladon's gaze laced with determination once again. Apparently, that was just round two. "I'm going with you."

Shit.

Magnus took a deep breath and closed his eyes, counting to ten. "I won't be able to get both of us in undetected. It'll be hard enough with just me because I don't have Wesley's ID card anymore."

"I'm going."

Magnus trailed his hand up Ladon's chest to the nape of his neck. He rubbed the strands of Ladon's hair between his fingers. "You can't, baby."

Ladon tried to pull away, but Magnus held him in place. Ladon didn't fight the hold but cupped Magnus' cheeks. "If you get hurt, I'll burn this city to the ground."

"You'll risk exposing paranormals?"

"I'd risk everything for you." Ladon's eyes shifted. His gaze held a hard edge that would've cut anyone who opposed him.

"Your priority needs to be Saint Lakes."

"I have my fucking priorities straight. Maybe it's you who has it backward." Ladon's jaw muscles ticced and he removed his hands, stepping back. Magnus followed him, trying to kiss him, but he pulled away. "Is this the last time?"

"The last time for what?"

"The last time you leave me behind."

Magnus averted his gaze. He wouldn't be able to tell Ladon what he wanted to hear. Ladon knew him well enough to detect a lie. When Magnus met his stare again, Ladon shook his head. "Ladon."

Ladon reached around his neck and pulled Magnus' hand away. He dropped it as if it was trash and walked over to the bed where Keaton still sat staring at them with watchful eyes as if they would bring him into their argument somehow.

The second Ladon lay on the bed, Keaton moved off it. His legs hit the other bed as he continued to back up.

"I won't hurt you. Ever." Ladon turned to meet Keaton's gaze.

Keaton's Adam's apple bobbed as he nodded. He still sat on the other bed and didn't take his gaze off Ladon.

Magnus rolled his eyes and walked to the bed. He climbed on top of Ladon, grabbing each wrist and holding them against the pillows. Ladon let him have his way but turned his head. "Stop with the tantrum."

"It's not a tantrum."

"I'm not your parents."

That last comment got Ladon's attention. "Stop bringing up old shit, Magnus. I mean it."

Magnus' let his eyes turn red. "I'll come back, and do you know why?"

Ladon remained silent. His gaze stabbed into Magnus' feelings as if they meant nothing.

"You're home." Magnus leaned forward and let his eyes glow blue. "You're home, Ladon. No matter what."

Ladon's fangs dropped. He pulled at his wrist until Magnus let go. As soon as he was free, he bit into his wrist and pressed the bloody wound to Magnus' lips. Magnus took it and drank.

Chapter Twenty-Six

The hotel room became Ladon's cage. His dragon was so close to the surface it took everything he had not to shift and fly after Magnus. It was Keaton sitting on the bed, trying to ignore Ladon's pacing and growling by watching television who kept Ladon in the hotel room.

Keaton looked at Ladon out of the corner of his eyes every few seconds or so. His stare held a caution that was unnecessary, although Ladon didn't say that. If he spoke at all, the words would come out harsh, and he didn't want to scare Keaton any more than he already was. Keaton would have to trust Ladon without the reassurances.

Despite Keaton's obvious fear, he kept darted his gaze from the door to Ladon every time he paced closer to that end of the room. Keaton wasn't very good at keeping his emotions hidden. They might not have been written all over his face, but the rest of his body language ratted him out.

Everything in him needed Magnus until it was all he thought about.

After Magnus' fangs dropped, they would talk about completing the mate bond, but it was pointless to discuss it until then. Magnus' health was more important than bonding. That still didn't stop Ladon from thinking how much easier it would have been if they had bonded. They'd have an inner connection that would allow them to talk to each other.

"You're not gonna leave me here alone, right?" Keaton crossed his arms over his middle, closing himself off to the possibility.

"No." Ladon stopped and sat at the end of the bed. By the gods, all the worrying had left him bone-tired, except no part of him could sleep through Magnus being out there on his own. A thousand dangers could befall Magnus, and they ran through Ladon's mind. The only thing stopping him was his limited imagination. He rested his elbows on his knees and put his head in his hands.

The bed shifted until Keaton sat next to him. A hand touched his back, patting him, providing comfort. "I've never had a mate. I guess that makes sense considering my age."

"Age doesn't matter. I'm only twenty years' old." Ladon's voice was barely above a whisper.

"You're lucky. You have Magnus and a clan as family."

"I'm lucky in a lot of ways." He thought about his family.

"He loves you." When Keaton said that, Ladon dropped his hands and turned, meeting his gaze.

"Yeah?" Ladon couldn't help but smile.

"It's all in the way he looks at you." In Keaton's business, Ladon would imagine, being able to read people was a necessity. It would keep him away from the johns with bad intentions. "You're all he sees."

"Well, I love him too. I want to shift and go after him, but I'd cause him more stress. Get in his way."

"He must be good at whatever it is he's doing, then." Keaton sat on his hands.

"He's very good at it." He didn't need Ladon flying along behind him like a shadow. Magnus had been right on that one point.

"Is he a cop or something?"

"He's an investigator for my clan." He was the single most important member of Ladon's clan because he was the only one who could do the legwork.

"Can I ask why your clan is investigating Jeffrey?"

Ladon sighed. "Human government officials know about paranormals. They've been pitting vampires and shifters against each other for years, although hid it well enough that we're just now figuring it out. My clan just had a battle with a vampire coven. We won the battle, but it was a close call. Too many died unnecessarily. On both sides." Ladon wouldn't speak of Lucas' role in the whole mess or the fae who they still had to find. Instead, he said, "This is the beginning of the end of our hiding."

Keaton sucked in a breath. His eyes widened. "Are you serious?"

"Very. It's a matter of time." Ladon had watched one of those documentaries which talked of strange sightings. It had shown video evidence of a dragon flying around. The dragon was real, but the commentator had blamed it on some remote-controlled fake. It was the same with the Bigfoot tracks. Someone on stilts with fake-looking feet fooling around with people's heads. And then there was Wesley's website, which had just as many nonbelievers as those who had seen a paranormal. "When the non-believers find out the truth, it'll be chaos. They may hunt us. If we don't make the right moves. Perkins' research means they expect a fight. He seems like he's testing shit just because he can but he's really building an army. Perkins probably only cares about the science but Senator Fowler and others like him know what they're doing."

Keaton let out a shaky breath. "Altering, how?"

Ladon shrugged. "I don't know exactly. All I know is they're creating humans that have the same strength and speed as a vampire. It's only a matter of time before they alter someone to have shifter abilities."

Ladon had thought about it a lot since Ramsey had given him the Alpha position. If they didn't make the right moves toward the humans, they would be in a war they weren't prepared for and probably couldn't win. That might have been the paranormal council's problem, but Saint Lakes was right at the center of the storm. Magnus, in particular, was in the middle and would remain that way if things didn't go right.

There was a knock on the door, which was a good thing because it broke Ladon out of his worries. He sniffed the air, wanting to know who was outside. It wasn't Magnus. He had one of the two keycards so he wouldn't have knocked. Even if he lost it, which wasn't likely, Magnus would call from his cellphone before knocking. It was just Magnus' way. Plus, Ladon didn't smell him.

Keaton stood to answer it, but Ladon grabbed his arm, stopping him. Ladon let Keaton go and stood. "Stay behind me."

Keaton took him literally because he grabbed Ladon's shirt and followed him. He peeked out of the small peephole and saw the front desk person standing there with the man who'd greeted them at the whorehouse.

The front desk man scowled as if it offended them somehow. He knocked again, insisting they open up.

"It's the greeter guy from the...um...your workplace."

Keaton cursed. "Mister wants me back, I bet."

Mister?

Ladon nodded and pulled open the door. He didn't even bother using the chain. No way was either one of the humans going to take Keaton anywhere he didn't want to go.

Ladon stood in the doorway, gripping the edge and his eyebrows raised. "Can I help you?"

"This man says you have a prostitute in your room." The front desk man swallowed, his Adam's apple bobbing when Ladon scowled. The whorehouse Mister, or whatever the fuck he was called, crossed his arms over his chest and smirked. "We have a strict policy not to cater to that type of behavior."

"The only people staying here is my boyfriend and another family member."

Keaton gripped his shirt even more.

"The other person isn't on the list."

"No, sir. We only met up a few hours ago. We're staying the night tonight and heading home in the morning. We'll pay extra for Keaton if it's a problem."

The front desk person tried to get a peek at Keaton, but Ladon blocked him from view. "I'll add him to the list."

Ladon smiled and nodded. "Thank you, sir. Very sorry for the mix-up."

The whorehouse mister scowled. Ladon shut the door, flicking the lock. "Shit."

"What?"

"There's no reason for that whorehouse guy to chase you back to here." How would he know? Magnus didn't use their real names to book an hour with Keaton, but Ladon had used his name to book the room. How would they have found Keaton? "I have to think."

When Ladon started pacing again, Keaton let his shirt go and climbed on the bed. He folded his knees up to his chest and wrapped his arms around his legs. "If me being with you guys is causing you problems—"

Ladon held up a hand, cutting him off. "I promised protection, and I won't break it."

"Mister won't give up."

"How well did he know Perkins?" Ladon stopped pacing, watching Keaton closely.

Keaton's eyebrows came together. "Jeffrey?" His eyes widened almost as soon as he spoke. He scrambled off the bed and began grabbing up every loose piece of clothing. It didn't seem to matter who the stuff belonged to. He grabbed one of Magnus' bags and threw stuff into it.

Magnus wouldn't like the way Keaton packed. And why that was the important thing, Ladon had no idea.

Ladon pushed Keaton aside. "Let me. I know how he likes things."

Keaton gave him an exasperated look. "We need to get out of here."

Ladon rolled one of Magnus' shirts. "Yeah. I've figured that out, Keaton. But I need a damn minute to process."

"You don't understand. Mister knows Jeffrey. They talk every time Jeffrey comes into the brothel." Keaton mumbled something under his breath about making a mistake but Ladon didn't have the time to roll that around in his mind.

Ladon let his eyes turn, and his fangs drop. He let smoke roll from his nose. When he met Keaton's gaze, Keaton's eyes widened, and he took a step back. "Magnus will come back to the hotel at some point. I won't leave him to that monster ever again. So we have a bigger problem than just Perkins."

Keaton nodded.

"Pack his computer."

Keaton practically ran across the room. He shut the lid and put it in Magnus' carrying case. "Can we call him?"

Yeah, Ladon wondered if that was a good idea. They had obviously pinpointed the room's location so calling wouldn't risk their exposure more than it already had. It might risk Magnus', though.

"By the gods, if Magnus were here, he'd know what we should do." Ladon had a new respect for Magnus' work. There were so many wrong moves they could make.

"Well, I think we should call him."

Ladon watched Keaton as he stuffed the computer charger into the case without coiling it up and using the fastener to keep the cord together like Magnus usually did. Ladon picked up the phone and then pointed to the cord. "Not like that. Magnus circles it around."

Keaton sighed and shook his head. "Fine."

Ladon dialed Magnus' cell number from memory. It only rang once before Magnus answered. "What's wrong?"

"I...I don't know what to do." Ladon sat on the bed, relieved just from hearing Magnus' voice. His knuckles were probably white from gripping the phone.

"Are you safe?"

"Are you?" Even though he could hear he was fine in his tone, Ladon needed the confirmation.

"Yes. I'm on my way back to the hotel right now."

"Don't come."

"Why?"

"The whorehouse greeter dude came with the front desk person." Ladon explained what had happened and that they were gone now. "We figured Perkins sent them."

"Yes. He probably did. Did you use your name to book the room?"

"You were there when I did, Magnus." In hindsight Ladon realized how stupid that had been and he fully expected Magnus to yell at him for it. It wasn't the right time for that, though.

"I wasn't in my right mind." Magnus sighed. "Okay. You're going to do exactly as I say. I mean it, baby. You are not in charge this time."

"Yeah...yeah, I'm okay with that." Ladon folded and rolled some more clothing.

"There's money in the inside pouch of my carrying case. I want you to take it and the computer."

"Leave the clothes and stuff?"

"Yeah. Not worth risking your life for them."

"Okay."

"Get out of the hotel. Don't use the front door. Try one of the side exits but be careful. Sniff things out to make sure no one's waiting for you."

"Yeah. Yep. Got it." Ladon motioned for Keaton to take the computer bag. Keaton grabbed it and stood by the door, waiting with the case hanging off his shoulder.

"There's a convenience store a few blocks from the hotel."

"How much is a block?" It might have been a stupid question, but Ladon was from a small town. Blocks didn't exist in Saint Lakes. Every location centered on one of three lakes. If someone asked where another lived, they said by North Lake or by Dewey Lake, or whatever. Not on X block. They didn't even give a road name.

Ladon could hear the humor in Magnus' voice. "Go north."

"North. Got it." He could figure out which way was north. Not too much of a problem.

"They sell burner phones. Buy one and call me back."

"Okay." Ladon sighed, trying to calm his nerves. "I'll call you in a few minutes."

Ladon had his hand on the doorknob leading out of the room when Magnus stopped him. "Be careful."

"As careful as I can."

"I love you." Leave it to Magnus to say the words for the very first time when everything in Ladon needed to hear it.

"Me too."

Chapter
Twenty-Seven

G   reen scales covered Ladon's hands, going halfway up his arms.
     They disappeared and then reappeared again to the rhythm of
his heartbeat. Controlling his dragon would've been nice, but it wasn't
in the cards. His dragon had an instinctive ability to fight that Ladon's
human side didn't seem to have, so maybe the half-shift would help
keep Keaton and himself safe.

A lot of shifters thought of their human forms as separate from the
other. Ladon didn't because both forms worked in tandem with each
other and had from his first shift. He knew the adrenaline would bring
out that dragon part of him. Instead of fighting it, he let it happen,
partially shifting even though he was in a human city.

"If I make it out of this alive, I'm letting Fane train me."

Magnus' instructions ran through his brain to the point they became instinct. They had to leave the room first.

Ladon edged the door open and sniffed the air coming through the crack. He didn't smell anything abnormal, so he took a step out. His muscles tensed. The carpet had large burgundy and tan flowers woven in the fibers all the way down the long hallway. The garishness made Ladon want to go back into the room again.

Maybe that was the point of having such ugly carpeting, so the customer didn't linger in the hall for too long.

Keaton held onto the back of his shirt, his arm an umbilical cord protecting him from every outside element. He wished all it took to keep Keaton safe was the connection.

Ladon stopped at the end of the hall assessing his senses. He held his breath before peeking around the corner but let it out almost as quickly when he didn't see anyone.

The staircase leading out was around a corner. Once they were outside, he'd shift if necessary, not that he wanted to. They were in a human city, which made shifting dangerous.

Ladon swallowed, wanting the fear to unclog from his throat so he could breathe again. He turned to Keaton, wanting to make sure he was ready for the exit. He worried his bottom lip between his teeth and his eyebrows drew together.

"Ready?"

"For what?" At the same time Keaton asked the question, he shook his head.

Ladon turned back to the door. "Never mind. Let's get out of here."

He pulled the door open slowly, looking for anyone who might've been waiting on the other side, but no one was around. He reached behind him and grabbed Keaton's hand when they stood at the top of the stairs, pulling it off his clothing. Keaton understood what he wanted and let him go.

"Sorry."

"No problem. Just makes walking down the stairs awkward."

There was only two flights and he could make them easily enough. He chose to go slow, using his nose to detect a threat.

When he arrived at the landing between, he stopped and peeked around the corner. The bottom of the staircase lay empty. Ladon went down and then sniffed the door leading outside.

His muscles seized up.

"Someone's outside the door." He kept his voice to a whisper, not wanting to alert the person on the other side. If they were paranormal, they may hear him anyway, but he had to take a gamble that they weren't.

He sniffed the air again, to see who the person was. A human. And Ladon was almost positive he was leaning against the outside wall to the door's right. He sniffed to make sure it was just the one human. Nothing on the other side, so he went back to the right side again, sniffing around. "I think he has a gun."

"How can you tell?" Keaton's eyes glowed red, and his fangs dropped. He kept his hands away from Ladon's shirt. Ladon was sure it was deliberate due to his fingernails turning into claws.

Ladon looked to the claws before meeting Keaton's gaze again. "I can smell the gunpowder." He took a deep breath. "Let me handle the human."

Keaton nodded. "What's the plan?"

"I have no idea." Ladon searched his mind for the best solution. By the gods, he'd probably have to fight, and he'd need to shift for that. If he got caught, they'd lock him up. If the humans didn't take him away for a science experiment first. "Act like we're drunk?"

Keaton drew his eyebrows together. "How will that do anything?"

Ladon shrugged. "It's all I got, okay."

Keaton shook his head. "I hope you know what you're doing."

Yeah, he did too. But maybe the acting would create enough of a diversion to throw the human off. Ladon didn't have a doubt he could take the human on, especially half-shifted. He didn't have to be good at fighting to do that but if the person knew how to use that gun then they might have an issue.

Ladon grabbed Keaton, wrapping his arms around his shoulders to keep his hands out of the human's direct line of sight. He pretended he needed help walking. He chuckled and tried to slur his words. "Liquor store's down the road, right?"

"No idea." Keaton chuckled as if he said something funny. As actors went, Keaton proved much better than Ladon.

Ladon pushed open the door hard enough that it banged against the wall. He expected it to either hit the human or for it to come back at him when the human blocked the attack.

Metal hit flesh and the human cursed.

Ladon chuckled and stumbled outside. He mumbled an apology all the while holding onto the fake humor, hoping to piss the guy off enough that he'd come away from the building. The last thing Ladon wanted was to burn the hotel down.

"Hey, mother fuckers." Metal clicked against metal. What the hell was that noise? Then he heard a sliding sound and turned just in time to see the guy put his gun in its side holster. The snap on the holster clicked into place when the human deemed them not a threat.

Ladon dropped his arm from around Keaton, who took a few steps away when he was free. Ladon turned completely. The human dressed all in black and wouldn't blend in with a crowd. He looked like a soldier in his cargo pants and a black T-shirt. The only thing he lacked was dog tags. He stood out even in the dark. Whoever hired the man didn't care about giving away their purpose.

The human stepped toward him as if ready for a fight hand-to-hand combat.

Ladon's heartbeat picked up. "Sorry about that, man."

The human's eyebrows came together, and he held his left hand up, studying something inside his cupped palm.

There was a moment when the rest of the world stood still. His own breathing was all he heard, heavy and shaky. A chill ran through him, even as his mouth built up heat and smoke came out his nose. He rolled his head around on his neck when the partial shift became uncomfortable.

The human's eyes widened. It was the only part of him that moved.

And then the world sped up again.

The man reached for his gun as if regretting putting it back. He fumbled with the snap, sweat beading on his brow, and he swore.

Ladon took a step closer as he opened his mouth. A steady stream of fire came rushing out, licking across the guy before the flames took hold.

The scream went straight to Ladon's soul. Ladon shifted back to normal as he stood there staring at the engulfed man, who reached out to Ladon as if asking for help.

Ladon took a step back and then another one.

Bile rose in his throat when the smell of burning flesh hit his nose. He turned, heading straight to the wire fence a couple of yards away. He trampled through the shin-high grass and weeds and braced himself with a hand on the fence. When the bile rose and spilled out of his mouth, he curled his fingers into the diamond-shaped holes. The thin metal dug into his flesh.

His stomach ached after he finished but he tried to breathe through it.

He wiped his mouth.

He turned to find Keaton staring at him with wide eyes, his face paler than normal. Keaton averted his gaze and ran from the scene. He slowed and waved his hand, silently commanding Ladon to follow.

The human's body lay surrounded by the orange glow, still and lifeless.

Ladon took another deep breath, willing the shakiness to disappear before running to catch up with Keaton.

Keaton turned back, concentrating on his direction. If they were heading north, Ladon had no idea. He relied on Keaton's sense of direction because he couldn't think past what he had just done. The killing had been quick. The whole process painless except for the wound to Ladon's soul.

They slowed down once they were on the sidewalk in front of a chain of small stores. Pubs and liquor stores were next to each other, along with restaurants that appeared dubious at best. When they came to a convenience store with bars on the windows and lottery signs glowing in the dark, Ladon pulled the door open.

He held it for Keaton, who entered but waited just inside, not getting far from Ladon.

Ladon nodded to the man behind the counter. "You got cell-phones?"

"Third aisle down." The man eyed them with suspicion. Ladon could feel his gaze even when they turned in the direction he indicated.

Ladon picked up the first phone he saw and then grabbed Keaton's hand, pulling him along.

The whole thing took less than ten minutes. It was as Ladon was paying that Keaton said, "I have something to tell you."

Ladon couldn't focus on whatever it was Keaton needed. Calling Magnus took center stage.

"I need a phone card too." Ladon nodded to the payment service cards that match the phone he purchased. They hung just behind the clerk.

The clerk turned and grabbed the one Ladon needed, putting it with his purchase.

Ladon handed the money over even before the clerk gave him the total. He shuffled from one foot to the other, impatience running through him. Tweaking with the need to talk to Magnus. It crawled through his skin until he itched.

The clerk mumbled a total even as he took the money from Ladon's hand. Ladon picked up the phone and the card, holding them to his chest.

The clerk handed him his change, and the receipt and Ladon made a beeline for the door.

The second he walked out he had the phone out of its box. He tried to turn it on, but his hands shook, so he handed it to Keaton. "You do it. Please."

Keaton took it. He fumbled with the phone, taking it apart. He held out his hand. When Ladon didn't hand over whatever the hell he wanted, he met Ladon's gaze. "Sim. And also, I need to tell you something."

"I heard you the first time." Ladon's tone sounded harsher than he intended. He handed over the only other thing in the box beside the information booklet. "Sorry. Just say it already."

Keaton fumbled with the phone again before putting it back to-gether. The screen lit up, and the phone made a noise, playing out a short little ditty that indicated it was going through the motions. "I'm supposed to take you to this house on the west side of the city. Jeffrey is waiting there with a bunch of those soldiery guys." Keaton did his thing with the phone and then handed it over as if he hadn't just told

Ladon he was a traitor. Not that the possibility hadn't crossed Ladon's mind.

Ladon gritted his teeth. "Why are you telling me this now?"

Keaton shook, and his shoulders came up to his ears. "What you did back there...it was brave. He probably would have killed us. And I don't want to die. I-I want to meet my mate."

Ladon took the phone from him. "They paid you to bring us to them?"

"Yes." Keaton looked away as if that fact shamed him. "I left the money in the hotel room on the bed. I don't want it now."

"Why?"

"You'd give your life for me."

Ladon nodded. "I said I'd protect you right from the start, Keaton."

"I know, but I thought that was something to say just to get me to do what you wanted." Ladon had seen the suspicion on Keaton's face. No one in Keaton's life had ever kept a promise. That fact had etched itself in the suspicion quite nicely.

"When I make a promise, I keep it." Ladon dialed Magnus' number, not wanting to discuss it any further.

Magnus answered after the first ring. "Ladon?"

Tears welled up in Ladon's eyes and clogged his throat, making it impossible to speak. He cleared his throat. "Yeah."

Keaton sucked in a breath and then put his arm around Ladon's waist, which was what he could reach. Ladon pulled him closer and held on, letting him know the protection would continue.

"Where are you?"

"I-I don't know. I had to kill someone." He sucked in some of the snot collecting in his nose and wiped the tears from his eyes.

"You did what you had to. So it's okay, baby." Magnus' voice was a balm for his soul. It went a long way to calming the panic.

"What do I do now?"

"Get somewhere safe. I'll come get you."

Keaton must have heard Magnus' end of the conversation because he said, "I know somewhere."

Ladon looked at him, studying Keaton's expression. By the gods, trusting Keaton could be the biggest mistake of his life. Keaton wouldn't have told him about Perkins' plan and his role in it if he were going to betray him, though. "Give Magnus the address."

Keaton rattled off a number and a street.

"Got it. Get into the first cab you see and take it. I'm on my way."

"Don't hang up." The thought of Magnus leaving him again set his nerves on edge.

"Okay but get moving." It was as if Magnus could see them standing in the middle of the sidewalk under the convenience store lights.

"Right." Ladon started down the sidewalk, heading away from the hotel because going back seemed like a bad idea.

Fucking hurry and find a cab.

"Talk to me, baby. Let me know that you're okay."

"I-I'm not hurt." But he wouldn't be okay until he got out of this mess and that wouldn't happen until he saw Magnus again. "I don't know how you do this all the time." He'd never been so scared. To say it wasn't his favorite feeling was an understatement.

"You're not alone."

"I feel like it." Ladon whispered the words, not wanting to say them but knowing they were needed.

Keaton flagged a cab down. The cab pulled up next to them, and they got in.

"Well, you're not." Magnus' voice held a hard edge that would have sent Ladon's back up under different circumstances. It gave him a warm feeling instead and calmed him enough that he heard Keaton rattle off the same address as before.

"We're in a cab."

"Good. I'll see you in a few minutes."

"Are you gonna hang up?"

"Not if you don't want me to."

"I think I'm okay now." Ladon still didn't want to hang up but he needed to pay attention to his surroundings.

Chapter
Twenty-Eight

M agnus cursed when he saw the rundown area surrounding the address. He drove through the front gates of the government housing where humans lived. A chain link fence surrounded several long two-story apartment buildings. The grass around the fence came halfway up. Whoever cared for the lawn either couldn't be bothered, or fear kept them from doing a thorough job. Someone had bent a section of fence just enough for a slim body to slide underneath. An abandoned guard's station sat in the center of the front gate with grass three feet high surrounding it.

The first thing Magnus saw when he drove inside was two men standing close together. One handed the other money at the same time the other passed him a baggie full of drugs. They didn't try to play off the exchange as anything other than what it was, fearing nothing, including the cops because they knew the cops weren't stupid enough to enter the complex.

Magnus sighed and shook his head.

Why the hell would Keaton bring Ladon here? Ladon was too young and way to naïve for the hood.

Past the second building on the right a woman smacked another across the face. That was all it took to get the tangle started. Where one started the other stopped, pulling at hair and clothing, punching between the pulling.

A better vampire than Magnus would have stopped to break it up. But even if his priority weren't getting to Ladon as quickly as possible, he still wouldn't have done anything to help.

Magnus pulled up in front of a building. They all looked the same, so he hoped he'd arrived at the right one. He shut off the engine and grabbed the paperwork and laptop computer he had stolen from Senator Fowler's office. He'd be lucky if he had intact windows by the time they left. The last thing he needed was the only tangible evidence to the senator and Perkins' crimes stolen. Not only that, but the laptop had evidence of paranormal existence, including pictures of a clan meeting. It wasn't Saint Lakes, thank the gods, so Magnus didn't care which clan. All he knew was the clan had at least one dragon shifter.

Magnus locked the door as he exited his car. Given the apartment's number, which started with a one, Magnus guessed it lay on the first floor, which was another safety problem Magnus couldn't do anything about. He'd grab Ladon and get the hell out of there. They'd get another hotel, maybe even drive out of the city.

Magnus found the right apartment and sure enough, ground floor. He rolled his eyes and raised his fist to knock, but the door swung open before he had a chance.

Ladon stood there with dragon eyes and his fangs dropped. His hands were half-shifted, scaly and clawed. It surprised Magnus that Ladon could even turn the doorknob with his hands like that.

His eyes were red-rimmed. The evidence of tears wrenched Magnus' gut. Magnus stepped into him, laptop and paperwork pressed against Ladon's side.

The door closed behind him and Ladon's entire body wrapped around Magnus.

He closed his eyes and pressed his cheek against Ladon's chest. He turned his face up to sniff at Ladon's neck.

"I've never been so scared in my life, not even when we rescued you." Ladon didn't even bother whispering it. Either no one else was in the room, or he didn't care if someone heard his vulnerable statement. Magnus didn't bother looking to check for others.

"Because you had Garridan there." Magnus' breath fanned across Ladon's neck. Something about it made his blood heat just enough that his lips acted all on their own, kissing the exact spot his breath touched. Ladon tilted his head as if asking for more, so Magnus did it again.

"And Bandos. Damian." Ladon moaned and tightened his hold around Magnus' waist. Magnus kissed him again. "Mmm, that makes everything better."

"Let's bond." They needed that above anything else. The connection was something Magnus craved more every time he drank from Ladon's wrist, and he wouldn't deny himself any longer.

"What about your health? Your fangs haven't dropped yet."

"You need me. That's all I care about." Magnus needed Ladon too. More than he had ever before.

"Spare bedroom is the door on the left." Keaton's voice came from somewhere in the room, not that Magnus paid even one ounce of attention.

Magnus needed to get Ladon somewhere horizontal. The end.

Ladon moved back just enough to turn. Magnus let him go but took his hand, letting Ladon pull him across the room.

It was then when Magnus' dick was hard enough to notice through his jeans, and his eyes glowed blue that he finally took in his surroundings. Keaton sat on a couch that had found a home in the center of the room. A television was against one wall. It looked as though it was on some nature station about bees or maybe the show was about honey. Magnus couldn't quite tell. Keaton was the only one in the room. His feet were propped up on a coffee table, and he didn't pay them any mind.

Magnus needed to have a conversation with him, but he forgot what about. He forgot about everything when Ladon led them through a door and into a small room big enough for a full-sized bed and not much else.

Magnus reached behind him and closed the door. The click of it brought home Ladon's silence, and Magnus' palms started sweating. When Ladon stood at the edge of the bed and turned toward him, the silence grew even more uncomfortable.

It took Magnus longer than he cared to admit, even to himself, to understand the reason behind the discomfort. Ladon hadn't ever had sex before.

Because he was only twenty years' old, young by even human standards.

Magnus cursed and closed his eyes. "Okay, we need to go slow."

"Probably." Ladon sounded nervous, so Magnus opened his eyes. He took a step in Ladon's direction, running a hand down his arm before taking the bottom hem of his shirt and pushing it up. Ladon smiled and lifted his arms. Magnus dropped the shirt onto the floor at their feet and focused on Ladon's chest muscles.

There wasn't one thing sexier than Ladon shirtless. Maybe if Ladon were all the way naked, but that was all.

He ran his hand over Ladon's hard pectoral muscles and then down his side when he leaned in to kiss the center of Ladon's chest.

When his hands reached Ladon's jeans, and he brought them around to the button, Magnus' fangs decided to drop. His gums ached right before he tasted blood in his mouth. He hissed and held on to Ladon's arm for support.

Ladon's arms came around him, holding him in a protective embrace. "What's wrong?"

"Fangs are finally dropping." The liquid in his mouth made him sound as if he were talking around water. "Guess we don't have to worry about how to get around that issue anymore."

"Nope." Ladon sounded relieved. Magnus hadn't realized how much Ladon worried about him until that moment when he finally gained full health.

"Hurts." At least it didn't hurt as much as they did back in the lab.

"Is there anything I can do?" Ladon kissed the top of Magnus' head, which was the part of him he could reach best.

He swallowed the blood pooling in his mouth and snapped his eyes open. He pulled back and met Ladon's gaze. The need to bite overtook him until his only focus was the pulse in Ladon's neck. "Yeah. Finish getting undressed."

Ladon unbuttoned and unzipped his jeans before pushing them down. At mid-thighs, Ladon kicked off his shoes, but by then Ladon's bare cock held his attention.

"You didn't wear underwear." Just knowing he'd been bare the entire time they had been together turned Magnus on even more. He didn't think his horny meter could go up anymore, but there it was.

"Didn't put them on after our shower this morning. They were dirty."

The pants came all the way off, and Ladon stood there with his hard length jutting out between them as if seeking Magnus.

Ladon sighed. "It doesn't work if just one of us is naked."

Magnus chuckled and pulled his shirt over his head. "Lay on the bed. We need to talk beforehand, and if I touch you, I'll forget myself again."

His shirt went down with Ladon's.

Ladon lay on his back, the mattress giving beneath his weight. He propped himself up on his elbows and watched Magnus.

Magnus kicked off his shoes and unbuttoned his pants. He unzipped them but left them on when he met Ladon's gaze.

Ladon licked his lips before smiling. He looked at Magnus as if he wanted to devour him. Magnus was the captured prey, and Ladon would feast soon.

Magnus chuckled. "I want to have intercourse this time."

Ladon grinned. "We don't call it 'intercourse' anymore, Old Man."

Magnus shook his head. "Shut up, Youngster and tell me what you like."

"I have no idea. Never done it before." Ladon's green eyes darkened with mischief. "See. It just so happens that I met my mate early in my life. I never wanted anyone after seeing him just one time. Wanna know why it only took one look?"

Magnus swallowed the lump in his throat and nodded. He took off his pants.

Ladon lost the smile. His gaze ate Magnus up again. "Because I fell for you. That first day. When my family held you captive in my yard, and you looked as if you would kill someone to get to me."

Magnus took his underwear off and climbed onto the bed, between Ladon's legs. He lay down, bracing himself on his forearms. "No more friend-zones."

"Thank fuck." Ladon flashed his fangs.

Magnus looked at Ladon's lips, wanting a kiss but he still needed to figure out what Ladon wanted. "I want it to be good for you."

"I trust you."

Magnus swallowed and nodded.

Finally, he lowered his mouth onto Ladon's, taking what he had needed. Ladon opened for him right away, giving over to Magnus, making it obvious that the friend-zoning was, in fact, truly finished.

For all that, Ladon was an Alpha in every other way, his submission was beautiful. Every lick against his lips and the way he followed Magnus' lead said everything.

Ladon moved his hands from Magnus' shoulders to his ass and then back up again, heating his blood with the glide of skin over skin.

All the months and years since meeting Ladon coalesced, turning into one moment, and all the wanting added up to a sum so overwhelming Magnus couldn't contain it.

He meant what he'd said when he spoke of making it good for Ladon. He wanted to make love, not take Ladon in a frenzy of need. But being inside him was what consumed his mind.

He broke the kiss, hissing at Ladon when he chased Magnus, wanting more.

Ladon scowled, his arms tightening around Magnus, holding him in place. "Calm down."

Magnus hissed again. "I can't."

Ladon flipped them over until he was on top. He grabbed Magnus' hands, lacing their fingers together and holding them above Magnus' head. His gaze never left Magnus'. "You need me to be Alpha?"

Probably or Magnus would fumble. He nodded. "I want you."

Ladon smiled. "Me too."

Ladon clearly didn't understand what Magnus the ferociousness of his want. He didn't get how it breathed hot and heavy in Magnus' blood. It wouldn't stop on its own. No point in telling Ladon that, though. His behavior showed it well enough. The lack of control wasn't something he'd experienced before. Not once in his entire life.

"I'm going to let one of your hands go. You're going to leave it right where it is. Understand?"

Magnus nodded again.

Ladon set him free only to reach over to the nightstand. He moved his body over just enough to look inside. "Let's hope there's lube." He rooted around. "Don't need the condoms. Can't get diseases and shit." The last part was something he said to himself. Magnus didn't give a crap if they used condoms or not. He just wanted the bite while he made love and he'd like to send Ladon over the edge of bliss while doing it. Condoms wouldn't stop that from happening. But Ladon was right. They didn't need them. Disease wasn't something a paranormal had to worry about. Only humans got disease from sexual intercourse.

Ladon came back to him with a tube in his hand. He held it up like a prize. "Ha!"

Magnus hissed and wiggled underneath Ladon, wanting to take it from him and use it to fuck Ladon with his fingers.

Of course, Ladon wouldn't turn it over. Damn it.

He popped the top of the tube and put some on his fingers. Magnus lost himself a little when Ladon reached behind himself, his hand disappearing.

"I want to see. Please."

Ladon's breaths came out in quick succession. He moved next to Magnus on his hands and knees.

Magnus didn't wait for Ladon's instruction. He was up and behind Ladon immediately.

Ladon had one finger buried to the knuckle. The surrounding muscles glistened with lube, inviting Magnus to join Ladon, so he did just that. He ran his finger along Ladon's, gathering a bit of lube before snaking a finger inside.

Ladon sucked in a breath and then moaned. He pushed back against their fingers.

Magnus calmed a bit as he focused on giving Ladon pleasure. His impatience waning just enough that he didn't feel like a barbarian ready to fuck Ladon with zero finesse.

Magnus created a steady rhythm. Ladon pulled his finger out, his chest flush against the mattress. Magnus made up for the absence by adding another finger. He curled them, massaging Ladon's prostate.

Ladon cried out, his chest lifting at the same time he pushed against Magnus' fingers. "Shit. Wh-what the…"

Magnus smiled. "I take it you've never touched that part before."

"No. Just…um…just fucked…ungh…myself in the shower."

Ladon was the one who set the pace. Magnus just had to hold still.

"By the gods, you're beautiful." It was him taking exactly what he wanted, with all those hard muscles and his ass on display. Magnus ran his hand over one of Ladon's globes, feeling the smooth skin. He came to Ladon's balls and cupped them. They were tight against the bottom of Ladon's hard shaft.

Magnus added another finger when he felt the muscles stretch.

Ladon moaned.

Magnus gripped Ladon's hardness, jacking him off at the same time he thrust his fingers in. Ladon moaned again, wiggling around and pushing back.

It took one more wiggle before Ladon rolled to his back. His eyes glazed over. "You. Now."

Magnus sucked in a breath at Ladon's dominant tone. Fucking sexy.

Magnus grabbed the tube of lube and coated his cock. He positioned himself, the head at Ladon's hole, pushing in just enough that he'd stay without holding it with his hand. He lay on Ladon, cupping his cheek with his clean hand before kissing him.

He didn't press in right away but let Ladon's body adjust to the initial invasion. Ladon cupped the back of Magnus' neck, his fingers threading through his hair. Ladon licked across Magnus' lips and moaned.

Magnus went a little deeper, giving in to his need.

Ladon panted. He gripped Magnus' nape, pulling him down until their foreheads pressed together.

"You okay?"

Ladon nodded. "Full."

Magnus nodded, pushing in a bit more.

Ladon closed his eyes, his knees going up around Magnus' waist. That was all the prompting he needed to keep going. He made sure to go slow, thrusting in small waves until he was all the way inside. By then they both were halfway to coming. He could see it in the way Ladon held his breath and then let it out when his lungs screamed.

Magnus thrust in, not stopping to let either one of them calm down. He didn't want to lose the beautiful edge he teetered on, so he did it again, gaining a rhythm, climbing up the hill of bliss. It was right there, still untouchable but close enough that he saw his own white-hot need.

Ladon let go of Magnus' neck. He tilted his head to the side in a clear invitation for Magnus to bite. That was all it took for Magnus to lose control again. When he struck, he went hard, gentleness a thing that didn't exist.

Ladon didn't seem to mind if his cry of pleasure was any indication.

Magnus welcomed Ladon's bite when it came. The second Ladon sucked his blood, Magnus orgasmed. He thrust hard, holding the position when the massive amounts of pleasure hit his core.

He had enough wherewithal to grip Ladon's cock, pumping it between them, not that it was needed because Ladon was already coming. He shuddered, growing sensitive at the same time Magnus' thrusts grew shallow again until finally, he stopped moving.

Ladon released Magnus, licking across the wound.

Magnus stayed right where he was. Even when satisfaction hit, he still didn't end the bite.

Ladon's dragon was a presence in his mind that hadn't been there before. It curled up into a ball like a sleepy cat.

Don't go to sleep yet. Magnus had to ask him if it was good first.

Ladon sighed. And wrapped his arms around Magnus. *It was great. Stop worrying.*

You think you can read my mind.

"We're connected now remember."

Magnus pulled his fangs out, licking the wound before lifting his head. "I've never been happier than right now." Very few times in Magnus life had he felt that emotion.

"I'm gonna try for contentment next." Ladon smiled.

"I'm very content, mate."

"And I didn't even have to try very hard."

Magnus chuckled and kissed Ladon.

He lay his head on Ladon's chest, snuggling against him until he was comfortable. "So, whose apartment are we in, anyway?"

"Keaton's."

Magnus shot up like a rocket. "Mother fucking gods damn it."

Ladon raised his eyebrows and just lay there. "Colorful language there, Old Man."

"By the gods, Ladon, get dressed. This place isn't safe." And not just because it was in the middle of the ghetto. "They'll track down Keaton here."

"Nah. Keaton made a deal with them. He was supposed to bring us to a different address." He had his pants halfway up when Ladon made that comment.

He opened his mouth to speak but couldn't figure out how to form words past the shock. Rage took over next. Magnus pulled up his underwear and pants, not bothering to zip and button them and flung open the door.

It was as he was stalking toward Keaton that he heard Ladon say, "Shit. Magnus."

A red haze covered everything, including Keaton, who sat on the couch with his back to them. The growl must have alerted him because he turned, his eyes widening. The little shit was smart enough to lie down, letting the couch cushions soften the blow. He still gave a distressed cry when Magnus landed on him. He wrapped a hand around the front of Keaton's neck but didn't squeeze.

Not yet.

"I'm gonna fucking kill you. Slowly. So that you have time to think about your mistake."

Keaton drew his eyebrows together. "Whatever I did, I'm sorry."

Magnus tightened his fingers just slightly. "You brought my mate into danger."

"Let him go. Now." Ladon's hand came down on his back and then snaked around his waist. Ladon pulled up, trying to lift Magnus off but Magnus just tightened his hold on Keaton to the point he made a choking sound. Keaton came off the couch with Magnus. "I'm telling you as your Alpha."

Ladon's breath fanned across the back of Magnus' neck. The warmth of his bare skin seeped into Magnus until he dropped Keaton.

Ladon duck-walked them back into the bedroom, shutting the door behind them and then leaning against it with his arms still around Magnus.

Neither one of them said anything. Anger consumed Magnus. He'd snap at Ladon if he spoke and that wouldn't do. Ladon wasn't the person who'd pissed him off.

Finally, Ladon kissed him below his ear. "He shares the apartment with a friend. The apartment is in the friend's name. Keaton's name isn't on any paperwork."

"And you trust him?"

"Yes."

"Why?"

"Because I didn't have a choice." Ladon kissed him again. "And I knew you were coming. You're good at reading people."

"If you wanted my help with Keaton, why'd you stop me?"

"Honestly?"

"Of course."

"Didn't expect you to get all pissed off and go after him. I thought you'd ask him questions."

"You didn't think I'd get mad that he put you in danger?" Magnus shook his head and sighed, rolling his eyes. "Let's just forget, for a minute, that we hadn't bonded when I first pulled into this apartment complex, which is the projects, by the way."

"Really?"

"Yes, Ladon. Really?"

"Cool." Ladon tightened his arms when Magnus growled and tried to get away. He chuckled. "I'm kidding."

"Well, I'm not. I want to kill that little shithead just for bringing you here." A part of Magnus had expected the protective instinct to kick in even more after they bonded but he hadn't expected the punch of it to hit him so hard.

"I think I'm equipped to handle a few poor humans." Ladon nuzzled into Magnus' neck. "Stop stereotyping everyone who lives here. They're not all dangerous."

"I care about *you*."

"I care about you too."

"I meant I only care about you. Not anyone else. Especially that little fucker—" Magnus was cut off by Ladon's hand over his mouth.

Ladon chuckled again. "Okay. I got it. But we're not going to judge Keaton just yet. We're going to clean up because your cum dripped all the way down to my ankles. After that, we're gonna talk to Keaton, and you're not going to kill him unless I tell you to."

"Fine," Magnus mumbled around Ladon's hand. He tried to pull away, but Ladon held on tighter.

"I think I got cum on the door."

The tension and anger ran completely out of Magnus. He chuckled, the anger finally leaving him. "Let's shower together."

Chapter
Twenty-Nine

There wasn't one reason for Magnus to keep Keaton alive other than obeying Ladon's order. He practically sat on Ladon when they took up a spot on the end of the couch. Keaton scrambled to the opposite end, as far away from Magnus as he could get and still sit on the only piece of furniture in the room. Why he didn't stand and run to the other side of the apartment was anyone's guess, but he braved it out. Comfort wasn't a priority with the way he leaned backward against the arm of the couch and his body tensed.

Magnus made sure to keep himself between Keaton and Ladon. Not that Ladon couldn't take Keaton if needed, but that wasn't the point. Protecting what was his from the threat. That was all that mattered.

His gaze remained narrow, and his lips curled, letting Keaton see his fangs.

"The only thing keeping you breathing is him." Magnus pointed his thumb toward Ladon. "Best remember that and answer every question truthfully."

Keaton nodded, his throat working to swallow down the fear.

"Now, where were you supposed to meet Perkins?"

"A few miles away on the west side."

Magnus nearly did him in right then, but Ladon must have felt Magnus' anger because he put an arm around Magnus' waist. "By the gods, you're a fucking idiot."

Keaton winced and averted his gaze. "It's safe here."

"Explain your logic," Ladon asked. The command was gentle, contrasting with Magnus' harshness.

"Well, Jeffrey wouldn't last ten minutes here. Even with all his soldiers. The people around here would take offense to all the black clothing. Word would spread and everyone with a gun would come out."

Damn it. That was probably true. The people around here weren't the soft kind. Even if they weren't of the criminal mindset and minded their own business, they still knew the score. Most lived a hard life, with even harder people around them. They knew how to survive and didn't like cops. They'd see Perkins and his men, and they'd fight or hide.

Too many people would get injured.

Magnus had firsthand knowledge. He might not have been poor starting out, but his mother had drunk herself sick. His dad couldn't sustain them on a fishermen's catch. Magnus had had time to venture into all the criminal activities. It helped put food on the table.

Magnus thought about their next move. "We should go home."

"Do we have enough to keep Perkins off your ass and out of Saint Lakes?" Ladon's question was a good one and not one he could answer definitively.

Magnus sighed. "I want to say yes."

"But…"

"But I didn't look at the evidence well enough to say for sure."

"But you have the evidence, right?"

"Yes. The senator kept dirt on Perkins. Probably an insurance policy since what they're doing in that lab is very illegal."

Ladon nodded. "I'd say it's time to ask for help."

Magnus smiled when Ladon pulled the burner phone out of his pants pocket. He dialed a number from memory. In a time where everyone relied on technology, and no one memorized phone numbers anymore, Ladon seemed to have all the important ones locked up tight and could pull them out when needed.

Magnus' vampire hearing allowed him to hear the other person on the phone. Ramsey's deep voice came through.

"Hey." Ladon rubbed at Magnus' side absently as if he had no idea he even touched Magnus that way. He used the gesture to soothe himself.

He must miss home. Had he ever left before?

"You okay, little brother?"

"Yeah. I miss you. And Fane. Everyone."

"We miss you too."

"I need your help," Ladon told him everything that had happened, but a condensed version. "I think we need to call the council. If Forrest is still there, can you have him call whoever and get them over here?"

"Perkins is dangerous. We need to get rid of him while we know where he's at. I think Forrest can talk Quidel into sending enforcers and I'll send Fane. He'll come up with a plan," Ramsey said.

Ladon let out a breath and smiled. "Are you making Vaughan fly him?"

"Yes. He'll be there as soon as Vaughan gets flight clearance. I'll let you know what Quidel says, but he'll want that information Magnus collected."

"I'll send it with Vaughan."

"You guys stay safe."

"Thanks, Ramsey."

"Love you, little brother."

"Love you guys." Ladon hung up the phone and met Magnus' gaze. "Now we wait."

"Just like that?" Keaton stared at them as if he were meeting them for the first time.

"Just like that." The Somersets were a resourceful bunch, and they stuck together. Those two things made them a formidable force. "It's too bad for Perkins and the senator." Magnus gave Keaton a narrow-eyed stare.

"What's too bad?" Ladon asked before Keaton had a chance.

Magnus didn't take his gaze off Keaton. "That they're on the wrong side. It'll get them imprisoned, and that's if they're lucky. Remember that, traitor."

For the first time since meeting Keaton, he raised his chin and gave Magnus a pointed look. "I'm not a traitor. Not even to Jeffrey. I was never on his side. It was all about the money, and he knew it. I'm loyal to Ladon and will be until the day I die."

It seems Magnus might just have hit a nerve. Good. It would let him know exactly where Keaton stood on things. "Why be loyal to Ladon?"

"Because he's keeping his promise. So I will too." Keaton met Ladon's gaze. "I won't betray you."

Ladon nodded. "I know that."

Magnus patted Ladon's knee even as he met Ladon's gaze. "You're a good Alpha."

"You don't think I'm too young anymore?"

"I'm still worried." Running a clan wasn't easy for anyone. Saint Lakes was anything but normal. They were in the center of trouble and with Lucas being special enough everyone wanted a piece of him, Magnus worried they'd never dig themselves out. Then there was the battle, which had only brought Saint Lakes into the spotlight, at least amongst paranormals. That wasn't necessarily a good thing because Saint Lakes wasn't equipped to handle whatever blowback might come.

The telltale sparkle that Ladon always got right before he teased entered his eyes. "Good thing I have an old man for a mate who will help when needed."

Keaton chuckled. "What's the age difference between you?"

Ladon opened his mouth to answer, but Magnus stopped him. "A lot."

"You don't look that much older." Keaton drew his eyebrows together but didn't comment further.

Ladon stood and stretched, his T-shirt coming up a bit, giving Magnus just a peek at skin. Ladon dropped his hands and then made his way around the couch. He chuckled, which confused Magnus, but not for very long. "He's ninety-two."

Ladon ran to the closest door. It banged shut behind him.

Magnus grinned. "Gotta pen?" He stood, looking down at Keaton. "Why?"

The door lock was a cheap one that would open with one push of a stripped-down pen. Magnus couldn't tell Keaton that because Ladon's dragon shifter hearing could pick up every word. "Pen?"

"In the kitchen. Drawer all the way to the right."

Magnus grinned as he walked into the kitchen. He pulled open one drawer before he found one full of abandoned objects. He grabbed what he needed and began taking it apart. Once he had the ink part separate from the rest, he walked to the locked door.

He fully expected Ladon to lean against it. Ladon was stronger than Magnus so Magnus wouldn't get the door open if that were the case. Magnus put the pen inside the hole and found the lock mechanism.

He heard Ladon chuckled from somewhere inside.

The lock popped open, and Magnus turned the knob, pushing the door wide. He lifted an eyebrow when he saw Ladon all naked and sexy lying on the bed with his hard cock in his hand.

Keaton chuckled, probably getting an eye full, which made Magnus growl. It would have irritated him, but he was the idiot who stood with the door open.

He shut it and turned the lock again.

Magnus pulled his shirt over his head as he closed the distance between them.

"I'm ready for you again, Old Man."

"Did you slick yourself up, Youngster?"

"Yep." Ladon pulled his legs back to prove it.

"You're not too sore?"

"Enough that I keep thinking about it and now I'm horny again."

"And you want me inside you? Not the other way around." Magnus ran his hand down the inside of Ladon's thigh.

"Yes. Next time we can do other stuff."

Next time. Those were two of the sweetest words.

Chapter Thirty

A calmness washed over Ladon the second he saw Vaughan and Fane walk through the door. Five council enforcers were with them. They all wore civilian clothes, which was a good thing given what Magnus and Keaton said about where they were.

Keaton nearly ran across the room to Ladon and Magnus the second he saw the big enforcers. Little did he know the most dangerous one in the bunch was little bitty Fane.

Ladon smiled at Vaughan and Fane, walking across the room to them. Keaton tried to follow him, but Magnus grabbed him when he took a step away. "You'll let him have a moment."

Ladon turned and met Keaton's gaze. "You're safe with Magnus."

"Yeah right." But Keaton looked like an energetic bobblehead when he nodded.

Ladon hugged Fane first because he was closest. "Thanks for coming."

"Ramsey made me." Fane's straightforward way of seeing the world had always struck Ladon as being super-cute, even if his honesty could be brutal sometimes.

Ladon chuckled. Ramsey couldn't make Fane do anything he didn't want to do. "That Ramsey. What a slave driver?"

Fane didn't get the sarcasm at all. "That's not true."

"I know. Just a joke." Ladon let him go and turned to Vaughan. "I'm fucking glad you're here, man."

Vaughan sniffed him. "Congratulations on finally bonding."

"Thanks." He didn't want to think about anything else but the fact that he had pieces of home so close he could hug them. He'd never thought of himself as a homebody, but he felt a sickness in the pit of his stomach that only home could cure. That knot loosened just a bit. Enough that he could think about what needed to come next.

He let go of Vaughan and turned to the enforcers. Most of them he remembered from the battle. They had come charging into the fray at the last minute, saving the clan like bear-shifting angels.

All of them tilted their heads downward, acknowledging him as an Alpha. He touched each one on the back of the neck. "Thank you for the help. We'll need it."

One stood in front of the rest, clearly the leader of the pack. "I'm Lexus." He nodded to the shifters behind him. "These are my guys. We'll follow your lead, Alpha."

"I know. I remember you from right after the battle. Thanks for coming to our rescue again." Ladon remembered the bear enforcers all sitting around watching a football game on television right after the battle, as if the carnage hadn't still lain right outside the door.

"Right. Dragon with a head injury," Lexus said as if the memory had just come to him.

Ladon pointed to Fane. "We'll all live longer if we follow his lead." The next question he asked Fane. "You okay with that, Fane?"

"I need to know if you want the enemy dead or captured."

Well, that was a good question. Ladon turned to meet Magnus' gaze. *I don't know how to answer.*

Perkins is expendable. We have his science and everyone he collaborated with. It's all in the paperwork. We need the senator alive. He's in the public eye way too much to kill him.

"Not the senator if he's even there. Magnus thinks we should keep him alive." Ladon held out his hand, asking Magnus to come with him. Keaton came too, grabbing onto Ladon's shirt again. It seemed to be the thing he needed, so Ladon let him.

Vaughan tapped Keaton on the shoulder, making him jump. He put his free hand to his chest. Vaughan smiled at Keaton and bent down to get at his level. Vaughan held out his hand as if knowing Keaton would understand that human greeting better than the traditional ones paranormals knew. "I'm Vaughan. Ladon's older brother."

"Keaton." He hesitated to take Vaughan's hand but eventually did, shaking it.

"You'll want to hang with me. I'll make sure you stay safe and get home."

Keaton took a step closer to Vaughan. "But I live here."

Vaughan pursed his lips and his brow wrinkled. "You're part of the clan now, Keaton. So your new home is in Saint Lakes."

"Ladon said that too."

"Yeah. You'll get used to us Somersets."

Ladon nodded when their gazes met. He turned to Magnus. "Let's all sit down, and Magnus can explain everything. Fane, you can get a plan together after?"

Ladon sat on the floor with Magnus right next to him. The bear enforcers pulled the chairs away from the kitchen table and brought them into the living room. Everyone else sat on the couch, including Fane, who folded his legs under him.

Ladon let Magnus tell them everything that had happened, starting with his time in the lab and the super-strength Anna had. He ended by saying, "We need to keep everything as quiet as we can. Paranormals are on the cusp of making breaking news on every television station in the world. And we have some major dirt on the senator. His collaboration with Perkins is enough to bury him. We have to be careful how we use the information. It's damaging to us as well. It's best to capture him. Blackmail works in our favor."

Fane closed his eyes the whole time Magnus spoke. As soon as he finished, he focused at Keaton. "You were to bring Ladon to the scientist, correct?"

Keaton hung his head and nodded. He folded his hands in his lap and laced his fingers together.

Fane got up from the couch. "Then that's what will happen."

Magnus came up off the floor like his pants were on fire. He stood in front of Ladon, blocking him from everyone else in the room. His hands were down to his sides, and he stood with his feet slightly apart. "Like hell."

Ladon sighed and stood, wrapping his arm around Magnus' waist before he went after Fane. Magnus wouldn't win if he started that fight and the last thing Ladon needed was an injured mate. Not when they had a bigger fight coming.

"I died for Ladon once. I'm prepared to do it again." Fane never moved from his spot. If he thought Magnus was a threat, he didn't let it show.

Is that true?

Yes.

Tell me what happened.

Ladon rolled his eyes. "First, I want to point out how annoying the over-protection is. There's a time and place for it. Now isn't one of them. Especially against Fane. So stop it."

Magnus' jaw muscles ticced, which was a sure sign he didn't like the order. Ladon didn't care as long as he calmed down. Magnus' behavior delayed things. The sooner they got a plan together, the sooner they could go home. "Not capable."

"Okay. So I sustained a head injury during the battle. Was unconscious and Fane protected me. He took a bullet to the gut, but Lucas fixed it just in time." Ladon still held onto Magnus even when he pressed against him as if he needed to feel more of Ladon's body.

"Thank you," Magnus spoke to Fane.

Fane didn't acknowledge the gratitude. Instead, he continued with the plan. "One of us goes ahead. Quietly. Hiding. Then Ladon and Keaton go. Ladon gives a signal when he's ready for everyone else." He pointed to Magnus. "You go back to the plane with Vaughan."

Magnus snorted. "That's not happening."

"Can you control yourself if someone hits Ladon? Because it may happen."

"No."

Fane nodded. "Then you go to the plane. Ladon will tell you he's safe through your link." Fane closed his eyes again when he felt satisfied with the plan.

Magnus' face turned red. He turned into Ladon's embrace and buried his nose in Ladon's neck. He didn't say another word. Maybe he knew how pointless it was to argue with Fane.

Chapter Thirty-One

I hate this plan.

Ladon sighed and rolled his eyes. *I'm aware.*

He kept an arm around Keaton's shoulder as they walked on the roadside. The gravel crunched under Ladon's feet. A gunshot rended the silence, but it was far off, so neither one of them acknowledged it. Keaton acted as if he'd never even heard it. He'd lived in the area long enough for the sound to have grown familiar, blending in with everyday life. It would be like the sound of the lake water lapping at the shore. As familiar as his own hand or his dragon counterpart. Hopefully, it wouldn't take Keaton very long to grow familiar with those things instead of gunfire and all the others sounds a city brought.

Where are you?

Walking still. Ladon wasn't too worried. Mostly because Fane was the one who'd gone ahead of them. If anyone could get in unseen and stay that way, it was him. Ladon had complete faith in Fane even if Magnus didn't. And the bear enforcers were just a street over, heading in the same direction. They didn't make their way over together just in case someone was watching. Staying hidden was the name of the game for everyone but Ladon and Keaton.

"I feel as badass as Magnus, but I'm scared all at the same time." Keaton shook his head. "It's weird to feel both at once."

Ladon chuckled. "You think Magnus is badass?"

"You don't?"

Ladon hadn't ever thought of Magnus with that term in mind before, but it did fit in several ways. "He's very good at his job."

"And ready to kill for you."

"That too." Magnus' protective nature surprised Ladon. Or rather, the ferocity of it. Thinking back to when Magnus had kidnapped Sage to get to Ladon, he probably shouldn't have. That had been before Magnus had found out he couldn't bond with Ladon until he'd shifted for the first time. He had threatened and fought for Ladon at every turn. It had worked, and then he had found out they had to wait.

"He does what he has to do." Ladon needed the reminder of that one thing sometimes. "Thanks, Keaton."

"For what?"

"For helping me remember to make sure Magnus takes care of himself. He focuses so much on me sometimes and forgets."

Keaton shrugged and turned right, down a road with a boarded-up restaurant on one corner and a lot full of two-foot-long grass on the other. The neighborhood hadn't improved during their walk, although they hadn't encountered anyone. "I think you'll take care of each other just fine."

"I think you're right." Ladon smiled.

The smile died when Keaton said, "It's the third house on the right."

We're coming up on the house.

Be careful.

Ladon sniffed the air, wanting to know if he could smell Fane. When he couldn't, his stomach twisted in knots.

They came to a house with white paint chipping off the wooden siding, giving the place a gray, blotchy look.

Ladon gripped Keaton's arm when unease crawled up his spine and made a home on the back of his neck. The thing about unease was it had patience and loved the anticipation of real fear. It twisted Ladon's stomach just enough for a solid knot to form.

"You're hurting me." Keaton's whisper did nothing to alleviate Ladon's tension.

Ladon didn't even realize how tightly he held onto Keaton. He loosened his hold. "Sorry."

The cracked driveway separated one house from another. The narrowness of the space made the area feel closed-off, with shadows in every corner but one.

Ladon shifted his eyes, wanting to see better. Dragon shifters didn't have the best eyesight, but they didn't have the worst either. Shifting to the dragon's sight was better than going with his human eyes.

Lights were on in the house, which shook Ladon's confidence a bit. By the gods, if he could've smelled Fane somewhere on the air he'd have felt better about the whole situation. He needed something to let him know Fane was nearby, but he also knew Fane was smart about most things. He wouldn't leave his scent floating around. Fane thought of stuff like that, especially if enhanced humans were around.

How many humans had Perkins altered, and were there any inside the house?

Someone came to the window overlooking the driveway. Ladon didn't know who it was, but he decided to play along to the pretense. "Who did you say lived here?"

Keaton cleared his throat. "Um...a friend from work." It wasn't a lie. Ladon would give Keaton that.

"I hope they have something to eat. I'm hungry." His stomach was knotted up. He couldn't eat if someone forced him, but the act might give them the element of surprise.

Keaton gave him a look that said Ladon's comment was unnecessary. And yeah, it probably was, but he was trying, damn it.

They went around to the back door and turned the knob.

Ladon leaned into Keaton and whispered in his ear. "Stay close but not too close. If I shift, I could knock into you by accident."

Keaton walked into the house first. Anyone who knew shifter behavior would've been able to tell Ladon was onto them as he kept his senses open, using them constantly. His hand was half-shifted until claws were in the place of fingers.

The pretense was a waste of time inside the house. It was too late to rethink the plan. *We're inside.*

Fuck. Okay.

The unease turned to fear, and suddenly Ladon didn't like the plan either.

They went through the kitchen which seemed to scream the nineteen-fifties with the orange and green paisley wallpaper above the wooden cabinets. The kitchen was closed off, with an arched doorway leading into the rest of the house.

The couch was visible, along with three people, Wesley being one of them. The other two Ladon didn't know, although he was sure one of them was the senator as his face seemed vaguely familiar. Ladon might have seen him on the news a time or two. Maybe. He wasn't sure because he didn't pay attention to politics. Owen was the one who liked it.

Wesley met his gaze and quickly averted it to his lap. Ladon could practically smell the guilt as they walked into the room.

A man sat in one of those antique armchairs that looked as though it belonged in front of a fireplace instead of next to the television. It was positioned so whoever sat there would see into the kitchen.

The smug smile on the man's face told Ladon it was probably Perkins. The third man on the couch came up and stood in front of the senator. He dressed in all black like the man outside the hotel. Three other men in black came out of hiding to surround the senator.

Perkins lost his smile when they did as if he thought he was the most important person in the room but found out differently.

Ladon smiled, his eyes narrowing. The unease took a back seat to anger. He used it as he walked farther into the room.

"Keaton. I see you did what I asked. Good boy. Now come over here and sit on Daddy's lap." Perkins patted his legs and smiled. He wasn't an ugly guy except for the oily quality to his smile and the lecherous way he eyed Keaton.

Every protective instinct Ladon had kicked in. Keaton was part of his clan, and more importantly, he was Ladon's friend.

"Get behind me." Ladon didn't whisper. Why bother when the show would get started as soon as Ladon gave the signal.

Magnus staying back at the plane with Vaughan had been a bad idea. Ladon would need him right after the shitstorm was over. *Come. Please.*

I'm already halfway there.

Ladon would have sighed in relief, but he wouldn't feel that until the end.

"You do realize he betrayed you." Perkins crossed his arms over his chest when Keaton followed Ladon's direction.

Ladon let his hands shift back to his human form before letting the claws and scales come out again. "You sure about that?"

Perkins' eyebrows drew together. He gripped the arms of the chair so tightly his knuckles were white.

Keaton fisted the back of Ladon's shirt.

Ladon sniffed the air, smelling Fane close by. The enforcers would be outside by now. All Ladon had to do was give the signal. Ladon wanted to know something first. He turned to Wesley. "You picked the wrong side. I'd like to know why?"

Wesley's face turned white, and he couldn't take his eyes off Ladon's hands. That was all it took for Ladon to know fear ruled Wesley's decision.

"It's not too late, Wesley. I'll protect you."

Wesley wanted to believe him. Ladon could see it in his eyes. He scooted to the edge of the couch and hesitated one second too long because the senator's arm shot out, coming across Wesley's gut, holding him in place. Wesley grunted when it made contact but didn't fight it.

"The paranormals will never accept you if they knew the truth." Senator Fowler knew he had Wesley right where he wanted him.

"It's not true, Wesley. Your slate is clean, starting now. We'll start over as friends, okay."

Wesley had tears in his eyes when he met Ladon's gaze again. One of the senator's goons pulled out his gun and pointed it at Wesley. Another pointed his at Ladon.

Ladon lifted his hands. "Let's not do anything that will get anyone killed."

And that was all the signal he needed for the storm to start.

Fane leapt out of a hallway, slicing the arm off the goon with the gun pointed at Wesley.

Glass shattered in another room and a bear roared right before five of them entered the room.

"Get back, Keaton." Ladon pulled his shirt over his head. He kicked off his shoes and dropped his pants, shifting as soon as he was naked. His body took up a quarter of the room, but his size didn't stop him from adding to the carnage.

A human in black pulled a gun on one of the bears, his back to Ladon, which was his mistake because Ladon came down on him with his mouth open, biting him in half. Blood coated his mouth and bones crunched before he spit the human out. The body fell to the floor in two chunks.

Ladon could feel Keaton's legs against his tail, which meant he was safe. Ladon's job was to keep him that way.

The senator stood, two men in black leading him out of the room. The senator had Wesley's wrist in his hand, pulling him along.

Ladon made a chuffing sound at Fane, who sliced through one of the men in black. The man made the mistake of pinning him in a corner.

Fane turned with his knife raised and ready to slice through the next enemy. One of the men in black turned with his gun pointed at Fane. He was about ready to get a shot off. The man in black was only two or three steps away, but that meant he had to leave Keaton.

Ladon made his decision, stepping toward Fane, biting into the man's leg, taking him down. The guy turned and the gun fired. Ladon roared when the bullet went through his thick, scaly hide. He let the guy's leg go in favor of stopping him from getting another shot off. He would have bitten his hand, but the man managed to pull the trigger again before he went limp. He saw a bloody hole on the side of his head. His eyes glassed over as the life drained out of his body.

Ladon looked over in time to see Magnus with a gun in his hand. His face was a mask of anger as he took another shot at the senator's last remaining goon. The man went down in a heap at the senator's feet.

Ladon forgot the pain in his shoulder when Magnus came over, standing in front of him, protective and steady. Ladon rubbed his head against Magnus' shoulder and chuffed.

It wasn't until Keaton cried out behind him that Ladon's attention changed. Perkins had somehow worked himself behind Ladon. He had a gun pointed at Keaton's head and kept Keaton in front of him.

Ladon shifted. The senator and Wesley were nowhere in sight. "Someone needs to find the senator and Wesley." He didn't care who went to look as long as someone did.

One of the bear enforcers shifted and came up beside Ladon. "Lexus and Benji are on it."

Ladon had a bunch of fucking questions about how they'd lost them, but they would have to wait for another time.

Keaton shook, and his face was ashen.

Ladon stood behind Magnus. He snaked an arm around Magnus' waist. Magnus was an excellent marksman. Ladon had complete faith in his ability to hit Perkins and only Perkins.

Perkins eyed Magnus' gun. "Let me go, and you can have this worthless little whore back."

Magnus' body loosened right before he pulled the trigger.

Keaton stiffened, and the muscles in his neck tensed even as Perkins' hand flew back. The gun clattered to the floor, metal scraping against wood. He cried out, releasing Keaton in favor of clutching his hand.

Keaton stood with shock clear on his face. He closed the distance between them, nearly running. He hid behind Ladon, pressing himself against Ladon's backside. He didn't seem to care that Ladon was still naked.

Magnus held the gun on Perkins and walked to him, squatting and pressing it against Perkins' head. "How many labs do you have?"

Perkins clutched at his hand. "The one your people sent up in flames."

Magnus grabbed Perkin's bloody hand and twisted. Perkins cried out in pain. "Is that the truth?"

"No. No! One-one more."

Magnus stood. "That's what I thought." Magnus turned to Ladon. "Get out of here and on the plane, baby. I'll be right behind you."

Ladon nodded even as he bent and picked up his clothes. He grunted when the gesture pulled at the wound on his shoulder. He took the time to cover the lower half of himself, but Keaton ended up helping him, doing most of the work. He pressed his shirt against his wound. Keaton wrapped an arm around his waist.

He turned to Fane. "You'll stay and watch his back?"

Fane nodded.

"The enforcers can come with me." Ladon was losing blood and fast. He needed someone to catch him if he passed out.

People like Perkins need to die, Ladon. They don't ask if what they're doing is ethical and they don't care about hurting people.

I know. It's part of the plan. I wish it wasn't you who had to do it.

Will you love me less?

You're fishing for an I-love-you. Ladon chuckled.

Always.

You know I do. They were out of the door and less than a mile away when the shot rended the air.

To Ladon's surprise he never lost consciousness. He didn't even make it to the plane before Vaughan started cursing. "Fucking shift, Ladon. By the gods, why'd you wait so long? Idiot."

Ladon had sweat covering his body even though a chill ran through him. "It's the middle of a human city. Idiot."

"And you're about ready to lose it."

"Stop yelling at me. Idiot." Ladon's legs gave out, and he went down like a stone. Keaton tried to keep him stable but couldn't. He nearly went down with him.

"Shit." Vaughan ran to him, kneeling enough to assess Ladon.

Ladon smelled Magnus. That was the only thing that let him know that Magnus was so close behind him. Magnus laughed, probably at some overly honest thing Fane said.

Ladon's vision blurred, turning black around the edges.

Magnus hissed, and then he was in Ladon's face. "Why the hell are you sitting on the ground?"

"Because I can't walk."

"Why?"

"Lost too much blood."

"What the fuck happened?"

"Got shot back there."

Magnus' eyes widened. "You were injured this whole time. By the gods, why didn't you tell me?"

Ladon shook his head. "Thought you knew."

"I wouldn't have left your side if I knew, baby." Magnus sat on the ground in front of him. He pulled his shirt over his head before sliding as close to Ladon as he could get. He wrapped one arm around Ladon's waist and cupped a cheek with his free hand. "Are you too weak to shift?"

Ladon nodded.

"Take the blood you need, so you'll be strong enough."

Ladon let his fangs drop and sank them into Magnus' shoulders. He took several swallows before he felt his vision return. Ladon didn't move away from Magnus even after he pulled his fangs out and licked across Magnus' wound. Instead, he pulled Magnus closer with his good arm and lay his head on his shoulder.

"You have to shift."

"Can I have one damn minute to hold you, please?" The pain made Ladon testy.

Magnus nodded. "As long as you're well enough now."

"I'm fine. Ready to go home. With you. Not being without you right now. And while I'm at it, you're not going on investigating trips alone anymore. Got it."

"Yes, Alpha." Magnus chuckled.

"I mean it."

"I know."

"He gets like that when he's tired." Who Vaughan was talking to, Ladon didn't know, and he didn't care.

"Shut up. Idiot."

"I'm not the one whining and throwing a tantrum like a toddler. Idiot."

"Do you guys always call each other idiots?" Keaton asked.

"Sometimes. Ladon hates it."

Ladon lifted his head to see Vaughan wrap his arm around Keaton's shoulder and lead him back to the airplane, which sat only a few yards away ready to go.

"Why do you do it, then?" Keaton didn't know Vaughan very well.

"Because it's fun. Why else would I call him names?"

Magnus chuckled. "He knows every button to press, doesn't he?"

"Yes. It's fucking annoying." Ladon lifted his head when he saw three bears shift halfway to the plane. "Are we still waiting for Lexus and Benji?"

One of the bear shifters turned. "We should take off. They'll report back to Quidel." Ladon knew Quidel was the leader of the enforcers and on the paranormal council.

Ladon nodded and lifted his head from Magnus' shoulder. He met Magnus' gaze. "Thanks for coming. You saved my life back there."

Magnus smiled. "So maybe you don't mind how protective I am."

"Maybe I don't." Ladon stood and moved far enough away that he wouldn't hurt Magnus when he shifted.

Chapter Thirty-Two

T he pillow Magnus rested his head on smelled like Ladon. The
sheets. And blankets. The air. Just that alone made him curl
up and shut his eyes. The bed held Ladon's warmth. The blankets
provided a cocoon of heat that Magnus never wanted to leave.

And then he realized Ladon wasn't in bed with him. That made
him shoot up like a rocket. He flung the covers off. They tangled
around his feet, holding him captive when he tried to get out of bed.

Where are you? Are you okay?

Good morning, baby. Oh, Magnus could sense the teasing. And it
was all he needed to know that Ladon remained safe. He probably
hadn't even left the house.

Magnus scanned the room, taking in his surroundings. He'd never
been in Ladon's bedroom before last night. Ladon had invited him
once, but the smell would have sent Magnus over the edge of horny,
and that hadn't been a good thing back then.

Magnus grinned. They had bonded, and that meant Magnus could get as horny as he wanted. Instead of getting dressed, Magnus pushed his underwear down and off and got back on the bed.

Do you have lube in here? Magnus pulled open the drawer of a nightstand and snooping inside. *Never mind, I found it.*

Holy crap. Hold on. I'm in a meeting with Ramsey.

Can't wait, baby. Your scent is everywhere. Makes me crazy from wanting you.

Liar and a tease.

Magnus chuckled. He squirted some onto his fingers. *I sure wish I had something bigger than my finger.*

By the gods, now Ramsey's looking at me weird. He could picture Ladon squirming around in his seat, trying to get comfortable with his dick straining against his zipper.

And just the thought of that hard cock revved him up even more. He brought his legs back as far as he could comfortably get them and rubbed a finger around his pucker, liking the way it felt with the slick.

He didn't even get a finger inside when the door opened, and Ladon stood in the doorway. He eyes shifted and his fangs dropped. He shut the door, the lock clicking.

He didn't wait for an invitation but pulled his shirt over his head, letting it fall to the floor. "Had to come clean to Ramsey. That's the only way he would let me out of the meeting." The whole time he talked Ladon unbuttoned and unzipped his pants, pushing them down and off. He had a small pair of bikini-type underwear. They hugged him in all the right places but did nothing to hide Ladon's hard length behind the red fabric.

Magnus grinned. "I like those."

Ladon wiggled his eyebrows. "I thought you might. Now tell me what you think you're doing interrupting my meeting like that, baby." The grin said just how serious Ladon wasn't.

"It's payback for not staying near me. I got worried." Magnus had a serious problem that had everything to do with Ladon getting shot. Thankfully, the bullet had gone right through him and hadn't hit anything major. Shifting a few times seemed to heal it up just fine. But it might not have gone that way and the *what-ifs* would haunt Magnus for a while.

Ladon discarded the sexy underwear and took his cock in hand. "We should go to your cabin and get your things today."

"You just want to see my collection of boy shorts."

"Absolutely." The closer he came the more his eyes zeroed in on Magnus' finger playing around his pucker. "I seriously get to be inside you?"

"Come here." His blood heated with the look Ladon gave him. He'd never felt so much like someone's favorite candy treat and the most cherished person alive all at the same time.

Ladon climbed between his legs and then slid up Magnus' body. The move was sensual and smooth. All other thoughts fled his mind when Ladon kissed him.

Ladon cupped Magnus' cheek. His other hand snaked down his side. Ladon lifted off him enough to get his hand between them. He pumped Magnus' cock a couple of times and then cupped his balls.

Magnus moaned into the kiss and then had to break it when his need built too high to do anything besides feel. Ladon kissed a trail along his jaw and then down to his shoulder. He licked across the mating bite, which sent Magnus even further into need.

Ladon smiled against Magnus' skin before licking his nipple. Magnus panted just from Ladon breathing across it. The anticipation heated his blood. When that wet heat covered it, he came off the bed, arching his back, wanting more.

Up to that point they hadn't played with each other's bodies too much. The stress of the situation was part of the reason. A larger part was them needing to bond. Back at home, they could explore all they wanted, and Ladon took advantage.

Magnus was happy to let him. His blood sang with each lick and playful bite.

Ladon focused onto the other nipple, and Magnus moaned so loudly everyone in the house probably heard. He didn't care. He just wanted Ladon to keep going.

Ladon didn't disappoint. He licked across Magnus' nipple again and then kissed it before moving to the center of his chest.

Another kiss.

Ladon touched Magnus' cock.

Another kiss and then a lick right above his navel. It was close enough to his cock that Magnus tensed. His blood heated. Ladon's breath fanned across the head of his cock and Magnus threaded his fingers through Ladon's hair. Time stopped as Ladon hung there, inches from his leaking cockhead. The tension built. "Please."

"I've never done this before." Ladon met his gaze. The uncertainty came through loud and clear in his downturned mouth.

Oh. Well, shit. Magnus tried to calm down, but his heart beat a wild rhythm. "Um...just a...um...watch your teeth. And use your tongue."

Ladon blinked at him several times. "That's it?"

"I'll like it. Promise."

When Ladon licked across the head of his cock, Magnus cried out. His body lost all its tension only to return when wet heat enveloped his hard cock. He couldn't think about anything else but all that pleasure coursing through him.

Ladon did exactly what Magnus told him only he took it to the next level, creating a tunnel that wrapped around his hard length deliciously. Ladon took too much at one point, choking. He pulled off. "Sorry."

"It's okay. It feels good." It felt like heaven. Or what Magnus' version of heaven would've been if he believed in such a place.

Ladon nodded and then started again, only he pressed a finger at Magnus' entrance at the same time.

"Oh yeah." Magnus pulled his legs back as far as he could get them, asking for more.

Ladon might not have experience with sucking cock, but he made up for it with enthusiasm. He even hummed as if it was the best thing he had ever tasted.

He set a rhythm with his finger that matched his mouth, adding another finger at just the right time.

Magnus couldn't keep his hips still. He tried to pump into Ladon's mouth, but an arm came across his abdomen, holding him down. Ladon added another finger and Magnus felt so full he could hardly breathe. Ladon stilled and pulled off Magnus' cock. "You okay?"

Magnus nodded. "You. Now you. Please."

Ladon nodded, pulling his fingers out and lay over Magnus.

Ladon was nervous. Magnus could tell by the way he swallowed as if the stress of the moment built up in his throat and he needed to get rid of it. "You'll tell me if it hurts or if you want to stop. Okay?"

"Yes. Yes. Just go slow." Magnus brought a hand around the nape of Ladon's neck, pulling him down until their foreheads pressed together.

Ladon's cock head pressed against Magnus' opening, pushing inside so slowly he thought the speed would drive him crazy. Ladon pulled back, meeting Magnus' gaze. His mouth fell open, and his eyes widened. "It's...oh...it feels..."

Magnus nodded. "A little faster."

Ladon pressed in a bit more. He moaned and pressed in all the way. He shut his eyes and bit his bottom lip. He pulled out just a little before pressing in again.

"Don't hold back, baby."

"I don't want to hurt you."

"You're not hurting me. Furthest thing from it." Magnus was about to come already.

Ladon drove in hard enough to scoot them both up the bed. Magnus grunted and wrapped his legs around Ladon's waist.

Ladon kissed him, demanding everything at the same time he gave. Ladon set a rhythm that staked a claim on Magnus, moving in and out of him without apology. Magnus couldn't do anything but go along for the ride.

When Ladon struck, it was without warning. The bite stung, and then an overwhelming pleasure took over, making him come. The heat exploded, sending him over the edge of pleasure.

Ladon stilled inside him before pumping in shallowly.

He shuddered and then stilled, pulling his fangs out. Magnus wrapped his arms around Ladon, holding him close, when Ladon collapsed on top of him.

They both sighed at the same time, which made them chuckle.

"You ruined me for the rest of the day," Ladon mumbled against his neck.

Magnus smiled. "I would apologize but..."

"Don't you dare." Ladon lifted his head. "Seriously, though. I have a clan meeting to schedule, but I want to know if you'd go somewhere with me before we go to your cabin."

"Why the clan meeting?"

"Ramsey wants to make me the official Alpha. The clan has to agree. It's what we were discussing before you took all my attention." Ladon lay his head back down, kissing Magnus on the cheek before snuggling in again.

"Shame on me." Magnus chuckled and wrapped his arms around Ladon, running a hand down his back.

"Yep. I might have to spank you later." Magnus could hear the teasing in Ladon's voice.

Magnus shook his head. "So where are we going?"

"I'm meeting a friend for ice cream in an hour. Think you can work yourself out of bed to come with. I'd like you to meet him."

"I wanted to sleep the morning away with you, though."

"You already did. It's nearly noon, so we can't lay here much longer. Alfie takes a nap at two o'clock."

Magnus would have asked questions about this Alfie fellow, but he knew Ladon well enough he didn't need the details. "If it's noon, does that mean we just had a nooner. Isn't that what you youngsters call making love in the middle of the day?"

"No one says that anymore, Old Man." Ladon chuckled.

Chapter
Thirty-Three

Ladon had commandeered one of the loungers on the patio before anyone else got out there, so he had Magnus between his legs, front to back. Magnus lay against him, and they both contemplated the stars. It was peaceful even with the rest of the family around them. Maybe especially because of the family. Their bickering and teasing brought comfort in ways Ladon hadn't realized until he had left on his little adventure.

And then Vaughan hit his shoulder. "Move over."

Ladon rolled his eyes. "There's no room. Go sit with Tim."

Tim sat on a lounger that was next to Kristin and Josh. Josh and he had made amends to the point that Tim came to dinner a couple of nights a week and Josh helped on the farm. Nothing like fighting in a battle together with death chasing everyone around to bring what was important into perspective. Things weren't perfect by any means but at least they were on speaking terms.

Tim's eyes were feline, and his fangs had dropped. That had everything to do with Keaton, who was in the house doing dishes with Sage.

"No way is that happening. That's drama and Anna is over there. She scares the shit out of me." Vaughan turned and to meet her gaze. "No offense."

Anna grinned. She sat on the chair next to Josh with her legs folded up and sweatpants on. The sweatpants made her appear more approachable but that was deceiving.

"Taken as a compliment. When are you sending me after Senator Fowler?" Her leg twitched a restless rhythm Ladon doubted she was even aware of, and her fingers played a silent song on her knee.

"I don't know that I am." He hadn't heard anything from the Paranormal Council. As soon as he did, he'd help however they let him. Sending out his own people stepped on toes, and with Saint Lakes on the radar, he'd rather not burn that bridge. And then there was the fact he still didn't know if he should trust her. Her loyalty hadn't extended very far where Senator Fowler was concerned, so it made Ladon question how far it extended with him.

Anna groaned. "Give me something, Alpha."

"I may send you and someone else to rescue Wesley Swenson." Ladon remembered the way his eyes had widened and the gray pallor to his complexion as he sat beside the senator. He hadn't wanted to be there. That much had been clear. As scared as Wesley was of paranormals, he would have come to Ladon if the senator had given him a choice. That alone meant Wesley needed protection.

Anna wrinkled her nose. "Fine."

Ladon lifted his eyebrows.

Upon seeing his expression, she said, "Yes, Alpha. When do we leave?"

Damian inched his way closer to Owen, who narrowed his eyes and crossed his arms over his chest. Damian looked at Owen as if he had crushed his heart in a fist. "I need someone to help me look for my brothers. We can rescue Swenson on the way. Was gonna ask you, Magnus, but Anna might do if she can investigate instead of kill."

Anna flipped him off as if he said something offensive.

No way would Ladon send Anna and Damian on a rescue mission together. Not without supervision. *Want to go with them, baby?*

I'd like to spend more time with you before going back out again. Meaning Magnus still had protective issues over Ladon getting shot and couldn't leave him yet.

Ladon grinned. *That's the reason you don't want to go. Riiiigghhtt.* Magnus chuckled.

Ladon grinned. "Rocky or Sully might be able to help with the investigation process." Ladon met Garridan's gaze to find out what he thought.

Garridan nodded. "I'll go over to their cabin tomorrow."

Anna sighed. "We can't go right now?"

Damian rolled his eyes. "Owen and I have to bond before I leave."

Owen glared right before he stomped his way off the patio and around the side of the house. Ladon had no idea where he intended to go but watching Damian chase after him like a lovesick puppy was comical.

Their voices faded but every paranormal on the patio heard their conversation.

"I might have to kill someone. You're way too delicate to see me do that."

Vaughan snorted out a laugh and said exactly what Ladon thought. "He thinks Owen is delicate. He has a lot to learn."

"Who said I wanted to go with you? And I'll show you delicate. Asshole."

"Aw, come on. Owen, slow down...ouch...damn it."

An eagle flew overhead, landing in one of the yard's maple trees. Damian came around the corner, limping his way to Owen.

Ladon tried not to laugh. Poor Damian had no idea the level of stubborn he was dealing with. Owen wouldn't give on any point and he wouldn't let Damian's way of thinking sway his point-of-view on things.

"What happened to your foot?" Ladon chuckled all the way through the question.

"Busted my toe." Damian didn't look away from Owen, who sat on a tree branch peering down. "Please, shift back."

Ladon chuckled and whispered to Magnus. "Wanna sneak out tonight? Make love under the stars in our usual place."

Magnus nodded. "I'm in."

****

Damian has been an assassin for a long time. It left him with a hard shell. He didn't think anyone could crack it. Can Owen Somerset break down Damian's walls. Click here to find out what happens next in the adventurous Saint Lakes series.

****

All battles leave scars. Some differ from others. ***Redefining Normal*** is yours FREE when you sign up for my newsletter. Claim your copy here.Or scan the QR code.

****

Honest reviews of my books help bring them to the attention of other readers. Leaving a review will help readers find the book. You can leave a review here: https://www.amazon.com/review/create-review/B01N5QOER2

About the Author

April Kelley writes LGBTQ+ Romance. Her works include *The Journey of Jimini Renn*, a Rainbow Awards finalist, *Whispers of Home*, the *Saint Lakes* series, and over thirty more. Since writing her first story at ten, the characters in her head still won't stop telling their stories. If April isn't reading or writing, you can find her taking a long walk in the woods or going on her next adventure.

If you wish to contact her, email authoraprilkelley@gmail.com.

Please visit her website at authoraprilkelley.com

Manufactured by Amazon.ca
Acheson, AB

11488336R00162